GORDON CASTELNERO

Toyful Love

To the kid in all of us

Contents

Chapter 1	1
Chapter 2	15
Chapter 3	26
Chapter 4	32
Chapter 5	44
Chapter 6	57
Chapter 7	68
Chapter 8	74
Chapter 9	84
Chapter 10	90
Chapter 11	102
Chapter 12	107
Chapter 13	115
Chapter 14	122
Chapter 15	131
Chapter 16	140
Chapter 17	146
Chapter 18	155
Chapter 19	165
Chapter 20	174
Chapter 21	185
Chapter 22	193
Chapter 23	200
Chapter 24	210

Chapter 25   217
Chapter 26   222
Chapter 27   231
Chapter 28   244
Chapter 29   250
Chapter 30   257
Chapter 31   269
Chapter 32   280
Epilogue   289

Chapter 1

In front of Perrinsville Elementary, located in the upper Midwest, clusters of kids swarmed the grounds before the morning bell rang on the first day of school. The parking lot was jammed with school buses and traffic from the incoming staff. A traditional flagpole waving the American flag in the early September breeze stood prominently on the grassy section of the campus. A team of boys played football on the grounds, while a group of girls nearby performed gymnastics.

Standing by the building's main entrance, a shabby-looking man in his early forties with a broom in hand welcomed the students with a smile as warm as the day. Sporting an untucked flannel shirt and a pair of faded jeans, he blended in well with the children—only his age and height set him apart from them. He was affectionately greeted by all the youngsters randomly: "Mornin', Henry!" "Hi, Henry!" "Hey, Henry."

Noticing the football game in progress, the janitor dropped his broom to run and catch a pass in midair. "Interception—Henry! First down!" he gleefully cheered. "Go out for a long one." Henry signaled to the boys on his team. "Hut! Hut! Hut!" As they scrambled, he started to fake them out by pretending to throw the ball before bouncing it off his left knee and kicking it with his right foot like a circus clown.

The boys in his immediate vicinity laughed, as the others chased the ball heading in the direction of the parking lot—where it hit a professionally dressed woman in her late thirties no one had ever seen before. Dr. Kristin Sharp was blindsided by the colliding pigskin that struck her face, causing her thick, black horn-rimmed glasses to fall on the ground faster than her briefcase and travel mug. Her purse slid off her shoulder as she wobbled like a Weeble to avoid eating the pavement.

"Whoa!" she screamed, trying to maintain her balance.

The boys stabilized her. "Sorry, ma'am." "Sorry, lady. It was an accident." "We're really sorry!"

Kristin pulled her purse back up to her shoulder. "Are you supposed to be playing football out here?"

"Yeah, we do it all the time," one of the boys answered.

"Hmmm...I see..." She bent down to retrieve her specs. "Will you be kind little gentlemen and help me pick up the rest of my things?"

"Yes, ma'am." The boys scooped up her items. "Here you go."

Dr. Sharp put her glasses back on and took possession of her belongings. "Please try to be more careful, so there doesn't have to be a new policy."

The boys looked at her strangely before disbanding.

On her way to the building, Kristin caught a glimpse of the girls' acrobatics on the grass. She stopped for a moment to observe their cartwheels, handsprings, and round offs. The image of them in contrast to the boys playing football reminded her of a bittersweet memory in her socially troubled youth—a memory she'd tried to suppress even as it unfailingly found a way to creep back into her mind.

Shrugging her shoulders, Dr. Sharp proceeded to the building's entrance just as the first bell rang. All the scattered students raced for the doors, nearly bulldozing her onto the sidewalk. Abandoned by the kids, Henry hid behind a tree like a juvenile delinquent—he had kicked the ball that smacked Kristin's face—but he also wanted to gaze at her in secret. His body had frozen like a block of ice, yet his heart had melted with joy. He soaked up every detail of Kristin's sophisticated appearance—her black pinstriped pantsuit, heavy glasses, and no-nonsense updo hairstyle—before she disappeared into the school. And with his head in the clouds, she was gone in an instant, taking his breath away.

* * *

Approaching a metal-framed glass door with OFFICE printed in white letters at eye level, Kristin juggled her briefcase and travel mug to free her right hand. Before she could clutch the door handle, she heard a voice coming from behind her. "Hold on; I got it." She turned around to see a mature plain Jane a few steps away, ready to open the door for her. Janet Goode, the longtime secretary and school nurse, greeted her new boss with a friendly demeanor.

"Dr. Sharp?" she asked.

"Yes."

"Hi, I'm Janet Goode," the woman said, extending her hand, "your secretary."

Kristin gripped her hand firmly. "Pleased to meet you."

"Let me get the door for you."

She opened the gateway, then motioned for Kristin to take the first step into the cramped executive suite of her new administrative post. Beyond Janet's desk, which was front and center and flanked by a small row of empty chairs along the picture windows on the right side of her station, two oak-stained doors were visible off the back wall, one open and one closed. The open door, on the left, led to a nursing station, complete with a reclining exam table, supply cabinet, copier, and kitchenette sink, which was home to a coffee maker that probably shouldn't be there. The closed door displayed a sign that read PRINCIPAL.

Inching toward her office, Kristin surveyed the premises with curiosity. "Looks like you have a makeshift infirmary...where's the nurse?"

"You're looking at her," Janet replied.

"Really?"

"Yep. I'm a jack-of-all-trades around here."

"Do you have a nursing license?"

"Sure do. I was an RN in my past life, you might say—"

"Past life?" Kristin interrupted with skepticism.

"Oh, I don't mean like a mystical past life."

"That's a relief," Kristin mumbled.

"It was a career path I gave up eons ago," Janet continued. "My heart is with the kids in this town, and since I don't qualify to be a teacher, I took the next best opportunity, and here I am. Do you want to see my license? It's current."

"That won't be necessary. I believe you."

Unloading the items she held, which had become a weighty burden by now, Kristin set them on one of the chairs by the windows. She proceeded to turn the knob, only to discover the door was locked. "Do you have the key?" she asked the secretary.

"No, I don't...didn't you get one?"

"No. Everything went down quickly with my hire and relocation. I didn't get a key, a tour of the school, or anything."

"No surprise to me."

"How so?"

"Our superintendent likes to keep everyone in suspense. The principal vacancy is just his latest cliff-hanger."

"That's a little over the top, don't you think?"

"Not if you're trying to keep prying eyes in the dark."

"Is that why he was so adamant about me not showing up until after the morning bell?"

"Bingo…mystery solved. He wanted to keep the lurkers on their toes, so there wouldn't be any gossip before this morning."

Kristin lowered her glasses. "Gossip?"

"This quaint little town is a dangerous rumor mill."

"It is?"

"Didn't you do your homework about this community before moving here?"

"Ah, no…should I have?"

"Where are you from?"

"New England."

"Well, I don't know much about the cosmopolitan societies in the Northeast, but when it comes to anything going against the grain around here, you'll be in for a wild ride."

"Thanks, I'll take that under advisement." The new principal immediately shifted gears. "Does the custodian have a key to my office? I'd like to get settled in there sometime today, please."

"He's right outside; I'll call him." Janet cranked open one of the windows to give a shout to the world's biggest kid, who had resumed his assigned duties. "Hey, Henry, drop the broom and come unlock the principal's office."

"Much appreciated," Kristin thanked the secretary, before taking a seat next to her leather bags. She gripped her travel mug tightly for a few sips of morning joe, waiting in anticipation to buckle down to her work. Deep in thought of what to do first, she was suddenly distracted by a tingling sound echoing from the vestibule.

As Henry shuffled his slouchy posture toward the office, a large bunch of keys dangled from his belt with enough jingle to mimic the sound of the Good Humor man peddling Popsicles from a tricycle on a hot summer day. Upon entering the office, his face lit up like a

Christmas tree at the sight of the *present* sitting next to the door, of which he held the key.

"Henry Hubbard," Janet said, "this is Kristin Sharp, our new principal."

Kristin stood up. "Pleased to meet you."

"The pleasure's all mine," Henry responded with a sliver of giddiness. "You have the key?"

"Yeah, I've got it here somewhere." His calloused fingertips sorted through the vast array of keys hanging from his belt.

Kristin hovered over him.

He stepped back without skipping a beat.

She automatically assumed the worst by covering her mouth. "Ooh, so sorry—coffee breath."

Sensing her embarrassment, Henry poked fun at her bashfulness. "No worries. The wicked taste of pepperoni and anchovies from my cold pizza this morning are about to steal your thunder, any moment now."

Janet, who had heard all his brazen wisecracks a million times, was stunned to watch the new executive "click" with the unfiltered janitor about inopportune bad breath as Kristin released a sheepish giggle.

Henry decided to feed off of his unexpected icebreaker with another shot aimed at a bigger laugh. "Oh, did I mention that it had garlic-flavored crust too?"

The well-educated, highly composed doctor of philosophy let loose an unrestrained cackle. In a jiffy, she asked a burning question like an inquisitive kindergartner. "You eat cold pizza for *breakfast*?"

"And a bowl of cereal for dinner," he bantered back with a childish grin, turning the key to unlock her door—in more than one way. "Now with the shell cracked and the door opened, welcome to your professional study miss...or is it mizz?"

"Neither—it's doctor!" she proudly affirmed.

Claiming her items from the row of chairs, she scurried into the office with authority. Worried that his ignorance had somehow offended her, Henry turned on the light switch and proceeded to the window to open the blinds. Meanwhile, Kristin placed her things on the freshly polished surface of the credenza and hutch combination behind her cherrywood desk. She sat in her black leather swivel chair to turn on the desktop computer. Just then, a blinding ray of sunshine burst across her desk, causing the honey blond in her hair to fade out.

She waved her hand like a commanding officer. "Close the blinds, please."

"Oh, sorry," he apologized, shutting the blades. "The morning sun can be a little strong. I'll just mosey along so you can start your busy day."

Before he reached the doorway, Kristin felt the need to understand his predisposed assumption about her. "Why did you presume that I wouldn't be a doctor and just a *miss*, or as you thoughtlessly stated—*mizz?*"

Henry turned to face the music. "I didn't mean anything by it. We never had a doctor at this school before. The only *piled higher and deeper* in the Perrinsville education system is the superintendent."

"He's a bright man."

"And he made a wise decision hiring you."

"I appreciate the compliment to cover your PhD cliché, but you don't know me. So how do you know it was a wise decision?"

"Well, doc…to be honest, we were all worried that Mizz Tater Tots was going to be the new boss. When Captain…err…uh, Mr. Hook decided to go on a permanent fishing trip, we expected Mizz Tater Tots to segue into this office. She's been salivating to sit at this desk for years, so she could be the first woman principal here. She's also power hungry."

"Mizz Tater Tots?" Kristin asked with a hint of nosiness.

"Yeah. She hates the label, but the kids have been calling her that for a really long time. She's not the most pleasant person to be around, especially if you're in her class. She's a control freak, so I think she kinda deserves it."

"Thanks for the warning."

"No sweat. Here's another little tidbit for your mental file: she's been fawning all over the superintendent for years. We had a large pool going on her getting the job."

"Does my employer have a personal relationship with her?"

"Oh, not anymore. Dr. Cake"—he caught himself as Kristin raised an eyebrow—"I mean Dr. Bakewell finally got tired of her charade."

"Do you have a nickname for everyone around here?"

"Kinda sorta. It's all fun 'n' games…nothing malicious." He glanced over his shoulder to Janet, typing on her computer. "Right, Miss Goody Two-shoes?"

"Hooray for Henry!" she hailed.

Kristin looked slightly puzzled at the quirky man. "Why did she shout hooray for you?"

The janitor's face suddenly gleamed like a freshly polished badge of honor. "Oh, that's in the spirit of my favorite children's book, *Hooray for Henry*. It was the first book I learned how to read, and it's been my life's story."

"Is it a dream come true or just the key to understanding you?"

"A little of both, kinda sorta."

Kristin rolled her eyes. "Don't you mean 'kind of, sort of'?"

"Yeah—whatever. I say 'face,' and you say '*le visage*'."

Expecting a more common analogy from him like, *I say potato and you say pohtaato*, Kristin was dumbfounded yet intellectually impressed by his inference about her preferring a more cultured sounding vernacular. In a New York minute, she became aware of the shrewdness underneath his yokel facade. Kristin knew he analytically read beyond her stoic expressions and saw everything she kept hidden behind her *visage*—a lifetime of overanalyzing simplicity.

"Well, I'll be curious to see what nickname you come up with for me." She winked. "By the way, did anybody win in the pool?"

"Just one."

"Who?"

Henry grinned with ear-to-ear satisfaction before waving adieu on his way out the door. Kristin waited till he was gone so she could take out her compact to check her face in private. Satisfied that nothing was disrupted by the mishap in the parking lot, she closed her compact, and there stood Henry.

She nearly jumped out of her pale skin. "Sheesh! You just about gave me a heart attack."

"I didn't mean to scare you."

"You must be part mouse; I didn't even hear you."

Henry held up the bunch of keys clenched in his fist. "I didn't wanna disrupt your self-examination with the sound of my keys."

"I would've preferred the warning. Anyway, is there something you need?"

He bowed his head. "I just came to tell you I'm the one who kicked the ball that hit you."

"Thank you very much. I really like a man who takes ownership of his faults."

"Well, I just didn't want you to get a bad first impression of our kids and a false impression of me."

* * *

Dr. Sharp spent most of her morning roaming the halls of the school in a self-guided tour to get acquainted with the facility. She stopped at every classroom to introduce herself to the students and faculty she now presided over. With only a few minutes left before the official end of the first day of school—which was half a day—Kristin realized that she needed a set of keys to her office and the building. Heading to the rear of the facility, near the incinerator, she paid an impromptu visit to the custodian's quarters and was stunned by what she discovered.

Near a wall of cleaning supplies stored in metal racks and cabinets, sat an elongated tool bench fit for the North Pole—a workshop worthy of Santa's seal of approval but filled with inventory from the Island of Misfit Toys, as the bench was cluttered with broken toy pieces. And seated on the stool, hunched over like a busy elf preparing for Christmas Eve, Henry put the finishing touches on a newly repaired doll.

Completely flabbergasted, Kristin was nearly speechless. "Oh my..."

Henry swiveled toward her with the doll in his hand. "Hello again; I've been expecting you."

"Really? Why?"

"You need keys to your office and the building, right?"

"How did you know?"

"I kinda withheld 'em, so you'd have to come see me."

"Should I be worried?"

"Nope—I'm just a kid at heart, as you can probably tell." He spun around on his stool like a spinning top.

"May I have them?"

Henry reached into the pocket of his faded jeans to remove a small keychain with freshly cut keys. He tossed them to her. She bent at her knees to catch the keys with both hands before they landed on the concrete floor.

"Good catch!" he commented.

The eleven-thirty bell rang. The sound of two hundred kids stampeding the halls, excited to go home for a free afternoon, overwhelmed Kristin. She worried about their orderly conduct. Taking a step into the hall, she shouted, "No running! Please walk. No running!"

"Aw, cut 'em some slack. It's only the first day."

"What if somebody gets hurt? I'm responsible."

"You'll never have to worry about the kids here—they're great! It's the parents and teachers that cause you a world of grief."

"Why do you say that?" she snapped.

"I've been at this institution of grammar almost all my life, except for middle and high school. I have yet to see a *really* bad apple. A few of them fall from the tree, but not enough to spoil the whole basket."

"Don't you mean 'the barrel'?"

"Ah, yeah—same thing. You get the idea."

"So, which teachers and parents should I be concerned about?"

"Talk to Janet. She's got the story on everyone around here—in and out of school."

"A regular pipeline of information?"

"More than you know."

Just then, a small first grader with a backpack slung over her shoulders wandered in. "Did you fix my doll, Henry?"

Henry, who'd quickly hidden the doll in his hand behind his back, asked, "Do you like to play hospital with your dolls?"

"Uh-huh."

"Do you remember what was wrong with your doll?"

"Her leg broke. My mommy tried to fix it and couldn't."

"What about your daddy?"

"He made it worse and bent her leg. He said he'd buy me a new one, but it won't be the same."

"Why not?"

"Because I want *my* doll."

"Well, it was a tough operation, but the prognosis looks good." He whipped out the doll with a finger bandage around its left knee. "I was able to bend her leg back and glue the plastic peg in her knee back together. You'll have to be careful for a couple of days for the glue to handle the stress of it bending back and forth."

"A couple of days?" The girl wilted like a flower. "I wanted to play with her today."

"You can…that's why I asked if you play hospital. Just pretend that she had an emergency and went to the doctor and got a bandage to make her leg feel better."

A glimmer of hope swept across the girl's face. "I can be the doctor too."

"Of course, you can," he agreed happily, giving her the doll.

"I have a toy doctor's bag"—she started to pet the doll's silky hair—"and I'm going to give her a shot when I get home."

"That's the spirit!"

"Thanks, Henry." She hugged him. "You're the best!"

"Have fun with her."

The little girl skipped out, talking to her doll along the way. "I'm going to take good care of you."

Kristin felt emotionally jarred by the performance she'd just witnessed, not knowing whether to applaud or cry. The endearing episode tugged at her heartstrings irrationally; her gifted mind could not process an ounce of logic. It was the second time in a single morning that she was haunted by some of the displeasures locked away in the vault of her cerebral memory bank.

"What you did for that little girl was incredible!" She wiped a tear from her eye under her glasses. "I can totally relate to that girl's dilemma."

"So can I."

"Is that why you have all these broken toys here?"

"It's what I live for," he humbly confessed. "Not everything in life is disposable. Sometimes I think kids are the only ones who get that concept. Things only have the value that you place upon them. Did you have a toy that was so precious your life seemed empty without it?"

She nodded timidly. "When I was that little girl's age, I *always* played with this really cheap cheerleader doll at school that was made out of rubber—the uniform too. You could bend and twist her in every direction imaginable. I wanted one of my own so bad and never got it."

"How come?"

"It was an old toy that the school had like forever. My mom shopped all over the place and couldn't find it anywhere. There wasn't an internet back then, so I was out of luck."

"Did it mean a great deal to you?"

"You're going to think I'm crazy, but when I was a child, I had unbelievable flexibility, like I was made out of rubber. Maybe on a subconscious level it's why I pursued cheerleading. And I was really *good* at it."

"Wow!"

"Yeah, 'wow' is right. I'm giving out way too much information."

"Your secrets are safe with me."

"I appreciate it, but I'm starting to get a little uncomfortable. I *never* reveal this much about myself to a stranger."

"I'm not a stranger—I'm your caretaker," he joked.

"And that's why I need to put the kibosh on this conversation." She went for the door, then turned back abruptly. "Tonight is the Parent-Teacher Meet and Greet. I assume you'll be back here to set up?"

"With bells on."

"Do you have a uniform?"

Henry looked himself over, drawing attention to his untucked plaid flannel shirt. "I'm wearing it."

"Did the school ever issue a custodian's work uniform to you?"

"Are you referring to the stiff-threaded ugly gray kind with my name sewn on the shirt?"

"Yes."

"The captain—"

"Mr. Hook," she horned in.

"Yeah, Mr. Hook ordered one for me a long time ago, and I ditched it."

"Why?"

"Uniforms represent an authoritative separation that clashes with my personal philosophy of being one of the kids. Besides my own duds are more comfortable."

"I think it's better if the custodian is visibly identifiable to everyone in the building."

"Uniform ID is for police and firefighters. Who needs a uniform to push a broom? Everybody in this town knows I'm just a plain old janitor."

Kristin stared him down. "Where I come from, a custodian looks like a professional maintenance worker. I would like that same image projected here. Are we clear?"

"Crystal."

"Do you still have the uniform?"

"It's around here somewhere."

"Find it and wear it, please. See you tonight."

As she strolled out the door, Perrinsville Elementary's permanent fixture plopped himself back on the stool, secure in his determination to free the bird she'd jailed in a gilded cage.

Chapter 2

Kristin arrived at the town's only supermarket in her newly leased luxury sedan—tuxedo-black metallic with flecks that glittered when kissed by the light of day. Pulling carefully into an available parking space among an array of assorted vehicles, she turned off the love song playing through her satellite radio before bringing the automobile to a complete stop. After gently placing the gear shift lever into Park, she took out her cell phone to delete her note to self: "Grocery store after school." Grabbing her expensive purse off the leather passenger seat, she was ready to tackle her mission.

Once inside the semicrowded market—still in her pinstriped pantsuit from school—the principal made it her first order of business to clean her shopping cart with a bleach wipe. Perusing the cart area, she felt miffed by the absence of a free sanitizing dispenser, which had become standard in all the grocery stores she patronized back in the Northeast. Never one to be without a plan B, she thumbed through her organized purse to withdraw a previously opened travel pack of hand sheets. Blind to the stares of fellow patrons coming and going, she began to polish the handle and basket rim of her chosen cart until the aluminum shone like glass.

Feeling a little smug about her perceived emergency preparedness, she discarded her soiled wipe in a nearby trash can and proudly wheeled her germ-free buggy toward the produce section. She set her purse on the cart's plastic child seat, then reached back into the bag for her grocery list and a fine-tip marker. Concentrating on the task at hand, she remained oblivious to her surroundings. The signage for organic produce conspicuously displayed above a wall stocked with fruits and vegetables caught her eye, and Kristin didn't see the water spot lying in her path along the refrigerated shelves. As she stepped forward, unsuspecting, with her eyes on her goal, one of the tips belonging to her kitten-heel shoes slipped on the moist tile, causing her to fall backward. "Whoa!" she screamed, losing her grip of the cart; her list and marker fell to the floor.

Before Dr. Sharp's body suffered a humiliating spill in the tradition of slapstick comedy, a pair of strong hands rescued her as the sound of a familiar jingle rang in her ears. Stumbling back to her feet, she turned to face her flannel-shirted hero—*Henry!*

"Are you okay?" he asked.

"I'll survive—thank you."

"I guess you didn't see the puddle on the floor?"

"I had no idea it was there. I never saw it."

"I could tell." He bent over to retrieve her lost items. "You looked like you were in your own little world."

"I was. Good thing you were here."

"That's twice now."

"That I nearly fell on my rump?"

"Yep! What are the odds? Oh, wait that's too easy; let me start over. What are the *calculable* odds?" he pitched like a fastball.

"Lucky…oh, wait. I don't believe in dumb luck, so *enumerable*, I'd say," she batted back playfully.

"Brilliant!"

"Because I saw *that one* coming a mile away."

"Now I know what things you see and what things you don't see."

"So you think," she uttered uncomfortably.

"Are you here for a full grocery shop or just a few things?"

"Since you insist on knowing my business, I just got settled, and my refrigerator resembles one belonging to a carefree bachelor—empty. And you?"

"I'm a carefree bachelor with an empty refrigerator."

"Ha-ha. I saw that one coming too."

Just then, the store manager appeared out of the blue. "Are you all right, miss?" the balding man asked in a panic.

"Well, it's about time you got here," Henry spouted. "Your poor response time could've cost you the store."

"I came as quick as I could, Henry."

"I'm fine," Kristin confirmed. "There's no cause for alarm."

The manager wiped his sweaty forehead. "Whew. I'm glad, miss."

"And it's 'doctor'—not 'miss,'" Henry interjected.

The old man looked surprised. "Oh?" He turned back to Kristin. "What do you practice?"

"I'm in educa—"

Henry chimed in again. "Her practice will be in lawsuits, over slips and falls, the next time you're negligent in cleaning up your messes. Where's the janitor?"

"I'm looking at him!" the man responded defensively, as though it wasn't the first time he'd had a confrontation with Henry.

Worried about so much fuss over nothing, Kristin put a stop to their bickering before other people tuned in. "Look, I'm all right, and I'm not going to make an issue over something that could've happened and didn't—okay?"

"Thank you," the manager said graciously. "I'll get a stock boy to mop up the floor."

Upon his exit, Henry mocked him to Kristin. "*I'm looking at him*'…I set up a good janitor joke to rib him, and the best punch line he could come up with was 'I'm looking at him.' That old prune has no sense of humor. He needs to get a personality."

"Please stop; this is getting shameful," she begged under her breath. "Can I please shop in peace?"

The softness of her plea sent a shock wave to his heart. For a man who was typically unabashed, he quickly became anxious over the idea of offending her—for the second time today. That kind of thought had never been a consideration to him before, but with Kristin it was different. He looked beyond her thick black glasses and carefully woven updo to unmask her concealed loveliness—the woman he knew she really wanted to be but didn't know how to bring out of herself.

Watching Kristin pick and choose which edibles to purchase, Henry saw an opening to rebound in a way that would appeal to her intellect without detracting from his goofiness. Observing her thorough study of grape clusters, he picked the roundest, firmest orange off the shelf. She was pleasantly startled by the smoothness of his voice over her shoulder.

"Why pore over sour grapes when you can have an orange?"

She twisted around to see the brightest orange in the store rotating like a celestial planet between Henry's fingertips.

"Put a little sunshine in your life," he continued, with a lighthearted wit that she found priceless.

Cracking a laugh, she plucked the orange from his hand to place in her cart. "You're funny." She bashfully winked at the poorly groomed man with approval. Pushing her cart to the vegetable shelves, she caught a glimpse of him snatching his partially filled buggy to catch up.

"By the way," Henry called out, "you're gonna have a ridiculously high bill buying that organic stuff."

"They're the best," she touted.

"That's a matter of opinion."

"Well, *I* can afford to pay a little more."

"And I'm going to make pennies scream in a way that'll bring tears to your eyes."

Kristin leaned over curiously to peek at the items in his basket. Before she could get a good look, he pivoted the cart away from her.

"Ah, ah, ah." He waved his index finger, grinning like a child on a scavenger hunt for buried treasure. "See you at the checkout."

Over the next half hour, Henry dodged Kristin up and down the aisles at every turn, until the moment of truth arrived at the cash register. His cart overflowing with enough groceries to feed a football team after a rigorous workout, he waited for the competition to show up. It didn't take her more than a few minutes to stroll into an empty checkout lane.

"Hey, Sharpie!" Henry shouted, maneuvering his cart in line behind her.

She glared at him in disbelief. "You were serious?"

"Of course. You thought I was joking?"

Her eyes nearly bulged through her glasses at the staggering number of items crammed into his buggy. *All that is for you?*

He waggled proudly before stretching his neck to see the height of her items barely at the rim of her basket. "Ooh—this is gonna be good!"

The cashier motioned for Kristin to start unloading her groceries onto the conveyer belt. One by one, she transferred her organic, all-natural, nongenetically engineered ingredient perishables to the middle-aged cashier, who passed them down to the youthful bagger at the end of the line. Every product from frozen dinners to beverages to yogurt bore a green seal compliant to the highest standard of nutritional value. As the last box of microwavable Mexican casserole—made with organic corn and beans—blipped by the scanning beam, the cashier announced the grand total, which appeared as big as day on the register monitor—$293.16.

"Whoa-ho-ho…that's almost three hundred dollars!" Henry ribbed. "I figured it was gonna be high, but—wow."

Kristin refrained from dignifying what she considered an exaggerated critique of her purchases. She removed a suede monogrammed wallet from her purse as the bagger loaded her cart, then clasped her credit card to swipe through the reader connected to the register. A second later, the robotic woman behind the counter yanked the long receipt from the register to hand to Kristin.

"Have a nice day," she said mechanically.

"Thanks—you too," Kristin responded, tucking the receipt into her fashionable purse. Just when the PhD thought she was free to roll her cart out the door…

"Wait—don't go yet," Henry begged. "You gotta see this."

"Must I?"

"Pennies scream and eyes will cry."

"C'mon, Henry," the cashier interrupted. "I'm supposed to go on break in a few minutes." She switched off the lane light.

"Okay…okay…" he mumbled before scooping out his smorgasbord of comfort food like a steam shovel. Bags of chips, packages of cookies, liter bottles of soda pop, boxes of crackers, frozen dinners of everything imaginable, from pancakes to garlic bread, burritos, and meatloaf—nearly all of it labeled as artificially flavored, right down to the Neapolitan ice cream sandwiches.

Watching this mass of processed junk—the kind that most kids relish—flood the back end of the counter like water through a broken dam was enough to make Kristin gag: *He actually eats all that garbage? Where does he put it all? I think I'm going to be sick.* Before she could say boo, the total flashed on the screen—$306.74. "Ha!" she jabbed at him. "Your bill is more than mine."

"Pennies scream and eyes will cry," he reiterated.

"Brace yourself, dear," the checkout lady added.

Henry dug into the front pockets of his jeans to produce a hodge-podge of coupons, discount cards, and store reward dollars galore. Kristin's mouth dangled open at the rapid price reductions on Henry's bill with the stroke of each coupon, card, and reward money across the scanner. As the numbers plummeted like the stock market crash of 1929, she folded her arms defensively, ready to digest the depressing outcome: *Please stop at fifty...twenty, now...ten—really? Oh no...$6.96!*

"There must be a mistake," Henry informed the cashier.

"I don't have all day to rerun these coupons again," she exclaimed.

"The gem doughnuts weren't one of the couponed items. I should be charged for them."

"Don't worry about it."

"Give me a minute to search my cart for them."

"You're going to take forever un-bagging to find them in the cart," she stated in escalated frustration.

"Not if the bagger helps me."

"Look, this is cutting into my break time, so the gems are free. Just pay me and go."

"As long as you know I wasn't trying to rip you off." He whipped out a tattered wallet that had seen better days to give her a five and two singles. "You can keep the four cents." He turned to Kristin, speaking in a low tone. "That way I at least paid something for the gems."

The principal looked dismayed. "Are we done?"

"After you," he said with a polite hand gesture.

Making their way out the door, Henry accompanied Kristin to her car. "Now do you get what I meant by pennies scream and eyes cry?"

"I assumed that was your angle. I just had no idea how low your bill would actually be."

"Impressive, isn't it?"

"You're definitely the king of extreme thrift shopping."

When they arrived at her car, Kristin used the remote fob from her purse to pop the trunk lid. "This is the end of the line for me."

"Let me put your bags in the trunk for you."

"I appreciate it—thanks."

"My pleasure." He handled her grocery bags like precious cargo from the cart to her spaciously clean trunk. "Last one," he announced prior to closing the lid. "I'll return your cart with mine."

"May I ask you a personal question?"

"Go ahead."

"Do you really eat all that junk?"

"Junk?" He pretended to be offended.

"I'm sorry, but I thought only kids lived on snacks."

"That's exactly who they're for—the kids."

"Oh?"

"Sure, some of it's for me...the frozen stuff and such. But the chips, cookies, and other treats I share with the kids at school."

"Why?"

"A lot of times they don't like what their parents give them for snacks or lunch."

"That's very noble of you, but don't you think that's up to their parents?"

"Yeah...if the parents around here actually took the time to *connect* with their kids, instead of being selfish with their time, they would understand them the way I do."

His declaration resonated with her on a psychological level impenetrable until this unexpected moment. Her reserve controlled her judgment. The store parking lot was not an environment conducive for exploring the intrigue she'd begun to experience with him. Dr. Sharp was unwilling to discuss such personal matters out in the open for any pair of prying ears to overhear. She deflected by glancing at her wristwatch. "I think it's time to say goodbye again."

He waved. "Until tonight's event..."

"Don't forget to wear your custodial uniform," she emphasized.

"Oh, that again. Is it really necessary?"

"Yes, I want you to look the part."

"Well, then, I guess it's show time."

"Good," she said with a smile, getting into her car. "See you at six thirty."

He saluted. "Aye, aye, Sharpie. I'll be there in full costume."

"That's the second time you called me 'Sharpie.' Is that *my* dedicated nickname?"

"Yes, ma'am."

"I'm not sure if I should be flattered or relieved, but I guess I'll take it."

"Don't worry, it'll only come from me. I won't let anyone else claim it."

"Okay, fine—I really need to go."

"Ciao."

Henry stepped aside with the carts, allowing the principal to back out of the space and drive away with the janitor in her rearview mirror.

* * *

On his way home from the grocery store, Henry eyeballed his custodial formal wear wadded up on the passenger-side floor of his twenty-year-old van. Having racked up over a hundred and fifty thousand miles on its engine, the old clunker continued to putt along in its dented and weathered body, which barely hinted at the original candy-apple red from its prime. The only apparent shine to his relic on wheels came from the silvery glossed duct tape used to mend the cracks running amok all over the black vinyl seats.

He'd bought the stripped-down van at a police auction when he was in his early twenties. And as long as his mechanical skills allowed him to keep the power train moving, he'd had no desire to buy a new vehicle—there was no one to impress and no monthly payment either.

Rounding the corner of Main Street in downtown Perrinsville, he spotted the hanging sign for Sheldon's Dry Cleaning and Alterations. Suddenly, a light bulb illuminated inside his head with a bright idea to get out of the uniform—literally. Henry stopped along the curb outside the storefront. Gathering his school-issued shirt and pants off the grimy floor mat, he slid out of the passenger seat and went into the cleaners, where there seemed to be no sign of life. Dropping his garments on the empty countertop, he cupped his hands together against the stubble around his mouth to simulate a megaphone.

"Hey, Shelly! I have a *creasing* matter for you to *iron* out."

"Always with the puns, Henry!" a man's voice yelled on his way to the counter. "You got a punch line for everything."

"Not for everything, Shelly."

The short man with dark hair in casual clothes looked perplexed. "*What?*"

"Not everything." Henry kept a straight face, then cracked a smile. "All my *material* here is *tailor-made.*"

Right on cue both men laughed for a few seconds as if their ribs were being tickled.

"What can I do for you, my friend?" Sheldon asked.

Henry displayed the shirt. "How fast can you loosen the seams around the arms?"

The tailor noticed the name patch. "Don't tell me you're going to start wearing a work uniform after all these years?"

"Of course not. That's why I'm requesting a few alterations."

"So, you *want* this to come apart at the seams?"

"Yep…and the seat of the pants too. How fast can you get them done?"

"Why? Is it urgent?"

"It's Parent-Teacher night tonight."

Sheldon squinted. *"Henry...*what do you have up your sleeve this time?"

"Hey, good pun."

"Yes, I can be clever too—ha-ha. What's the purpose of loosening the stitching of your uniform?"

Henry backed up to the door in baby steps. "You know, I've got a van loaded with groceries waiting to go home. My ice cream has probably turned into buttermilk by now." He grabbed the door handle. "Can I get them in an hour?"

"They'll be ready."

"You're the man, Shelly—*press on!*"

Chapter 3

Inside the school's cramped ladies' room, Kristin refreshed her makeup in front of the mirror above the double sinks, opposite two pink toilet stalls. It had already been a long busy day for the new principal. Her only break was the grocery shopping earlier that afternoon, and she never had enough time to change her clothes or powder her nose—she had too much on her mind. After unpacking her edible purchases at home, Kristin raced back to her office to type out the agenda for tonight's meeting and email it to the staff.

In the half hour remaining till curtain time, she needed to conceal any sign of stress with a coat of confidence from her compact. Removing her glasses to spread the makeup evenly around her eyes, she placed the plastic frames on the counter next to her purse. While rubbing the pancake pad in small circular motions across her face, she realized her updo could stand a little remodeling. After finishing her face with lip gloss, Kristin removed the pins from the back of her hair to let the long honey locks fall freely below her shoulders. Before she could take out the hairbrush from her handbag, the door flew open—leaving her vulnerable and exposed to the scrutiny of whomever entered the facility.

Longtime fifth grade teacher, Alma Tater, stomped in like a drill sergeant searching for a delinquent recruit. "There you are! I want to have a word with you," she barked at her startled superior.

Unlike Kristin's visible display of prim and proper, Mizz Tater Tots, as referenced by Henry, wore brash and brazen like army stripes. She was the complete antithesis of classiness—a frumpy woman who had been the pride of Perrinsville High School decades ago. Anticipating hostility, Kristin snatched her glasses to shield herself from the imminent altercation. Without batting an eye, Mizz Tater flashed a sheet of paper in her boss's face.

"You must really have it in for me!"

"I don't know what you mean," Kristin responded innocently. Glancing at the document, she noticed it was her email about the meeting agenda.

"First, you steal my job—"

Kristin stood her ground by cutting her foe off at the knees. "How could I steal your job? I never heard of you until this morning."

"Your job is supposed to be *mine!* Now I have to suffer further embarrassment by playing lunch maid!" She tossed the paper, in contempt, at the PhD's feet.

The blatant lack of respect directed at Kristin reminded her of all the schoolyard bullies she'd dealt with throughout her lifetime. Aloofness always worked to her advantage when handling such audacious individuals. Kristin had also worked hard to get to where she was today, making personal sacrifices along the way, and she felt every bit entitled to the office she held, despite the obvious objection. But in contrast to the irate teacher, the principal would not tolerate any kind of insubordination. She turned back to the mirror to repin her hair.

"My decision is final, and unless you have *business* to conduct in here, I'd like you to leave."

Alma winced. "I've got my eyes on you."

"And I'm watching you too," Kristin fired back calmly, as her declared nemesis retreated out the door in a hissy fit.

* * *

Janet Goode struggled to carry the heavy oak-stained podium onto the stage of the empty auditorium. Her predicament was witnessed by Fred Pace, the school's six-foot, golden-blond gym teacher, who was first to arrive for the assembly.

"Let me help you with that," he shouted on his way to the stage from the seating area.

The secretary froze in place upon recognition of his booming voice. As the town's former all-star sprinted up the side steps of the stage in his red sweatshirt, with PERRINSVILLE embroidered across the chest in white letters, and matching shorts, his irresistible smile and raw machismo overpowered her.

"I got it," Fred said, lifting the boxy rectangular stand with ease.

"Coming to my rescue?" she flirted.

"Just being helpful," he replied indifferently, as he set the podium down center stage, in front of two rows of folding chairs reserved for the faculty. He then plugged the cord for the attached microphone into the floor outlet next to the stand. As he fiddled with the mic to test it by blowing into the wind screen, the secretary examined his darkened tan still fresh from summer vacation.

"You wear summer very well, and oh, by the way, that's my favorite time of year."

"Mine too," he agreed rather coldly, paying no attention to her.

Before Fred could say *testing one, two, three*, Kristin entered the venue, cradling a vinyl folder in her left arm and leading the first group of incoming parents and students to the vast array of empty seats.

"Who is that?" he mumbled out of the side of his mouth.

Janet frowned. "Didn't you meet her this morning?"

"Obviously not!" he snapped. "I wouldn't have asked if I did. Quick—who is she?"

"Dr. Sharp, our new principal."

"Oh yes. I heard she was looking for me, but we didn't connect."

His fixated attention toward the figure of authority was a bit much for Janet. "She's not for you, Freddie."

"How do you know?"

"She's the quiet, shy type."

"My specialty," he bragged.

"I've known you for a long time, and I've seen a lot of ladies in your life come and go. What you need is an extrovert who can complement your robustness."

He steered away from Kristin for a second to jeer at Janet's plainness. "And that would be *who?*"

"Well, *me* of course," she blurted in the heat of the moment.

"Why don't you take your bubbly personality to the cleanup man? He needs someone his own age to go play with after school."

The condescending implication that she couldn't do better than Henry only added insult to injury to Janet's ruffled feathers. Ready to give him a piece of her mind, she was suddenly thwarted by the principal.

"Janet," Kristin called out, coming up the set of steps to the stage. "Can you round up the staff? We're going to begin promptly in ten minutes."

"Oh, okay. I'll go make the announcement on the PA."

"Great."

Janet scowled at the object of her affection. "I'm not done with you."

"You are for now—see ya."

He waved a fond farewell to Goody Two-shoes, without a shred of remorse over the pain he'd just inflicted on her. Seizing the opportunity to make a lasting impression on the new boss, he thought of a diversion to get her attention at the podium. When she opened the folder to review her notes, he immediately obstructed her vision.

All she could see was a bronzed hand lowering the microphone to accommodate her height.

"How's that?" Fred asked.

"That's perfect." She lifted her chin to the gym teacher towering over her with a gleaming smile showing pearly white teeth. "You're perfect!" she voiced unexpectedly on a hot mic for the entire auditorium to hear. Giggles spread throughout the audience faster than a flu bug. The public admission of her immediate attraction to the handsome jock reduced her to a mousy schoolgirl wanting to crouch behind the podium. Noticing her mortification, Fred quickly turned off the microphone.

"Sorry about that," he apologized. "My thumb must've tripped it during the adjustment."

"Did I just say what I think I did?" she whispered.

"That I'm perfect?" he gloated. "Yes, you did."

"I'm so sorry…it was very unprofessional of me…I'm completely embarrassed."

"What for? I liked it."

"But I don't even know you."

He offered his hand, "Fred Pace—phys ed teacher."

"Dr. Kristin Sharp—principal," she replied, shaking his hand firmly.

"That's quite a handshake for such a soft hand."

"I was taught that a firm handshake is a sign of assuredness."

"Then are you *sure* about our meeting now, since we missed each other this morning?"

She looked at him starry-eyed. "I'm sure we won't miss each other again."

"I heard that you're new in town."

"I am."

"I'd be glad to give you a guided tour of Perrinsville."

"I'd like that."

"Tomorrow night good?"

She nodded giddily. "Sure."

Unable to take their eyes off each other, they became oblivious to the action around them: teachers and staff taking their seats, parents and kids packing the auditorium, and a dejected Henry standing in the shadows of the stage wing wearing his custodial uniform—watching his new love fall prey to someone he knew was a wolf in cotton sweats.

"Attention!" Janet broadcast over the loudspeaker. "All faculty and nonfaculty staff, please report to the auditorium immediately. The Parent-Teacher Meet and Greet begins in two minutes!"

Chapter 4

As the Parent-Teacher welcome speech wound down in the auditorium, Kristin placed another checkmark by the agenda item previously discussed with a red felt-tip marker. The "Early Drama and Forensics Curriculums" topic was complete, leaving one unchecked header, "Quiet Time."

"Lastly, before I dismiss the faculty," she glanced over her shoulder to the occupied rows behind her, "to their classrooms for the Parent-Teacher Meet and Greet with the students, I'd like to wrap up with my new cafeteria policy, appropriately called 'Quiet Time.' What exactly is that? Well, it's a policy to make sure kids have ample time to finish eating. Many students today are not eating and just throwing food away because they're so busy chitchatting for the entire period. And I understand—I was a child too. Therefore, to ensure they consume all their lunch, two teachers will be monitoring the cafeteria, each wearing whistles around their necks. For the first fifteen minutes, children will be allowed to socialize as normal. At the fifteen-minute mark, the monitors will blow their whistles to start"—she air quoted—"'Quite Time.' No talking will be allowed. The students will use this time to finish eating their lunches.

"I've assigned the monitoring duties to our computer lab teacher, Mr. Maloney," she motioned for him to stand, "and fifth grade teacher, Mizz Tater." She pivoted to confirm both teachers' stance before turning back to the microphone. The assigned monitors gave a brief wave to the audience.

Still reeling from Alma's shocking confrontation in the ladies' room, Kristin couldn't resist the temptation to inject a lighthearted joke at her adversary's expense. "And just so you know boys and girls, I chose Mizz Tater, in particular, because I heard she's *one tough cookie.*" Her attempt at double-sided humor fell flat with the parents like a sad trombone—*wah wah waahh*—but many of the kids laughed anyway, as the gag was geared to their level.

"Now if anyone is caught talking during Quiet Time or exhibits any acts of delinquency, such as throwing food, they will be sent to"—Dr. Sharp air quoted again—"'the wall' by a monitor. What's the wall? It's the inside wall of the lunchroom by the doorway. They will stand there until the lunch period is over and help the custodian clean the cafeteria while the rest of the student body is enjoying their midday recess."

Kristin turned to the staff row to look for Henry and noticed that his seat, at the left end of the back row, was vacant. Perturbed by his absence, she clutched the sides of the podium's desktop and leaned toward the microphone. "And speaking of our custodian...*Henry?*" She scoped the auditorium—no sign of him anywhere. "Has anyone seen Henry?" she openly asked bewildered.

All of a sudden, the kids erupted with cheering laughter! Henry entered from stage left as a sad-clown-faced mime. Strapping a wireless microphone headset and transmitter for sound effects, to his uniform, he hobbled into a comedy act mimicking Kristin's new lunchroom policy. He started out by seating himself at an invisible table, pretending to yuck it up with imaginary friends. His comical grimaces and smooth hand gestures ignited the kind of hysterics reminiscent of an old-time Saturday matinee featuring silent-movie shorts but with the addition of his personal sounds, à la Jonathan

Winters—everything from food crunching to beverage chugging and the Quiet Time whistle.

He then satirized Mizz Tater on future patrol, exaggerating her movements to resemble a robot with a stern face to boot. It wasn't hard for everyone present to figure out the butt of his joke, including Alma herself, sitting in a huff, beet red. As the pantomimed antics progressed, it was evident to Kristin that the only attendees amused were ages ten and under. The adult guests sat like bumps on a log, as did the faculty. Their boredom screamed, *He's at it again. When's this torture going to be over?* Even though it wasn't in the script and completely juvenile, the validity of his prank managed to get a few involuntary giggles out of Kristin here and there.

By the time Henry got to "the wall" part of the sketch, in true mime fashion, he simulated floor sweeping and scaling a glass wall. Finding a few smudges on the window plates, he pulled out a fictitious rag to clean them. He imitated a rubbing noise as he wiped in circular motions. Thinking he was all done, Henry did a quick double take and discovered a smear he'd missed—way up high in the corner. He stretched his right arm but could not reach the spot. He jumped and reached, jumped and reached again, and again. On his final try, the stress on the seam of his sleeve tore off to his synced effect of a material slash. Kids roared with laughter, as Henry comically reacted to the awkwardness of his torn sleeve. In his attempt to mend the bad sleeve, he ripped his good sleeve in the crossover. Once again, he created the audible illusion of a tear on impact—the shrieks grew louder!

With severed sleeves hanging by his wrists, the out-of-uniform janitor realized his make-believe rag was missing. Conducting a search for it, he slipped and fell on a pretend banana peel—*whoopsie-daisy*—he landed flat on his rump. Thud! By now, the schoolkids were ready to roll on the floor—with grown-ups ready to give Henry the hook. Sensing the discomfort of her staff, Kristin fought to hold back her own childish *tee-hees*.

For the grand finale, Henry ended his impromptu skit by standing up, rubbing his sore backend, then bent over to pick up the "rag" on the floor. Right on cue, he split the seam of his pants to the most embellished laceration sound imaginable. Rapidly covering the seat of his trousers, he smiled at the audience like a blushing buffoon and skedaddled off stage—receiving a thunderous applause from the entire student body.

Torn between distress and admiration, Kristin wrestled with her mixed emotions. Put off by the destruction of the uniform and the mockery of her new rule, a part of her wanted to fire him for the outrageous stunt. Yet, she found herself, once again, envying his unique bond with the schoolchildren—a special connection she spent a lifetime trying to achieve. All the course work and seminar training she'd completed over the years had failed to prepare her for the kind of relationship with kids that came naturally to *him*.

During the mass departure from the auditorium, Kristin overheard a conversation between Alma and another teacher. By the tone of their exchange, it was apparent to her that both ladies exhibited a contemptuous attitude about their students' beloved caretaker. She stalled the collection of her meeting notes in order to tune in to their disturbing comments.

Alma smirked. "Another clown show by the town jester."

"Last year it was sleight-of-hand magic…the year before, rubber ball juggling," the other teacher added.

"Remember that monologue he gave on pop culture trivia?"

"Where he pretended to be a game show host?"

"Yeah, I thought that was a royal joke. Every year he succeeds in topping himself."

"I know. He's a living comic book and a walking encyclopedia of useless information."

"I'm just waiting for the school to be slapped with a lawsuit because of Henry Hubbard."

"Won't happen, Alma. As much as we hate him, the kids love him—that's the only thing saving him from being swept out with the rest of the trash."

Kristin's jaw hit the floor. The maliciousness behind those remarks were more than she could stomach. She knew just how misguided people were in their perception of someone a little different like Henry. Kristin recalled the jealousy from her fellow cheerleaders who couldn't duplicate her rubbery moves—*Showoff!* She also heard the echoes of her college roommate, alienated because Kristin pulled high grades while she struggled—*Quit being so smart! Know-it-all!*

Remnants from Kristin's past began to subconsciously attract her to Henry. On a more conscious level, her preoccupation with appearances prevented her from getting too personal with the eccentric maintenance engineer. She had an image to project, one of status and authority that had taken her years to procure—a quirky janitor would turn her into a laughingstock.

Standing alone at the podium in the now empty auditorium, she hastily took out her cell phone and composed two messages:

Henry—Please stop by my office in the morning.

Hi Fred—I'm looking forward to tomorrow evening :)

* * *

The next morning, Kristin reported to school bright and early before anyone else arrived. Dressed in a solid white pantsuit and sporting a decorative butterfly brooch on her left lapel, she set her travel mug of hot coffee on the credenza before tucking her briefcase and purse on the floor underneath the wooden desk. Dr. Sharp wasted no time in gathering all the student records from the lateral file cabinets in the reception area, stacking them neatly on her desk in multiple piles. Given the limited space on her desk, the folders were piled so high that when she sat down, she was up to her eyeballs with work.

By the time school started, she had barely made a dent in the mountains of manila concealing the cherry surface of her desk. It wasn't long afterward that she heard the familiar tingle of keys outside her door and the voice attached to them.

"Mornin' Miss Goody Two-shoes," Henry greeted.

"Good morning," Janet replied. "That was quite a performance last night."

The janitor beamed with delight. "You know me, I'm a laugh a minute…at least to the little rascals."

"And some of us squirrely adults too. We're not all sticks in the mud—"

"Like Tater Tots," he interjected.

"Oh, you should've seen the look on her face when you split your pants."

"Could you see the steam coming out of her ears?"

"And from under her collar as well," Janet laughed.

"She needs to *rent* a sense of humor," he joked before getting to the point of his visit. "Is the boss in? I got a message that she wanted to see me…probably about last night."

"I hope you're not in trouble."

"Hope not either."

"Although, I did notice her chuckling a little bit."

His eyes widened.

"Just a little," she added.

"I'm sure it caught her by surprise."

"Well, you won't know standing here talking to me; her door's open—go in."

"See ya later."

Henry's slouched physique froze at the entrance to Dr. Sharp's professional domain. His heart was warmed by the ray of light streaming through the window, engendering a halo effect over an intricately braided updo worthy of being on the cover of a bridal magazine. Looking past the heavy frames resting comfortably on the tip of her delicate nose, he saw the beauty of her eyes as she focused on the papers in her manicured hands. He knew the image she projected to most was that of a dedicated working woman, but to Henry she resembled his idea of a heavenly angel. He reverently knocked on the solid wood door to get her attention.

Kristin raised her head. "Good morning."

"Hey, Sharpie, you wanted to see me?"

"Yes, please sit down," she instructed him while pushing her thick frames back up to the bridge of her nose with her index finger. She closed her open folder and set it aside on her desk pad, as the meekly whiskered king of plaid flannel occupied an empty chair like a delinquent sent to see the principal for discipline.

"Looks like you're drowning in a year's worth of work," Henry said.

"I'm just reviewing each of the student files to acquaint myself with them."

"There's an easier way to do that. Just talk to them. They're good kids; they'll tell you whatever you wanna know."

She glared at him slightly miffed. "That's not what I mean. I'm assessing all their academic strengths and weaknesses—"

"They'll tell you that too," he interrupted. "They're not ashamed to say if they like reading and hate math, or vice versa—"

"You're not understanding," she interposed condescendingly. "I'm cross-checking the school board's reports against the actual student files—get it?"

"Sounds like a migraine headache to me."

"I don't see it that way."

"If you don't mind my saying so, I think you do many things the hard way."

"I'm very detail driven, and I take my work quite seriously."

"No offense to you, but somehow I think this goes beyond your work. I think you take everything a little *too* seriously. You might want to loosen up a little."

Kristin folded her arms to rock back in her chair. "Like the way you loosened out of your uniform last night? Which by the way, is why I wanted to see you."

"I had a feeling that was the reason for this summons."

"I suppose that was a clever way to get out of wearing your uniform?"

"One stitch at a time."

"So, your gag in destroying a school-bought-and-paid-for uniform, not to mention making a mockery of my Quiet Time policy, was worth making a public spectacle of yourself?"

"Hey, I could've gone into full Soupy Sales shtick and capped it off with a pie in the face, but then the real janitor would have to clean up the mess."

"Soupy what?"

"Not 'what'—who. Soupy Sales was only TV's greatest comic genius, whose brand of humor was aimed at kids; but adults also laughed at him."

"Never heard of him...must've been before my time."

"More like our grandparents' time. Good humor is ageless."

"Well, as upset as I am about the uniform, I saw how engaging your act was with the students, so I can't fault you for that."

"I told you how I felt about uniforms—that's not who I am."

"Fine, your point is taken. You can stay as you are."

Henry clapped his hands in victory. Kristin leaned inward to ask the question that was really at the core of her irked curiosity—the deplorable statements she'd overheard between Alma Tater and the other teacher.

"Why did you disrupt my presentation?"

"Every year, Parent-Teacher night is always the same boring mumbo jumbo that kids have to suffer through."

"My speech was not boring; it was informative."

"With all due respect, Sharpie, your speech was the same as all of Captain Hook's snooze fests. There's no reason the kids should have to sit through what seems like an eternity because the school has never made other arrangements for them. I know it's purposeful for the parents, but I heard enough complaints from the kids, many years back, about how they dread sitting through the principal's speech. So one year, I decided to jazz it up at a random moment with an unplanned sideshow for them."

"You should've heard some of the comments I listened to afterward."

"I'm sure I know who screamed the loudest. I know the teachers and most of the parents hate it, but I'm immune to their insults and innuendos because the joy it brings to the children is worth every bit of embarrassment to me."

"Well…when you explain it that way, I think you did an outstanding job. I have to admit it was pretty funny."

He bowed like a master showman.

"But why did you mock my lunchroom policy? You couldn't have known about that in advance."

"True. I was gonna to do something else, but your QT rule made a better segue."

"You thought it up that fast?"

"Kinda sorta."

She shot him a blank stare.

"I just made it up as I went along," he continued. "Sorry if I rained on your parade."

"You did."

"Try not to take yourself so seriously. It's okay to laugh at yourself sometimes."

Before the principal could respond, her desk phone rang. Taking a quick glance at the caller ID, her eyes sparkled when the name *Pace, Fred* flashed across the screen. Her overanxious reaction extinguished the fire in Henry's belly.

"Excuse me," she told him, while trying to compose herself to answer the phone professionally. She cleared her throat and picked up the receiver in a calm, well-rehearsed manner. "Dr. Sharp speaking…" The boom of the phys ed teacher's manly voice caused her to melt like butter, making it obvious to the janitor that he was toast.

"I've been thinking about you too"—she carried on in a girlish tone—"I can't wait till tonight…I braided my hair for you…"

The revelation about her hair delivered a devastating blow to Henry. He couldn't fathom why she exerted so much time and energy to prepare an elegant hairstyle for Fred—the biggest flirt in town and a lifelong antagonist who had demeaned him since childhood.

The sight of Henry, still in her office, looking like a bump on a log, eavesdropping, compelled Kristin to politely shoo him away. He dragged his sunken heart out the door.

* * *

Determined to stop his crush from getting flattened like a mat on a gym floor by Perrinsville's most notorious PE instructor, Henry spent the rest of his workday figuring out a strategy to use on Kristin. He was near the front of the school when the perfect solution suddenly popped into his head. While pushing a trash barrel down the enclosed glass corridor, with the parking lot in plain view, he noticed the close proximity of her car and his van. Knowing it wouldn't be difficult to stop his clunker from starting—*the old potato-in-the-exhaust pipe bit*—he gambled on her mechanical naivete to trick her into believing his vehicle couldn't start—ingenious!

Shortly after the kids vacated the school, Henry sat in his van, patiently waiting for Kristin to leave the building. He knew she wouldn't stay long because of her date with Fred. His only fear was they might exit the building together, causing his plan to backfire. Nevertheless, he knew how much of an egotist Fred was when it came to impressing the ladies. He would be the first one out of the gate to get home and change from his gym sweats to his *working* threads—especially when trying to impress a high-class woman like Dr. Sharp.

Without skipping a beat, Fred flew to his red sports coup like a bat out of hell. He sped off, leaving everyone else at the parking lot in the dust. Another half hour went by, and still no sign of the principal. Henry started to feel plagued by a nervous anxiety that only grew with the passing of every minute. Looking in his side-view mirror, he spotted her white pantsuit approaching the lot. Time to put the plan into action. He started to crank the motor that he *knew* wouldn't turn over. Again and again, he tried to no avail. Kristin couldn't help but notice his quandary. Just as their paths were about to cross, he popped the hood release and leaped out of his eyesore on wheels.

Raising the hood, he staged an engine exam. "Ah-huh…just what I figured," he diagnosed aloud, stopping Kristin in her tracks.

"Having trouble?" she asked courteously.

"Oh, this bucket of bolts has seen better days. I think it's time to replace the starter. I can only nurse it along so many times."

"Are you going to call a tow truck?"

"No, I can fix it. I just need my tools at home."

"Don't you have tools here?"

"Yeah, but not my socket set—that's at home."

"Oh…"

"I really hate to ask, but would you mind driving me home to get my tools and bringing me back here?"

Kristin shuddered. "You want me to what?"

"Drive me home and back?"

"Well, I have plans and don't have much time."

"I don't live that far and won't take up much of your time." He held up two fingers on his right hand. "Scout's honor…please?"

"All right," she exhaled, "let's go."

Chapter 5

Upon arrival at the Hubbard dwelling, Henry persuaded Kristin to come inside while he retrieved his socket tools. Entering the caretaker's disheveled bachelor pad, the principal was overwhelmed by the number of oddities belonging to her kooky subordinate—starting with the hand-me-down furniture. Everything—from the couch to the coffee table and the lamps—appeared to be from a generation long ago; not to mention the tattered condition of the furnishings. Multiple strips of the same silver duct tape used to conceal the torn upholstery in his van were mending the worn-out fabric of his sitting pieces as well as the flattened faded carpet.

If the chaotic state of the house and its fittings didn't clash enough with her refined habitat, the décor proved to be even more disconcerting to her. Nostalgic superhero-movie, TV, and music memorabilia was everywhere—walls and all. And smack dab in the middle of his foundation wall was a conspicuous display showcasing his extensive arsenal of vintage toys—the home's only items in mint condition. In many ways it was like a twilight-zone experience for her, the unexplainable cross between reality and fantasy. Only it wasn't hers—it was *his!*

Before she could catch a breath to mentally process Henry's life-size time capsule, the opening act of his home entertainment called on the landline—*ring, ring.*

"Excuse me while I get that," he said.

"Sure."

He picked up the receiver belonging to his archaic push-button telephone on the rickety end table by his couch. "Hello?"

"Hi, I'm Kevin from the Dude on the Roof—" the voice on the other end said loud enough for Kristin to hear.

"I'll bet he's on top of things," Henry bantered.

A tiny grin fractured her stone face.

The solicitor continued his script. "Dude on the Roof is a reputable—"

"Then you won't catch him lying in the gutter," Henry zinged again.

"Of course not, he's—"

"Married or shingle?"

Click—the caller hung up abruptly.

Kristin covered her twitching mouth to block a fleeing giggle. Her passive gesture didn't go unnoticed.

"So much for tonight's phone funnies," Henry joked.

"There's a way you can get rid of those annoying calls."

"Why would I wanna do that?" he questioned in a nanosecond of seriousness.

"You mean, you *want* these annoying calls?"

His lips curved into a smile.

She pushed up her sliding glasses. "*Why?*"

"It's my nightly entertainment."

"It is?"

"Oh yeah, I look forward to 'em."

"For what possible reason?"

"They're like a game to me."

"How?"

"I never know who it's gonna be or what I'm gonna say, so it's a real challenge for me to see how fast I can make them hang up on me."

"Isn't that rude?"

"Ah, yeah...but I don't care."

"Why don't you politely tell them you're not interested in what they're selling?"

"That never works."

"Try it sometime."

"You know, I could also hang up, but that never stops them from calling again to wear me down."

"Regardless, I believe in the diplomatic approach."

"Then I guess it's my turn to ask, *why?*"

"Those calls are recorded, and you never want your off-color moments to become a headline."

"Funny you should mention that...guess who called last week?"

"A newspaper?"

"Yep! After the lady ran through her whole pushy sales spiel, I told her, 'Sorry...I'm illiterate; I can't read.'"

"*Henry!*"

"Well..."

"I do have to say, that *is* pretty clever. I doubt they'll ever call you again."

"And that's the whole idea...to get them to quit wasting my time by frustrating them and wasting their time. Someday, you'll appreciate the method to my madness."

Kristin walked toward his vast toy collection with an unguarded curiosity. "Where did you get all these?"

"Oh...," he said, joining her at the display, "most of them were from my childhood. I couldn't stand to part with them, just like everything else in this house. The ones in the boxes I bought at toy conventions—my favorite place to shop. Some of the others, that obviously don't fit my personality and gender, were unclaimed toys I found around school and other public places over the years; so I just fixed and cleaned them. They make nice gifts for the less fortunate kids."

"I'm amazed," she whispered joyfully.

"I take great pride in giving toys to kids, and my collection goes beyond this room. These are just the ones in the best shape. I have about every kind of toy imaginable between here and my shop at school."

"You do?"

"Yep, my purpose is to accommodate any request. If someone says, 'Hey, do you have this?' I can say, 'Yeah, I do.'"

She turned to look him in the eye. "Can I ask you a sincere question?"

He shrugged as if to say, *Can I stop you?*

"Why do you do what you do?"

"What do you mean?"

"What compels you to be into kiddie things?"

"Because, deep down, all grown-ups secretly want to relive their childhoods. We all wanna be kids again."

"I think you're confusing fantasy with reality," she asserted like a paid-by-the-hour shrink.

"I'm not the one who's confused. Their fantasy *is* my reality. *You* should try it sometime; it keeps you young."

"I don't want to relive my childhood. I'm proud of my accomplishments, which wouldn't have happened if I lived in the past."

"I'm not living in the past either."

"Who are you kidding?" She pointed to many numerous mementos around his living room. "Your house is like a shrine paying homage to your childhood."

"There's a simple explanation: when I was a kid, my parents were too busy to pay attention to their only child—*moi*. I spent much of my time alone and was forced to entertain myself. So, rather than cry about it, I chose laughter and dazzling entertainment to keep me company. I found strength in superheroes, hence all the memorabilia. I listened to music when the TV was off, and the best friends I had in the whole world were my toys. That's why I refuse to part with them."

"What about the furniture?"

"This is the house where I grew up, and the furniture belonged to my parents and my grandparents before them. When my parents passed away unexpectedly after my high school graduation, this is all I had left to remember them by. I know it's all very old and looks like junk to most people, but to throw it away is like throwing my parents away."

"I think you're taking that to an extreme."

"Yeah, extreme comfort. Please have a seat on the couch."

"I really don't have much time."

"Just for a second," he pleaded.

"Okay." She took a seat on the end of the sofa daintily.

"*Really, Sharpie?* Sit back and relax."

She scooched back.   Much to her surprise, it was incredibly comfortable! "Oh, my…how's this possible? I thought I was going to fall into a sinkhole."

Henry sat himself on the armrest at the other end of the couch. "The upholstery and cushions are the originals, and I can't find those patterns anywhere, so they'll just have to be—duct tape and all. But I was able to redesign and replace all the springs and internal parts to improve the comfort. I did the same with the chairs and the seats in my van."

"Speaking of which, shouldn't we get going?" She stood up. "I've been here a lot longer than anticipated."

"What's the rush?" he asked, knowing full well why she was pressed for time.

"I have plans."

"What type of plans?"

"I don't think that's any of your concern."

"Is it a date?"

"You don't need to know."

"I know you don't know anyone in town, so why don't you let me show you around this evening?"

"I can't do that."

"Can't or won't?"

"I have a reputation to maintain. It won't look good for the principal to be out painting the town with the—"

"*Janitor!*"

"I have a standard when it comes to men, and I'm sorry, but I'm not willing to compromise."

"You think I'm not in your league?"

"I think you're very nice, but I date *men*, not *boys*," she stated rather matter-of-factly.

Henry lowered his head like a scolded child.

"I'm sorry if I hurt your feelings. Just because I'm not interested in you romantically doesn't mean we can't be friends. I think you're incredible…just not for me."

He rubbed his runny nose. "We're connected, Sharpie. I understand you more than you realize."

"That's why we'll be great friends."

"The let's-be-friends speech is never what a guy wants to hear."

"Have you ever thought about Janet?"

"Goody Two-shoes?"

"Yes, she's single."

"You have no idea?"

"About what?"

"She's been pining over Fred Pace like forever…"

Kristin's bifocals nearly shattered.

"…and everyone in town knows it."

"They do?"

"Yeah…and he doesn't give her the sweat off his back."

Growing increasingly uncomfortable, Kristin decided to end the conversation. "Please get your tools, so we can go. I don't want to be late."

"For Fast Freddie?"

She turned away from him.

"I have a confession to make."

She glanced back at him, chewing on her lip.

"I knew you were going out with Freddie tonight."

"You did?" She folded her arms. "How?"

"I saw your reaction to him last night in the auditorium. Just like everyone else, I heard you call him *perfect*."

"I was caught off guard."

"I can assure you, he wasn't. Fast Freddie is always on the move because he never lets a pretty face go unnoticed."

She was peculiarly flattered by his complimentary dig but refused to yield to his warning.

"He'll be all paws trying to hook his claws into you before saying goodnight," Henry added.

"I'm not that kind of a girl—I'm a lady."

"Well, he's that kind of a guy. He's got quite a rep for playing cat and mouse, except he's a hungry lion, and you'll be the cheese standing alone, if you get my drift."

"If that's true, I know how to handle guys like him."

"Do you?" he objected. "Wanna know why he ignores Janet? Because she's not vain enough for him. He targets women he *thinks* are insecure, so he can be their prince in shining armor."

"It's knight in shining armor."

"That again? Whatever—same thing."

"What's your point?"

"Brief backstory: Freddie *used to be* the big man on campus—a real Doug Simpson, if you're familiar with that famous episode of the *Brady Bunch*."

"Marcia's *'ow, my nose'*…yes, I lived it yesterday. Where's this going?"

"Well, *something suddenly came up* and sacked his chances at pro football in college due to a broken shoulder. Since he can't play any other sports—he's damaged goods—the only game plan Freddie has left in his playbook, besides vulnerable women, is a suntan. He's been out of commission so long that his coarse hands morphed into the softness of a baby's behind. He also *used to be* the coach at the high school—can you guess why he's no longer there?"

Kristin's ears heard enough of Henry's Fred bashing tangent. "I don't want to know, Henry. I will not listen to gossip for a very good reason—I *know* what it's like to *be* the subject of gossip."

"I know that feeling too—you heard it yourself last night."

"Then I don't have to explain to you why I dismiss it. I reserve judgment until I can draw my own conclusion."

"And my conclusion is to spare you from an awful lot of grief that comes with *him*."

The principal made the executive decision to put an end to their tit-for-tat exchange. Her eyes projected the optics of insecurity and frustration straight through the lenses of her thick glasses. "I don't want to be rude to you in your home, but my love interests are really none of your business."

Fearing another possibility of alienation, Henry conceded defeat. He understood the battle was lost, but he was determined to win the war. "I'll go get my toolbox. Please wait here."

She agreed as he exited through the kitchen to the attached garage. Agitated, Kristin began to pace by the front door. After a few minutes, or what seemed like an eternity in her mind, he returned with his socket kit in one hand and his other hand behind his back.

"I'm sorry if I upset you. Will you accept a peace offering?"

She shrugged nervously, concerned about what might be up his sleeve.

"This is for you." He whipped out an old rubber cheerleader doll—the very same one she told him she always wanted as a kid but could play with only at school.

"Oh my!" she cried, placing her hands on her cheeks in a prism of conflicted jubilation. "How did you get this?"

He placed it in her hands. "I'll never tell; it's my secret. Do you like it?"

"Of course, I do—I love it!" she exclaimed tearfully. "Come here." She embraced him with loving gratitude.

"Shall we go?"

"Uh-huh." She nodded before removing her black spectacles to dry her watery eyes. The full beauty behind her eyes was revealed to Henry, in validation of his unique ability to pry open the oyster-shell casing of her bright pearl. As much as her date with Fred hurt him, he couldn't risk losing her by being too critical of the has-been sportsman. He needed to trust her. His faith in their special bond reflected the timeless cliché about all good things coming to those who wait.

Stepping outside into the warm afternoon sun, Kristin got an eyeful of the weeds and wild bushes in the front yard that went undetected by her preoccupation on their way in the house. "Do you have any gardening tools?"

"Just a lawn mower, why?"

"You've got a lot of weeds, and your shrubs look like they're having a bad hair day."

He grinned. "Hey, good one about the bushes."

"The weeds will kill your lawn. Have you thought about pulling them?"

"Heck, no."

"Don't you do that at school?"

"Nope. A landscaping service hired by the school board does that. Besides, who *likes* to pull weeds?"

"I do," she replied humbly.

"Really? Why?"

"I find it therapeutic."

"Well, that's one way of getting to the root of your problems."

She broke up in laughter, as they headed toward her car parked along the curb.

* * *

Kristin stepped into the immaculate kitchen of her newly purchased home tucked behind a colorful country scene of tall maple trees, just a few miles away from downtown Perrinsville. She prepared a fresh brew of gourmet coffee like a trained barista and poured it into her *Teacher of the Year* ceramic mug. She needed the extra perk to help shed the degree of aloofness that earned her a doctorate in loneliness with men. Noticing a few drops of java spilled onto the hardwood floor, the obsessive-compulsive side of her reached for a paper towel to quickly wipe up the mess before it stained the urethane finish.

After venturing to her harmonious bedroom, Kristin set the cheerleader doll against the mirror on top of her neatly organized makeup table. Proceeding to the closet, she opened the louvered bifold doors to inspect the options of attire for her date with Fred. Desperately wanting to ditch the uptight image she'd personified since adolescence, Kristin selected a few skirts and dresses that had never been worn and tossed them on the bed's fine-thread comforter.

After kicking off her heels and removing her suit jacket, she gazed at the legless garments, contemplating whether or not to wear one of them. In doing so, she thought back to her teenage years when kids teased her about her thin legs. One memory, in particular, came to the forefront in her mind. Kristin recounted a day when she stood on a street corner waiting for the traffic light to change, with a backpack, a denim skirt, an oversize jacket, and her signature glasses. Three athletic boys, at the opposite corner, started mocking her. She couldn't hear what they were saying but was humiliated by their bird flapping arm gestures. It was *that* kind of teasing that added to the building of a fortress around her heart—one brick at a time.

As Kristin held the dresses against her clothed figure in front of the full-length mirror, she reflected back on her love life—post PhD—how she had struggled in healing the haunting wounds from her *nerdy girl* years. She'd tried to present herself as a sophisticated woman early in her career, a woman she thought would be desirable to all men, particularly the alpha types who had taunted her. She miscalculated her assumptions of them miserably. The brawny dudes who always caught her eye only wanted to play the kind of games without rules and boundaries. She'd called foul on them one too many times, and she became known as *Strikeout Sharp* among the school district's male population.

Kristin tossed the dresses back on her bed. Taking a seat in front of the mirror at her makeup table, she evaluated her intricate updo and horn-rimmed glasses. Removing the specs from her face, she set them aside and took a hard look in the mirror before unpinning the braided tails crowning her head. She then opened the top drawer of her table to pull out a small plastic case with unused contact lenses. Glancing at her cocooned reflection, she wondered if tonight was the right time to break the shell around her and set a beautiful butterfly free.

With "forty" looming around the corner, her dream of marriage and starting a family, while balancing a successful career in education, had not come to fruition. The idea of it reminded her of her preschool commencement ceremony—little kids all dressed up in caps and gowns proceeding to the stage during a recording of "Pomp and Circumstance." Upon receipt of their diplomas, each child was asked what they wanted to be when they grew up. They spoke into a microphone held by the principal for the parents in the audience to hear. Many of the kids said they wanted to be doctors, nurses, police officers, firefighters, teachers, or the occupations of their parents. When it came time for a tiny, shy, honey-blond girl named Krissy Sharp to answer the question, she replied, "A mommy."

That early remembrance, permanently etched in her brain, drew Kristin's attention to the rubber cheerleader doll standing at the base of the mirror. She picked it up to bend its limbs in imaginary backflips across the tabletop. The pleasure derived from playing with the toy was satisfying. Much of that fulfillment stemmed from the selfless manner in which it was given to her. She had told Henry about it only yesterday, and today she had it! Kristin had to admit that only *he* truly understood its value to her—not because she'd always wanted it but because she *related* to it. The doll symbolized the happiest period in her life. A time before the ugliness of her peers altered the course of her destiny.

Kristin had never encountered a person like Henry Hubbard before—so simple, yet intriguing and endearing. He appealed to the hidden kid in her by doing thoughtful things for her, in the spirit of a child. Even his off-the-cuff whimsicality was worthy of relationship consideration. As hard as she'd tried to socially connect with men—and she did try, really hard—none of them ever took a second to understand her—until now.

Her only dilemma was that Henry didn't fit her mold the way Fred did. She'd have to do a lot of chiseling to get her perfect sculpture. He was a fixer-upper project that may never become the manly work of art she saw in Fred. Even though Henry had touched her heart this afternoon, he lacked the maturity and social status she desired in a romantic partner. The scenario was too mortifying for her to bear—she had basically told him so this afternoon.

Peeking at the hands on her watch, she panicked—*Fred will be here in five minutes!* Back to reality, she swiftly pinned her hair back up, grabbed her glasses, and scooped up the skirts and dresses to throw back into the closet. Rushing to the dresser, she pulled out a crisp pair of jeans from the bottom drawer and a black V-neck pullover shirt from the top drawer and changed faster than a runway model.

Chapter 6

Inside a rented one-bedroom apartment, Fred admired his pseudo masculinity in front of the bathroom mirror above his vanity. The countertop held a cluttered mess of lavish skin and hair products, along with an assorted choice of expensive colognes. He spent the bulk of his free time nurturing the illusion of his former self—an alpha male champion—to look like the ultimate gift to women. Every dollar of his income was blown on the excess of showy items: high-end fashion, priceless jewelry, and flashy cars.

Dressed in comfortable jeans and a red crew-neck sweater, with the sleeves pushed halfway up his tanned forearms, he detailed the follicles of his golden blond hair—not a single one of them out of place—with the pricey styling gel on his fingertips. And with a few quick smiles in the mirror, at varied angles looking back at himself, his illustrious facade was complete.

Stepping into the compact living room—a hall of fame unto himself—the phys ed teacher inspected the monument of his youthful glories. Not an inch of wall space was bare, as he literally framed the room with action shots of himself playing every sport conceivable. Only a massive display case stood apart from the domineering "photo-finish" gallery. From the floor to the ceiling, the exhibit showcased a hoard of medals and trophies, all bearing the name Fred Pace. The careful preservation of artifacts from his glory days of old, was all that was left of a hometown hero who struck out in the game of life, but in his mind, he was still a legend.

Moments later, he hopped into his sport coup parked in the building's resident carport. The illumination from daylight savings time provided enough brightness for him to don a pair of black shades like Joe Cool. Feeling confident and cocky about his ability to woo his new boss, he shifted the car in gear and raced off into the sunset. The directions Kristin provided to him were discarded, as there wasn't a part of town unknown to Fred. He soon pulled up her driveway right on time.

Hearing the sound of a car door slam, Kristin threw on a simple one-button blue blazer made of velvet to match her jeans and contrast with her black V-neck shirt. The butterflies in her stomach intensified until she heard the hard knock on the heavy front door from his strong hand. *Boom-boom-boom!* Her eyes glistened from the commanding bangs reverberating off the solid oak. Snatching her purse, she rushed to the door but stopped short from answering it until he knocked a second time—*boom-boom-boom!*

Kristin opened the door with a sense of control that hadn't existed a moment ago. Despite the natural anxiety inside her, she knew better than to greet her date like a skittish schoolgirl. She listened to the rationale of mind over matter and chose to answer like a consummate professional—"Good evening, Fred."

"Hey, there," his stentorian voice replied. "I love your braids; you look like a princess."

That's all she needed to hear before her professional composure turned into jelly.

"You have a tasteful house," he continued, looking above her head.

"Thanks. Let me give you the tour," she blurted before realizing the potential consequences of inviting a man she just met into the sanctity of her private domain. *Please, please, please say no,* she hoped.

"Maybe another time, *babe*."

Kristin raised her eyebrows. *He didn't try to take advantage of me AND he called me 'babe'!* Those four words brought immense comfort to her—at least for now. She wanted to think highly of him. It didn't matter that he registered a thousand degrees Fahrenheit on her internal thermostat; she needed assurance that he would be different from the others she'd previously dated. The ones who would've jumped at the invitation without wanting to leave.

"Like my ride?" he asked pointing to his coup.

She nodded joyfully.

"Let's split before we lose the light." He took her by the hand with his chest out and chin up. "I want to give you a personalized tour of Perrinsville."

* * *

Kristin had had no idea that the personalized tour really meant everything *Fred*. Fred did this here; Fred did that there. Fred scored his first touchdown on this field…he practiced basketball on that court… hit his first home run on that diamond…earned his letter from the games played here…and so on. It was enough to put her feet to sleep, especially his recital of the speed records he set in football, basketball, and track that earned him the nickname "Fast Freddie." She'd known there'd be a degree of shallowness with him, as was her experience with most jocks, but this bigheaded ham was over the top with himself.

By the time they sat down for dinner in a corner booth at Darlin' Darla's Steakhouse, one of the classier and busiest restaurants in town, Fred finally changed the topic from himself to Kristin. She was blindsided while reading the menu when he apologized for monopolizing the conversation, before blatantly asking, "So what's your story, babe?"

Kristin peered above her menu to stare him in the eye from across the table. "Why do you keep calling me 'babe'?" she fired back.

He shrugged. "You don't like it?"

"I do." She folded the menu to place it on the table and leaned toward him. "I've just never had anyone call me anything like that before."

"You're kidding?"

"No, I'm not."

"Oh, c'mon. I can't believe a babe like you hasn't had other guys in your life."

"Just my father."

Fred cocked his head. "You've never had a boyfriend?"

"I've dated a lot of guys who wanted too much too soon—so no, there's never been a man that I could say was my boyfriend."

Just then, Darla, the owner of the establishment, approached the table to give a warm welcome to Fred. She was an older woman with the inviting country hospitality of a rocking chair on a wooden porch. "Freddie...how's my favorite customer?"

He stood to give her a big old bear hug. "Just fine, darlin'."

The proprietor peered at Kristin with keen interest. "Who's *this* cup of sugar with you?"

"Oh, this is our school's new principal, Dr. Kristin Sharp," he said before sitting back down.

"Pleased to meet you," Kristin said warily.

"I thought I knew just about every girl Freddie's ever brought here," Darla broadcast.

"Ah, just how *many* has he brought here?" Kristin inquired, staring at her date's reddened ears.

"I'm sorry, honey. Did I say something I shouldn't have?" Darla responded like someone who, having set a house on fire, stands across the street to watch it burn. "We still idolize Freddie here in Perrinsville. I like to think of him as our real-life Roy Hobbs."

"Who?"

"From the movie *The Natural.* You know, the one with Robert Redford? Doesn't Freddie look like Robert Redford?"

"A little bit—yes."

"Well, I don't have to tell you that our Freddie is still *the best there ever was.* That's why the school board hired him to coach all the high school teams here."

Kristin suddenly recalled how she didn't want to hear Henry's explanation about Fred's demotion. Now was the perfect time to get it from the horse's mouth. "So, how did you go from coaching high school sports to teaching elementary gym? Isn't that a comedown for someone like you?"

Fred squirmed. "Long story—not now."

"Oh, Freddie…everybody knows about your awful breakup with Alma Tater." Darla's attempted lifeline turned into a sinker. "That woman was a jinx. She's the reason you got injured in college."

"You and Alma?" Kristin grilled Fred.

Fred waved his hand at Darla to stop burning him at the stake. "How about taking our orders?"

"Oh, sure, I'm so sorry. Hope I didn't embarrass you."

By this point, Kristin didn't know whether to stay out of courtesy or pity. Either way, the date had become more than she could swallow.

"Do you want your usual hungry man special?"

"Yeah."

"And you sweetie?"

"I'll have a small Caesar salad with very thin chicken strips, please," Kristin said softly.

"Any drinks?"

"Just water," Fred said.

"I'd like a glass of lemonade."

"Okay, y'all, they'll be coming right up." Darla smiled. "It was nice meeting you, doctor."

The PhD nodded shyly. "You too."

Before exiting, the older woman turned to Fred with a motherly warning. "You be a good boy tonight and treat this one proper—she's a keeper. I can tell." She gave him a wink.

Fred pivoted to Kristin with a gusher of sweat beads dripping from his forehead into his yellowed brows. "I hope you're not taking her seriously?"

"Just watching a mama bear protecting her cub from the spoiled pots of honey."

"Look, I hope you don't think I'm a narcissist."

"After that self-promoting tour and the paid commercial from the reputable owner of this fine establishment, why would I think anything else?"

"You're joking, right?" His confidence dwindled by the second.

"Look, in all fairness, I don't want you to put on a front to impress me. You're an incredibly handsome man who knocked my socks off at *hello*. But one of my biggest pet peeves is phoniness. I know I'm one of hundreds of women you've likely pursued, and I will not be the last. So please stop with your sales infomercial. Your script may fly with others, but it's turning me off."

"I'm hurt"—playing the victim—"Why would you say that?"

"Because I don't want to go on the same *standard* date as your others. Maybe that's why I've been single for so long. I want my dates to be unique. I want a man who's off-the-charts *different*. One I can discover connects with me on a level like no one else can. Make sense?"

"I will find a way to be *that* man," he pleaded.

"You need to start by slowing down—waaay down—not with a blitz of your glory in one night. Just be yourself."

"*I am.*"

"Then you've got some work to do."

Over the course of the meal, Kristin began to tune out Fred's empty small talk. As the sound of his voice faded into muffled garble, she inadvertently thought about Henry—the beta male personified by his lack of maturity—a big step backward by her conventional standard, and yet a perfect touchstone for her emotional emancipation. She realized that her declared qualifications pertaining to Fred were more applicable to Henry, thus creating further internal conflict for her to sort out.

At the end of the evening, Fred pulled his sleek set of wheels up Kristin's driveway. She couldn't wait for the date she'd wanted so badly to be over. The muscle-bound strong man turned out to be a titanic disappointment. His to-die-for looks and social status were the only redeeming qualities of interest to her, yet they fell way short of what her heart was churning and burning for. If she could take a few pieces of Henry and plug them into Fred, she'd be all set. But that would be an impossible task, and one she wasn't ready to wrap her brain around—at least not tonight.

A few days ago, the new girl in town had zero romantic prospects, and now she had two polar opposites, both wanting to be her man—wow! After turning one of them away earlier this afternoon, Kristin was on the cusp of doing the same to the other one, especially when she caught him shutting off his car motor. *If he's expecting to stay, guess again.*

"How 'bout that house tour you offered?" Fred reminded her.

She demurred. "Not now…maybe in another lifetime."

"What! Why?"

"It's a school night," she kidded dryly.

"Funny—I almost believed you," he chuckled naively.

She toughened her tone. "I wasn't trying to be funny."

"You're not going to invite me in?"

"Nope."

"Did I do something wrong?"

"It's time to say goodnight. Thank you for an evening I won't ever forget."

"Well, if you're not going to invite me in, then I guess I'll say goodnight." He leaned toward her with closed eyes and puckered lips—a sight very familiar to Strikeout Sharp!

She raised her hands to block his slick move. "Ah, what are you doing?"

"Giving you a kiss."

"No—you're not."

"Oh, c'mon…why don't you take off your glasses and let yourself go."

Kristin wrinkled her nose. "They're staying on. I'm not ready for this."

"You look like you caught a whiff of bad breath," he said, mistaking her facial expression. "I'll take care of that."

Fred dug into his pocket for a dissolving breath strip that he popped into his mouth with rapid precision, making it apparent that he'd practiced this drill many times before.

She deemed him utterly clueless. "It's not your breath, *coach*. I'm not going to give you a *kiss and tell* story to share with your buds about how you scored a point with the new girl in town—who happens to be your employer."

"Is that the kind of man you think I am?"

"I've been down this road too many times not to miss the signals."

"It's just a kiss. I'm not asking for anything more."

"Sure, you aren't," she remarked skeptically. "A kiss you think will progress into a smooch-a-thon."

Playing the victim again, he asked, "Is that what you think of me? I'm hurt."

"Sorry." Her face turned stone cold.

Fred noticed her right hand inching toward the door handle and thwarted her escape with a swift grab of her wrist.

"If you won't let me kiss you properly, then allow me…"

He attempted to kiss her hand. She jerked it away before his lips touched her delicate skin.

"Hey, what did you do that for?"

Kristin flexed her authoritative muscles. "As of right now, I'm not speaking to you as your date; I'm speaking as your superior. If you don't stop now and say goodnight, I'll accept your resignation on my desk tomorrow morning—are we clear?"

He slumped back in sticker shock. "You're going to fire me?"

"Not if you behave like a good little boy and play nice."

Fred was offended and, at the same time, more determined to win her affections. No one had ever rejected him like that before—at least not on the first date. It typically took three or four dates before women got his number and complained. By that point, he didn't care because he was done with them too. Yet Kristin was in a league of her own. In one night, she called out his braggadocio and resisted his temptation. He didn't know how to deal with her but sought to be the victor at the finish line. For that to happen, he needed a time-out to formulate a new game plan.

"Goodnight, then…I'm sorry if I came on so strong," he said haltingly but with sincere regret.

"Apology accepted—good night."

She exited his car and hurried to her door, as he politely waited for her to get inside safely. Waving goodbye upon opening her door, she whisked inside, shutting the door behind her. Hearing the sound of his car drive away, Kristin dropped her purse on the floor and breathed a sigh of relief. *Henry was right,* she thought, *"Fast Freddie is always on the move because he never lets a pretty face go unnoticed."*

* * *

Kristin avoided Fred for the next several days. His calls to her office went unanswered. His texts on her cell were automatically deleted. When she passed him in the halls, there was no eye contact and nothing said, other than "Good morning, Mr. Pace," in response to his friendly greetings. If not for the fact that she was aware of the role appearance played in avoiding gossip, he wouldn't have gotten the *good mornings*. She needed to be distant—at least until she could internally process his presumptuous impression of her. Thankfully, she didn't have to fight him off, unlike his forerunners who scared the bejeebers out of her.

Dr. Sharp blamed herself for letting her guard down just enough to be defenseless against the big man on campus. This was in sheer contrast to the dude at the bottom of the food chain—Henry. He was easy to shoot down without hesitation. As an educated working woman, there was no *logical* way she should or would allow herself to date a janitor, especially a childish one. Fred on the other hand, was her *sensibly* well-constructed dreamboat. A tug of war between her public and private identities was the kind of battle she wasn't ready to engage in at this juncture in her life. For now, her vessel's unexpected navigation through the *tunnel of love* had slipped back on course toward the flagship that anchored her in Perrinsville—a fleeting career.

Meanwhile, the threat of being fired at the awful end to their date eerily reminded Fred of his previous accusers. Like Kristin, they also claimed to have accepted his apologies for his cheekiness, while circumventing him at every turn. His exercise in poor judgment pained him in every brush he had with Kristin. Vowing never to be that weak again, he hatched a plan after days of pondering to get his boss canned and dependent on him. Fred knew he couldn't execute it alone; he'd have to enlist the services of an accomplice. There was only one candidate he could bank on to be equally as devious as himself—his bitter ex-girlfriend, Alma Tater!

67

Chapter 7

Sunday morning was quiet. Most of Perrinsville's citizenry attended church, while others spent the hours relishing the *spirit of rest* at home or out for breakfast in one of the town's many family diners. During this time of tranquility, Alma met Fred at a roadside coffeehouse several miles outside town where no one would see them together. The location for their discreet meeting came at the insistence of the gym teacher, a precautionary measure to provide plausible deniability should there be any threat of collusion.

With fresh coffees in their hands, the former premier couple of yesterday found an empty table in a far corner, away from the mainstream traffic of customers who might overhear their scheming.

"Thanks for meeting me here," Fred said as they sat down.

"Get on with it," Alma barked. "I'm not here for the coffee or company, so this better be good."

"You're still feisty as ever," he snickered.

"You said on the phone you had a plan for me to be the principal..."

He nodded.

"So, what's your plan?" she asked.

"How's your relationship with Bob Bakewell these days?"

"I'm sure you know it's on the fritz"—she scowled—"probably for good this time."

Fred gloatingly smiled.

"It's no secret I'm angry at him about his new hire."

"Can you patch things up with him?"

"Why?"

"So you can access his office."

"Why?"

"So you can snap a picture of Dr. Sharp's résumé."

"Why don't you just look her up on the internet? I'm sure her résumé is posted on one of those business sites like LinkedIn."

Fred rolled his eyes. "I've already done that. Other than our school's website, which doesn't have anything we don't already know, she doesn't have a social media presence to be found anywhere."

Alma squinted. "Ooh…the plot thickens…tell me more."

"I want to know where she came from, where she worked, went to school—"

"Save yourself some trouble, just ask her."

"I can't."

"Why not?"

"It will be too obvious."

"Out of character is more like it," she quipped.

"What's that supposed to mean?"

"I'm referring to your incapability to show the slightest interest in anyone's life other than your own."

Fred sneered.

"I'm sure it didn't take her more than two seconds to figure that out," she goaded.

"Then you obviously know why I can't ask her those kinds of questions. Her résumé will serve the purpose for what I need."

"Then what?"

"I'll dig into her past for some dirt."

"I highly doubt you'll find a skeleton in her closet. That's probably why Bobby hired her. He thinks I've got a lot of baggage."

"Well, I'm not looking to find a skeleton in her closet."

Alma pursed her lips before taking a sip from her paper cup.

"I'm aiming to put one there," Fred crowed.

Alma nearly choked on her beverage. "Are you joking?"

"Do I look like it?" he replied in his best poker face.

"Didn't you just go on a date with her?"

"Yeah." He started to drink the java in his cup.

"So, let me guess…hmmm…she didn't fall for any of your *legendary* moves either?"

Her scathing remark cut him down to size.

"Is she going to file a complaint like *all* the others?"

"I don't think so," he responded sheepishly.

"But something's coming down the pike, or you wouldn't be sitting here with me—right?"

Old feelings of frustration in dealing with Alma's domineering personality brutally cascaded over the washed-up athlete, as if he were a barrel at the bottom of Niagara Falls. He tensed to avoid acrimony in his composure. It was that inherent quality of nastiness in her that drove him to terminate their high-profile relationship when he left for college—she controlled him. Leaving town gave him the liberation he wanted to play the field.

Yet, for Alma, the public humility of being dumped by the superstar of Perrinsville sent the former beauty queen on a downward spiral of short-lived relationships with men more interested in her as *arm candy* than someone to meet their mothers. It wasn't until she started teaching at the elementary school, years later, that she met a tenacious colleague with an ambitious goal of becoming the district's superintendent—Dr. Robert Bakewell.

"Look, are you going to help me or not?" he demanded.

"What's in it for you?"

"I want to get married."

Alma laughed right in his face. *"To her?"*

"I'm serious!"

"Oh, I'll bet you are," she cackled.

Fred gritted his teeth. "Little wonder why you're still single."

"I can run circles around that *poindexter*. She's sooo not your type. What's the attraction?"

"Kristin's the kind of woman a guy wants to bring home to meet the family."

"Like I'm not!"

"You're complete opposites."

"You bet we are—I have no tolerance for egomaniacs."

"Like me?"

"Who says you're not as dumb as you look."

"You really need to quit blaming me for all your problems with men."

"Why shouldn't I blame you? I'm the living embodiment of heartache and broken dreams..."

"And unending misery," Fred said under his breath.

"Because of the empty promises from men, I'm alone with no children—my job is all I have left. So, if I'm not marriage material, then neither are *you*."

"Stop!" His fist pounded the table loud enough to attract the attention of the shop's barista. "I guess this was a big mistake." He got up to leave.

"Sit back down, Freddie," she urged him with visible satisfaction that she'd gotten under his skin in mere seconds. "My fun with you is over. Tell me your plan."

"You'll help me?" he asked, taking his seat.

She nodded. "I want my job, and I want it that bad!"

Fred scooted in and motioned for his new partner in crime to do the same, so he could reveal the details of his conspiracy.

"She's from hundreds of miles away from here," he explained. "No one anywhere near here knows her. No one has seen her before this week, except Bob and the Realtor who sold her the house."

"What are you getting at?"

"How thoroughly does Bob screen his candidates during an interview?"

"I'm sure he checked her out and verified her résumé and references. He's not an amateur," Alma affirmed.

"I'm not saying he is, but what if there's something in her past that's worthy of a scandal?"

"Like what? She's too introverted for anything like that."

"It's always the cupcake types who you never suspect of being a home-wrecker."

"Don't *you* have experience in that department?"

"Ha-ha." He faked a smile. "I tried to kiss her, and she resisted to the point of threatening my job."

"Uh-huh...I figured as much."

"The way she reacted to me was so automatic, I'm betting this is her standard operating procedure on dates."

"Smart girl."

"Spoken like a typical woman. But guys don't see it that way; to us it's an insult."

She winced. "Too bad for your bruised egos."

"That's exactly what I'm driving at. There's got to be a few bruised egos in her past that would love to even the score."

"How are you going to find them?"

"That's where her résumé comes in. Once we find out where she worked, we'll place a few anonymous complaints to the local gossip column pretending to be scorned marrieds whose lives she turned upside down."

"That's insanely devious." The corners of her mouth curled up. "The press here is hurting so much, they'll print it at face value."

"Exactly."

"Bobby will have a stroke when he reads it."

"He'll be so afraid of the school board's reaction—"

"She's history."

"He'll be in such a panic that he'll appoint you to her position."

"What will you do?"

"I'll be there to pick up the pieces of her broken heart."

"How do you know she'll let you?"

His forehead furrowed. "Who else does she know around here?"

"Doesn't matter. She can still refuse you and skip town."

"Not if I pledge to fight the board to get her job back."

"To take *my* job away?"

"Certainly not. I want her to *think* I'm fighting on her behalf, so she becomes dependent on me."

"How long can you keep that sham going? As much as I don't like her, I doubt she's stupid enough not to see right through you."

"Not if I can get her to fall in love with me first."

"Of course…you never change, it's all about you." Alma raised her paper cup admiringly for a congratulatory toast. "Fast Freddie's always on the move!"

Chapter 8

On Monday morning, Alma Tater wasted no time reaching out to Superintendent Bakewell to execute her role in phase one of Kristin's impeachment. The thought of finally getting what she believed was owed her had kept Alma up most of the night. The coveted title of Principal Tater was no longer a dream but an opportunity to usurp power. She despised Kristin for living the life that she wanted—especially the historical bonus of being the district's first woman principal. It took her years to save face from the public humiliation of being dumped by Fred Pace, and yet it required an unholy alliance with him to avenge her failed candidacy to run the elementary school.

Bob Bakewell maintained an unbroken crush on Alma. She was the kind of woman he daydreamed about in his youth—a glamor girl worthy of unending admiration. He knew back then that she would never give a studious geek like him a friendly "hello" unless she was desperate for a math tutor. Her fall from grace, along with her sagging appearance, made Alma approachable for a guy like Bob, who still saw the image of Perrinsville High School's homecoming queen every time he laid eyes on her. Just like Fast Freddie before him, Bakewell struggled to calm Alma's stormy nature—hence their long-standing on-and-off-again romance.

After avoiding Alma's calls throughout the day, Bob found himself unexpectedly detained outside the Board of Education building by his ex-flame, while he locked the door at the day's end.

"Always the last to leave," Alma commented.

"And always the first one to arrive."

"I've been trying to call you all day."

"I know."

"So why didn't you return my calls?"

"After the way you blew up at me," he retorted, "I wasn't sure what you wanted, so I thought it would be wise to let you cool off for a while—a very long while."

She caressed the lapels of his single-breasted suit. "Oh, Bobby...you know I'm just full of hot air sometimes—"

"You mean all the time," he shot back.

"I want to apologize."

"Really?"

"Mmm-hmm. How about we go back to your office and bury the hatchet with style?" she flirted.

"How about we not." He pulled her hands down. "The cleaning lady is in there. Besides you look like you're up to something."

"Guilty as charged," she confessed disingenuously. "I wanted to congratulate you for making the right decision in hiring Dr. Sharp."

"I'm glad to hear you acknowledge that," he responded, blind to her manipulation.

"You know how much I wanted that job."

"I do."

"I'm sure you had valid reasons for bypassing me—"

"None of which you cared to hear when I told you that I hired someone else," he interrupted.

"I was in shock."

"You said you'd never speak to me again."

"Can you blame me?"

"No, but I did it for the good of everyone."

"How's that?" she asked, genuinely stunned.

"You know how much I hate gossip."

She nodded.

"I didn't want people to think that you got the job because of our special relationship. I take my appointments seriously, and to ensure impartiality to the school board, I thought it best to hire a fresh face from outside the community."

Alma turned away from him in a reflexive move to digest the hard truth.

"Kristin's credentials are impeccable," he touted. "I couldn't have found a more flawless individual if I was granted one by a genie in a bottle."

Disgusted by Bob's rave review of her nemesis, Alma realized that she was running out of time to get into his office. Since she couldn't tempt him to let her in, she quickly figured out an alternate route to access his suite—*the cleaning lady*.

"I have to go to the little girl's room." She wiggled and pointed to the metal framed glass door. "May I?"

"If you must...but I'm locking the door behind you, so you'll have to find the housekeeper to let you out."

"She shouldn't be very hard to find if she's still in your office."

Bob withdrew his keys from his coat pocket to let Alma enter the building.

"You're a lifesaver," she said as he held the door for her.

"Good night." He waved before locking up.

Cutting through the lobby, Alma conjured up an excuse to give the cleaning lady to justify her reason for entering the superintendent's office suite at this late hour. Upon arrival, she startled the cleaning woman, who was about to vacuum the carpet in the secretarial area, with a knock on the open door.

"Excuse me?" Alma announced.

The woman nearly jumped through the ceiling. "Oh, geez!"

"Suzy…isn't it?"

"Mizz Tater, good evening. What are you doing here?"

"I have a late meeting with Bob," she fibbed.

"You do? He just left. Didn't you see him?"

"Ah…no, I was just in the restroom," she falsely claimed.

"You can probably catch him in the parking lot if you hurry."

"I think I'd rather call him." Alma lifted her cell phone from the pocket of her corduroy jumper. "Uh-oh…my phone's dead. May I use the phone on Bob's desk?"

"Are you going to be long? I'm behind schedule."

"It depends on how much he has to say after I read him the riot act for standing me up."

"Give it to him *good!*" Suzy chuckled, aware of their rocky relationship.

"Go ahead and vacuum. I'll just close his door for a little privacy."

"Understood."

"Can you let me out when I'm done?"

The housekeeper nodded then flipped the switch on the commercial-grade upright vacuum cleaner.

Displaying a sinister grin, Alma proceeded into her estranged boyfriend's office. Shutting the wooden door, she was free to rummage through his files. It didn't take her more than a minute to figure out where to start looking—she knew Bob's organizational habits intimately—right down to the password of his computer. Without a shred of guilt, she occupied his desk and moved the wireless mouse to illuminate the monitor. As soon as the password-protected box appeared, she entered his dog's name and birthdate. *I always warned him about his easily predictable passwords*, she laughed to herself.

After a few clicks of the mouse, Kristin's résumé flashed on the screen. In rapid precision, Alma whipped out her fully charged cell phone to snap a picture of the document just before the cleaning lady shut off the vacuum. Fearing exposure, Alma raced to click out of the file, log off the computer, and hurry out of the office.

"Suzy…" she called out upon opening the door. "Can you escort me out of the building now?"

* * *

Glued to Monday night's pro football game on the wall mounted TV in his darkened apartment, Fred found his attention suddenly diverted by the ringtone from his mobile phone, indicating a text message had been received. Grabbing the device from the cluttered coffee table he routinely used as a footstool, he opened the message with great expectation. The note simply read, *Your turn!* Beneath the wording was the photo he had tensely awaited. Spreading his index finger and thumb over the screen to enlarge the image, he couldn't help but cheer when he saw the name Kristin Sharp, PhD, in big bold letters—*touchdown!*

Fred worked feverishly till the wee hours of the morning perusing websites belonging to the schools listed on Kristin's résumé. Seated at his small kitchen table, which he'd converted into a makeshift home office, he pecked on the keys of his laptop, while making notes with a pen and paper pad. He studied the male faculty members at each institution, paying particular attention to the ones most resembling himself. With a scribbled laundry list of names completed, he then cross-referenced their social media accounts for pictures, postings, something—*anything*—that might tie at least one of them to the object of his affection.

The thrill of the chase gave him an adrenaline rush—the kind he experienced before his football injury benched him for life. He loved the excitement of pretending to be an amateur private investigator, hot on the trail of a few juicy leads. Finding a conduit to his boss's love life proved to be a tougher job than he originally assumed. Not a trace of her could be uncovered through evidentiary photographs. It was time to go fishing into the depths of the unknown, hoping to reel in a "live one."

Based on the social media profiles of Kristin's former colleagues, Fred decided to start with the longtime bachelors and recently married men approximately the same age as her, all of whom were still at the schools where she had worked with them. He strained his brain to remember the details about her past love life. All he could recall were the few crumbs she'd dropped over dinner at Darla's about never having a boyfriend because of guys who wanted too much too soon. His narcissism surfaced from the pleasant memory of her saying how much he knocked her socks off at "hello"—deliberately omitting the part about her wanting an off-the-charts different kind of man.

Caught up in his own arrogance, which wasn't hard for him, Fred composed a bogus email claiming to honor Dr. Kristin Sharp for becoming Perrinsville Elementary School's first woman principal, under the pretext of a "surprise" banquet. He identified himself as the organizer of the event, soliciting testimonials from her former colleagues to be read as part of the celebration. The note included instructions to keep this request confidential and reply within seventy-two hours. Pleased with his plan of action, he copied the faculty email addresses posted on the school websites to send each of the unsuspecting contenders their own copy from his personal email.

The next few days were real nail biters for the burly phys ed teacher, as the hours passed without a nibble at his email bait. Constant nagging from his partner in crime for a progress report didn't help matters either. His mind had become a ticking time bomb ready to detonate at the end of seventy-two hours. There was no contingent plan in sight—at least not in the immediate future. He cringed at the emptiness of his in-box. The preoccupation of checking his phone increased from every hour between classes to every few minutes during class. Even the schoolchildren noticed that Mr. Pace wasn't paying much attention to their misbehavior.

Deflated by his part in the scheme he masterminded, Fred relaxed in a hot shower at his apartment on Thursday night. Dreading the wrath of his former girlfriend, who was banking on their principal's removal from office, he found himself fresh out of leads and ideas. Wrapped in a terry-cloth bathrobe, he decided to retire to bed early, but not without a swig of coconut water from the fridge. During the seconds in which he consumed the beverage, the beep of a received email pinged from his laptop on the kitchen table. Slamming the water bottle on the countertop, he dashed to the table with revitalized energy.

The email was from a name not on his list, Clifton Spencer. *Who's that?* he thought. Yet, the subject line was a forwarded response to his email, *Testimonial for Dr. Kristin Sharp*. After opening the message, Fred's face lit up like a kid in a candy store. His wish had come true—a grievance letter from someone with an ax to grind. It read,

Mr. Pace,

I was forwarded your email by a friend who thought I should see this. I cannot believe that your school hired Kristin Sharp, and I'm even more baffled that you would honor her with a banquet. I worked with her many years ago when I was a teacher and know her very well. She is undeserving of your consideration. My reasons are too many to list, but let's just say that this prudish tease cost me my job and ruined my life. Don't give her the time of day.

Regards,

Clifton Spencer

"I hit the jackpot!" Fred shouted, jumping out of his chair as if he'd won the lottery. He quickly wrote back to ask for a phone discussion, and within the hour both men were talking up a storm.

Clifton vented to Fred about his long pursuit of Kristin, only to be publicly rejected. He explained that he was a science teacher at the middle school where Kristin landed her first teaching position, before switching to elementary education. He claimed that she was notorious for leading men on and giving them nothing in return. He told Fred about how she was branded Strikeout Sharp because no one ever got to first base with her—especially him! His endless pining grew into an obsession, and then she filed a harassment complaint against him. He laid out the details of his firing and how he'd never been able to get another teaching position—thanks to her!

"I've been reduced to unskilled labor in a warehouse ever since," he cried.

When the lengthy call finally ended, Fred referred to the notes he'd jotted down. *Spencer's story is perfect!* All he needed to do now was make a few creative edits: Strikeout Sharp was changed to Homerun Sharp because a date with her was like hitting a "grand slam." *She threw curveballs to her girlfriends in order to steal their boyfriends. She obsessed over another teacher who filed a complaint against her. She changed schools as part of the settlement to avoid termination....*

Oh, the lies he invented were guaranteed to implicate Perrinsville's school board in a damaging scandal that would take years to repair. The personal harm it would do to Kristin gave him pause, and for a moment he rethought his dubious strategy. But it was quickly dismissed as a necessary evil for him to come to her rescue.

* * *

Fred waited till Saturday morning to drive outside the county to purchase a burner phone—the next phase of his plan. He needed an untraceable number to contact the editor of the *Perrinsville Gazette* for an exclusive phone interview. Even though he knew he could call from a blocked number, he wanted a valid phone number should he have to leave a message to be called back—a precaution to help legitimize the fictitious allegations. As he suspected, the editor was unavailable at the time of his "concerned" call that afternoon.

"I heard that your school district hired Dr. Kristin Sharp to be the principal of your elementary school," Fred recorded on the editor's voice mail in a disguised tone. "I really must warn you about what kind of highly unethical person you have administering your kids' education. She's not who you think she is. Call me at…." *Click!*

Confident in the editor's temptation to entertain what appeared to be a major scoop, at least for a small town like Perrinsville, Fred lay low in his apartment, waiting for the return call. Early the next morning, he was awakened by the ringing on his burner phone.

"Hello," he answered, struggling to overcome his grogginess in a fake voice.

"This is Brice Hurst from the *Perrinsville Gazette*," said the man on the other end of the phone. "You left an alarming message in my voice mailbox yesterday."

"Yes, I did…thanks for returning my call."

"Whom am I speaking to?"

"I'd rather not say, I want to remain anonymous in case of retaliation."

"Okay, I'm going to need a lot of details. Let's start from the beginning."

"Homerun Sharp loves to play the field…"

The two spoke for nearly twenty minutes before wrapping it up.

"These are very serious allegations for me to print just on your word alone," Hurst explained.

"Your community needs to know," Fred insisted, still in character.

"I agree. But to cover myself from a libel suit, I will print this as a special editorial 'opinion' piece that will appear on the front page. So if she claims innocence, I'll give her the space to submit an op-ed. How's that?"

Fred took a moment to think carefully about his response. His knowledge of the paper being a borderline tabloid was slightly debunked. He was in no position to reveal any of his prior convictions about the *Gazette* without raising Hurst's suspicions. He had to play ball—even if it meant giving Kristin the opportunity to refute the editorial. Yet, he knew all too well the emotional reaction of the school board. They would take it as the truth because it was on the front page of the newspaper.

"Works for me," Fred answered.

"Thank you for the story," Hurst replied before ending the call.

Fred sighed after hanging up with the editor. He sprang out of bed with a zest for life he hadn't had in years. *Time to call Alma and tell her the big news,* he thought with a tight grin from ear to ear.

Chapter 9

Monday morning kicked off the first of many themed days peppered throughout the year to celebrate school spirit. Today's theme—pajama day. Kids arrived in a variety of their favorite pj's, along with many of their teachers. A firm believer in boosting the morale of the student body, Kristin agreed to participate in the school's long tradition by donning a pair of pink fleece jammies with a kitten print pattern on the top and bottoms. She had bought them special for this day, as well as puffy kitty slippers and hair curlers. The idea of a pajama day animated her wish to be respected by the students she governed, so it was a no-brainer for her to be vested in today's event.

What the principal presumed would be a happy occasion this morning was greeted with saddened hostility. She entered the reception area of the front office with her purse over her shoulder, her briefcase in one hand, and her travel mug in the other. Noticing Janet's engrossment in the morning paper, she cleared her throat to get the secretary's attention.

"Ahem," she muttered.

In red plaid pajamas, Janet projected a solemn gaze at her jovial boss twirling around like a fashion model, showing off her school spirit.

"Well…what do you think?" Kristin asked proudly.

"Homerun Sharp?"

Kristin misinterpreted the meaning of Janet's reference by taking it as a compliment. "Oh, thank you. I guess I did hit a homerun with this getup."

"No…" Janet clarified, "not your duds—your dudes."

"I don't get it. What are you talking about?"

"This!" Janet waved the newspaper in front of her face. "Is it true?"

Dropping her briefcase and purse to the floor, Kristin took the early morning publication from Janet's hand to glance at the front-page headline: "Elementary Examination Should Cry Foul!"

"I don't get it. What am I supposed to see?" she asked, lowering the paper to sip her coffee.

"Don't stop at the headline—read the article."

"Okay…" Kristin continued to drink from her thermal mug as she dived into the story. "…better known to her colleagues as 'Homerun Sharp'!" The burning flash from the incendiary words she just read caused her to spew her brew onto the paper. "Homerun Sharp!" she wailed.

"Is it true?"

"Please don't tell me you believe this lie?" Kristin contested, handing the soiled paper back to Janet with a jittery hand.

"I find it hard to believe myself," the secretary admitted, fanning the wet paper before setting it on her desk. "But you have to understand that no one in this town knows you or anything about you. When it comes to these kinds of scandals, it's typically the quiet ones who are the culprits."

Kristin stood aghast. "The exact opposite is true. Yes, I had a reputation among the men in my school district once upon a time."

Janet's eyes widened in anticipation of some risqué confession.

"I had a couple of unflattering nicknames from cruel people whom I tried to impress. The first one goes back to childhood, and the second, which is where this lie came from, I was branded as 'Strikeout Sharp.'"

"Why?"

"Because I never let any of the *players* get to first base with me," she proclaimed unequivocally. "I don't play those kinds of games—never have and never will!"

"I believe you," Janet conceded with her hands in the air.

Hotter than a pistol, the doctor gathered her belongings and marched into her office at the sound of the morning bell. "I'm going to call that rag and read them the riot act till Sunday."

"I should warn you that the superintendent called just before you came in, and he's on his way over to see you."

"Don't tell me he's buying into this yellow journalism?"

"Eeeee…I don't know," Janet fudged.

"Then I'll be ready to get in the thick of it with *Dr. Cakewell*," she affirmed at her office door.

"That sounds like something our comedic custodian would say."

"It's going to take a janitor to clean this mess up," she responded in sarcasm.

Just as Kristin set foot into her office, Janet called out to her. "By the way, I'm sorry for ruining your morning. You *do* have the best pajama ensemble on staff."

"Thank you—you're forgiven," she shouted back.

No sooner did Kristin get settled at her desk than her superior barged in to toss his copy of the *Gazette* at her. Dressed in a power business suit, Dr. Bakewell confronted his new hire on the most awkward day of her career—pajama day. Appearing in pj's and slippers, with curlers in her hair, was unimaginably humiliating for the career woman who had worked incredibly hard to earn this coveted position. And now she looked more like a schoolgirl about to be grounded by her father after being yanked out of bed first thing in the morning. The ironic imagery was too much for her to bear.

"Can you explain this?" he asked her pointedly.

"Please sit down," she said, surprisingly calm.

He seated himself comfortably across the desk from her.

"I don't know where this bogus story came from, or why it was printed, but I assure you that none of it is true."

"My phone has been ringing off the hook all morning from board members, city officials, and angry parents ripping into me for hiring you."

"I sure hope you defended me."

"As best I could—"

"What does that mean?" she interrupted.

"I told them I'd speak to you."

"That's all? You didn't defend your decision to hire me?"

"I told some of the more reasonable personalities that I checked you out thoroughly and you came highly recommended."

She held up the paper. "Then why give any credence to this libel?"

"There are people in this town who think if it's in the news, it must be true—"

"So everyone here is *that* gullible?" she interjected.

"I didn't say everyone, but some of the big names on the school board will run and hide at the very hint of a scandal."

"Are you one of them?" She stared him in the eye through her heavy horn-rimmed glasses.

"I'm sorry, Kristin, but they kind of own me, and I cannot allow the fine reputation of our good school to be further smeared in the press."

"It won't—these are lies!"

"Can you prove your innocence?"

"How's someone supposed to prove they didn't do something," a deep voice bellowed from the reception area.

Both Kristin and Bakewell turned their attention to the door as Fred Pace charged into the office, sporting his usual athletic sweats. The manliness of his perfectly timed entrance plunged Kristin into further embarrassment, being the only one in this critical scene basically undressed—figuratively and literally. Sitting before two fully clothed men in her pj's, she felt like an unmade bed. It didn't matter that it was pajama day; it was the principle of it that mattered to her. One man was hurling accusations while the other came to save the day, and she was caught in the middle of them without clothes on. To help conceal her discomfort, she grabbed a binder from her desk to snuggle against her chest like a protective teddy bear.

"What are you doing here, Pace?" Bakewell inquired.

"Yes, why aren't you in class?" Kristin added.

"This isn't like a high school," Fred said as a reminder to both of them. "My first class doesn't start till nine."

"Then why are you here?" the superintendent demanded.

Tension between these two men was obvious to anyone in their presence. Kristin wished she had a knife to cut the thickness of it down to size. These extreme opposites shared a common thread—Alma Tater. Both had unpleasant histories with her, and both were afraid of her in their own way. Like everyone else in town, Kristin knew what they had in common and she couldn't blame them after getting a taste of Mizz Tater Tots's charming personality on the first day of school.

"I heard about the article and came to give my support to Dr. Sharp," the gym teacher pledged.

"I can handle myself—thank you very much!" Kristin defended vigorously.

Bakewell turned his focus back to Kristin. "Keep in mind that I'm compelled to launch an investigation into this allegation."

"So am I. It's my name that needs to be cleared. I intend to call the writer of that filth." She reached for the phone receiver on her desk.

"Then you'll have to do it from home."

Kristin froze. "What are you saying?"

"Yeah, what are you getting at?" Fred chimed in, pretending to be confused.

The superintendent stood to deliver his decision from a position of strength. "Pending the outcome of an investigation, I have to suspend you till further notice—effective immediately."

Kristin leaped to her feet in bewilderment. "You can't be serious?"

"I'm very sorry. Please get your things together."

"You want her to clean out her desk?" Fred butted in.

"You're not fired, just suspended, so you don't have to get everything."

"I can't believe such a bright man is reacting so stupidly to an ugly rumor," Kristin uttered tearfully, as she collected her purse, briefcase, and mug.

"C'mon, Bob, give her a break," Fred pleaded. "You're condemning her with no proof of anything."

Bakewell shrugged. "It doesn't matter; it's the seriousness of the charge. Until it's proven otherwise, she's suspended."

"With pay?" Kristin asked.

The superintendent avoided eye contact. "I'm sorry."

Dr. Sharp proceeded to the door with her items in hand. "I sure made the wrong decision to come here."

Bakewell halted her. "Please leave the briefcase here."

"Why?" she scorned.

"I can't allow you to take any school files with you during the suspension."

Her jaw hung open. "Really!"

"I just want to go through it first, and then I'll have Janet return it to you."

She trembled in disbelief and made a mad dash out of the office.

"I'm on your side. I'll call you later," Fred yelled to her deaf ears but to the frequency of Janet's antenna. The busybody secretary stewed at her desk, simmering in conflicting emotions.

Chapter 10

Henry wandered down the hall in a printed T-shirt resembling a pajama top, unaware of the day's news dump. Heading toward the main office, he spotted Kristin tearing out of the building in her jammies and curlers, visibly upset. His first thought was she must've had an emergency, but that was quickly nixed by the visual of Fast Freddie and Dr. Bakewell exiting the office with long faces. As the two men responsible for her demise silently parted ways, Henry made a beeline into the executive suite.

"What's shakin' Goody Two-shoes?"

Looking like a nervous Nellie, Janet ignored his friendly greeting.

"Something wrong?" he asked before making light of the mood. "I know it's pajama day, and we look like we should still be in bed, but it's morning and time for school."

"Don't *you* know?"

"Know what?"

"Didn't you see the morning paper?"

"You know I never read that fish wrap."

She cracked a faint smile.

"Is there something you want me to see?"

She handed him the soiled paper. "I think you better read the editorial on the front page."

He took the paper and focused on the massive coffee stain. "Looks like I'm not the only one who barfs at Hurst the Worst's scandal rag."

"Just read it, please."

Henry scanned the article. Angered by the content of the printed word, he crinkled the paper into a ball and tossed it into the wastebasket at the foot of Janet's desk. "I don't believe a word of that trash."

"Me neither."

"Is that why Sharpie booked out of here like yesterday's news?"

The secretary nodded.

"Is that why Cakewell was here?"

She nodded again.

"Did he can her?"

"Not exactly. She's been suspended pending an investigation."

"An investigation into what? He believes that garbage?"

"Yes and no. From what I overheard, he's been pressured by the board and others to investigate the charges."

Henry raised an eyebrow. "Charges? What charges?"

"Okay, I misspoke—allegations. He wants her to prove they're not true."

"How is she supposed to prove her innocence from a pack of lies?"

"That's what Fred said."

"I saw him step out with Cakewell. What was he doing here?"

"He came to support her."

"And just in the nick of time, I bet. A little suspicious, don't you think?"

"I don't know what to think. I read the paper and confronted her about it."

"Aw, no."

"I feel so guilty for jumping to conclusions."

"What did she say?"

"She denied everything, and I believe her."

"You should. If anyone is close to that kind of behavior, it's the tall man with the spectacular tan, who was just in here. That's more *his* style."

Unable to contain her passion for Fred, Janet snapped at Henry. "He's not the ogre you always accuse him of being. You don't understand him the way I do."

"I don't see him the way you do either."

"What do you mean?"

"I'm not as blasé as I look. I've seen the way you stare at him whenever he's around."

"You *know*?"

"C'mon, Goody Two-shoes, that cat got outta the bag a long time ago."

She seemed befuddled. "Ooh...so they do know, huh?"

"Yep...and everyone knows he doesn't give you the time of day either."

"Oh, my gosh! How did I not see that?"

"When's the last time you cleaned your radar screen?" he chuckled.

Janet slapped his arm playfully, as they shared a laugh together. Their lighthearted moment was short-lived when Alma Tater barged in.

"Really?" she scoffed at them. "Why aren't either of you working?"

Henry turned to her with a quick rebuttal. "Why aren't you in your classroom Tater Tots?"

Janet giggled.

"My kids just went to art class. And if you call me Tater Tots again, you can sweep yourself to the unemployment office." She pointed her finger at Janet. "That goes for you as well."

Her out-of-the blue hostility left Henry and Janet speechless.

"I am to be addressed as Mizz Tater—got that?"

"Why are you coming at us with both barrels blazing?" Henry dared to ask.

"Effective tomorrow, I will be running this institution."

"Says who?" Janet wanted to know.

"Superintendent Bakewell."

They stood agape at the shocking revelation—*Alma Tater, principal? Say it isn't so.*

"I came here to tell you," she eyed Janet, "to find a sub for me." She then turned to Henry with a bark. "Since you're here, make yourself useful and clean my new office."

Henry saluted her like a parodied foot soldier. "Aye aye, ma'am."

To their horror, they watched the interim superior officer strut into the principal's office and take possession of the leather chair, as if it were a throne.

"Don't get too comfy," Henry declared, moving toward the doorjamb. "Your time in that chair is temporary."

"Wanna bet?" Alma challenged.

"The true queen of this school will be back to claim her rightful place."

"Not if I can help it," she asserted. "And by the way, I'd like you to get rid of all the remnants of my illegitimate predecessor—today."

Alma's emotional "high" gave way to an unintended consequence picked up by the custodian. Her careless slip-up was enough of a clue for him to suspect that she was somehow tied to Kristin's demise, along with Fred. It wouldn't surprise him if they were in it together. His intuitiveness about their motives allowed for the logical possibility of a truce between them. He just needed to figure out the logistics of their scheme to expose them.

"Henry…" Janet beckoned.

He swiveled to approach her, leaving Alma alone to wallow in her fantasyland.

"I'm supposed to take Dr. Sharp's briefcase to her house. I don't think I can face her if I have to take the rest of her stuff from the office too."

"I'll do it," he enthusiastically offered. "What's her address?"

* * *

Henry left school before lunch to return Kristin's belongings to her beautifully landscaped house. Inside her picture-perfect home, the falsely accused educator continued to sob on her living room sofa. Still in the pajamas and curlers she purchased for spirit day at school, she was alarmed by the knock on her front door. Kristin was unaware of Henry's van parked at the end of her driveway—the sound of his approaching vehicle had been drowned out by her sniffling and crying.

Unwilling to relinquish the security of her fetal position on the couch, she ignored the knocks, hoping the trespasser would leave. The knocking persisted, and before she could think straight, a familiar voice called out to her.

"Hey, Sharpie…it's me, Henry. I know you're here. Please come to the door."

"This is not a good time," she yelled. "Please go."

"I have your stuff from school."

"Leave it on the porch. I'll get it later."

"I heard what happened, and I believe you're innocent!"

She wiped the streaming tears from her eyes and reached for her glasses on the tasseled rug covering her hardwood floor.

"I want to help you. Please come to the door."

Composing herself, Kristin went to the door to open it just enough to put her head out, keeping her body hidden from his sight.

"I thought Janet was coming to bring my briefcase."

"She was too ashamed of herself to come, so I volunteered."

"What's with the box in your arms?"

"I can explain if you'll let me in."

"I'm not dressed."

"I already saw you in your jammies when you left school in a hurry."

"That was different…it was for pajama day."

"So?"

"I don't feel the same anymore. I'm uncomfortable standing here in them now."

"Then I'll wait till you get dressed. Okay?"

"It will be a while, and I'll feel better without the rollers in my hair."

"Take as much time as you need. I'll just sit here on the porch till you're ready."

"You're such a gentleman," she complimented.

"Try not to say that too loud. I have a childish reputation to maintain," he kidded.

After shutting the door, Kristin went into her bedroom to fix her hair and change into a pair of jeans and a sweater. Despite having the blues, she refused to let herself be in the company of a man without looking presentable. This also included a fresh application of makeup. Ready to face her guest half an hour later, she returned to the door and invited him inside her feminine dwelling.

"Oh, wow!" the shabby man blurted at the elegance of the hostess and her home. "What a perfect vision of loveliness."

Kristin smiled at him with modesty.

"My castle could sure use your touch. Maybe sometime—"

"Please put the box down and have a seat," she interrupted, steering him back on course to avoid a calamity in troubled waters.

As he set the box on the floor of the foyer, she checked out his printed T-shirt with a subtle adjustment of her glasses.

"Interesting shirt," she remarked obscurely.

"I wanted to show my spirit like everyone else."

"I don't think I've *ever* seen a T-shirt with a pajama print."

"Now you have," he said with a grin. "I've got a drawer full of them for just about every occasion."

Why am I not surprised, she thought. "Oh, where are my manners," she motioned him toward the living room, "please have a seat."

The world's biggest kid moseyed over to the couch where she'd been bawling for hours.

"Do you want anything to drink?"

"Nah, I'm fine."

"Okay, let me know if you change your mind." Kristin sat next to him on the sofa. "What's in the box?"

"All your stuff from the office."

"I thought I was just suspended. Does this imply I'm fired now?"

"Ah, no."

"Then why is all my stuff here?"

"Because Tater Tots is occupying your office now."

Kristin fumed. "What!"

"That's just how I feel, and so will everyone else at the school when she makes her grand announcement tomorrow morning."

"Bob never said anything about her filling in."

"He has a history with Alma. Sometimes I think he's afraid of her."

"I had a run-in with her in the ladies' room on Parent-Teacher night. For all intents and purposes, she threatened me."

"No surprise there. I told you when we first met how badly she's wanted that job."

"She can have it then."

"No!" he snapped. "Please don't throw in the towel."

"I'm tired of fighting mean girls. It's been my life's story. I'm thinking of going back home."

"You can't—isn't this your home?"

"I want it to be. I love it here, and I love my new job. I had so much I wanted to do for the school and the kids here—nothing was out of the realm of possibilities."

"That's why you *must* stay. We need you."

"How do you know? You really don't know much about me."

"I don't have to know much about you to feel what a genuine breath of fresh air you are. The best thing to happen to the kids in this town is *you*."

"Please…I'm nothing special."

"Oh, really? Then why is *someone* working so hard to publicly trash your good name?"

"I don't know. I've been trying to figure out the source of that fake story."

"Any leads? No pun intended."

"From the details, it sounds a lot like a guy I dated and dumped many years ago. But he wouldn't know where I am today."

"Maybe he looked you up on the internet?"

"I'm a very private person. I'm not on social media anywhere."

"Even the school's website?"

"All that's there is generic information about me—nothing specific. I didn't get my picture taken yet, so there's no photo of me. I know I'm not the only Dr. Kristin Sharp in the United States, so without a picture, Clifton—that's his name—would be afraid to call the school. He's done enough damage to himself."

"Maybe someone from your hometown told him?"

"Impossible. When I took this job, my exodus was on the QT."

"If you don't mind my asking, why?"

Kristin turned away to lament. "Because I wanted to get away from everyone and everything I knew. I could've been a principal in the district where I worked, but I wanted a fresh start somewhere else far, far away. Too many painful memories back in New England."

"Again I ask, why?"

"It would take a lot of time for me to explain."

"I'm not going anywhere."

"What about your job?"

"They won't miss me. Besides, the iron maiden doesn't start till tomorrow anyway."

"I hardly know you. I'm not ready to bare my soul to you."

"Whether you realize it or not, we have a connection—I feel it."

"I have to be honest with you; I doubt I'll ever see you as more than a friend."

"And that's what you need right now—a friend."

"Can you live with that?"

As heartbreaking as her perception of him was, Henry knew if he attempted to push for more at this stage, he'd lose her entirely. If friendship was all she could offer, he'd take it—for now.

Henry gently patted her shoulder. "I'll always be your friend. But I have to admit that what you're describing is a bit mysterious, and it almost gives credibility to the accusations in the article."

"I was never called *'Homerun Sharp.'* I was cruelly known as *'Strikeout Sharp'* because of my prudishness when it came to crossing the line in dating."

He secretly sighed with relief. *A girl after my own heart.*

"I've never had a real boyfriend. I'm not capable of being the kind of woman most men are attracted to. Remember when I told you on the first day of school how wiry I was as a kid?"

"Uh-huh."

"That's partly because I was a super skinny child. I had boney legs, and everyone used to call me 'Bird Legs.' It was much worse than *Strikeout* because it went to my body image—something I couldn't control."

"Sorry to hear that."

"I can't tell you, Henry, how much I hated it! It just about killed my self-esteem."

Henry gave her a compassionate once-over. "You don't have bird legs. You're a beautiful, smart, and successful woman who can easily prove all the naysayers wrong."

"I'm so tired of fighting the Alma Taters of the world. I've been in the school system long enough to accurately predict the future personalities of kids: who will be the jocks, the burners, the mean girls, the tomboys…. There will always be another Alma out there thinking she can walk all over a nerd like me. So what's the point?"

"The point is, I've also been in the school system long enough to make the same predictions, but I have hope for their futures. Not everyone has to be a prisoner of the labels like the ones plaguing you. The best way to cast out those spells is through solid leadership, like the kind you wanted to implement here in Perrinsville. That's exactly why you must stay and fight. You're trying to run away from your past, and Tater Tots is inadvertently using that fear to create her future."

The wisdom in Henry's words resonated with Kristin. She continued to listen with a sense of intellectual infatuation that was unexplainable because it was coming from a clownish janitor.

He continued, "You are an educator and a darn good one if Bakewell hired you. He's not a stupid man—a spineless one in this case—but not stupid when it comes to picking the very best person to lead our school. Don't let Tater Tots become the latest thief to steal your identity."

His argument won her favor!

"Okay, counselor, I'll fight the storm," she declared. "Just so you know, I'm not getting paid during the suspension, and I put all my money into moving here. I'd have to call and beg my parents for assistance, and the answer from them will be to go back home."

"I can help you. I've got money to float you till…"

Kristin lifted her nose in the air. "I won't accept a loan from you or anyone else."

"Do you have enough to get by for a little bit?"

"That depends on what you mean by a 'little bit.'"

"I have a pretty good hunch someone planted that story to set you up."

"Alma?"

"No doubt. Who else would benefit from your removal? And she may not be alone."

"Who do you suspect?"

"Before laying my cards on the table, I need to find a way to expose her."

"Maybe Fred can help?"

The mere mention of *that* name was like fingernails going down a chalkboard to Henry. He cringed at her suggestion, wondering if he should reveal his suspicion about the gym teacher's involvement. "Why do you think he can help?"

"He was there when I was getting the boot."

"So…"

"He came to my defense and stood up for me."

"Uh-huh."

"He's not a fan of Alma's, either, but he obviously knows her very well."

"You believe he might know something?"

"I didn't think much of it earlier, but he seemed to show up at just the right moment to intervene."

"Don't you find it odd?"

"Maybe he figured Alma was the culprit and tried to stop it."

"Fast Freddie never misses a trick."

"He's supposed to call me later. Do you want me to tell him about our suspicions?"

"*No!*"

Kristin squirmed from what she thought was an overblown reaction. "Why not?"

"That'd kill everything."

"How? If he can help, why not?"

"Please trust me."

"Do you think Fred's mixed up with Alma?"

"I don't know what to think." He skirted the issue to throw her off the scent. "You know the old saying about loose lips sinking ships? Let's just keep this between us, okay?"

She nodded her head in agreement. "When he calls, I'll just act like I did when you showed up and see what he says…if he says anything at all."

"Good girl." Henry prepared to leave. "Well, I better get back to school. I have a lunchroom to clean with the kids sent to *the wall*."

Kristin stood and laughed at his emphasis on "the wall" from her Quiet Time policy. "I'm really glad you came over. I feel much better."

"That's what *friends* are for." He hugged her goodbye.

Chapter 11

Vowing to save Kristin's career, Henry paid a visit to Eugene Maloney in the computer lab after the school bell rang. Affectionately referred to as "Mr. Baloney," he was the district's tenured computer-science teacher and resident geek. Like Henry, he was a bit quirky, but more in the traditional stereotype of a nerd, rather than an overgrown child. Their shared statures of being the kind of kid who was never picked to be on a team, of any kind, blessed them with a solid friendship of mutual trust. If there was anyone Henry could confide in to help him restore Kristin's honor, it would be Eugene Maloney.

"Wassup, my man?" Maloney asked, failing miserably to be cool—especially in flannel nighties.

"Bad news, pajama boy."

"Very funny," he leaned back in his ergonomic chair. "Is this about the rumor that's buzzing around here about Dr. Sharp?"

"Did you read the story?"

Maloney fished out a crinkled copy of the newspaper from his circular file. "It was hand delivered to me by Tater Tots. She personally informed me that she's permanently off lunchroom duty after today."

"This reeks of a setup."

"You don't have to convince me," he agreed, tossing the paper back in the trash can. "I heard about the incident in the office this morning."

"Sharpie doesn't deserve this—"

"Neither do we," Maloney interrupted. "It's going to be torture around here with Tater Tots running the show."

"No kidding."

"Have you talked to Dr. Sharp?"

"Yeah, I went to her house this morning."

"How is she?"

"Devastated."

"I can imagine."

"This whole thing just smells like Tater Tots."

"You think she's behind it?"

"I *know* she is. I just have to prove it."

"What are you going to do?"

"That's why I'm here. I need your computer savvy genius to help me get to the truth."

Maloney stood to shake Henry's hand, sealing their new partnership. "We'll be the news hawks this town deserves."

"I knew I could count on you."

"What do you want me to do?"

"Later tonight when everyone is gone, I need you to come back and plant a little bug in the principal's office computer and phone."

Maloney's pupils dilated. "Won't we get fired for that?"

"We're gonna get fired by Tater Tots sooner or later anyway."

"She can't stand either of us."

"So, look at it like a race. Let's see who gets who fired first."

The computer teacher laughed out loud.

"I'll be back here to let you in and serve as lookout just in case anyone shows up unexpectedly."

"Got it."

"And put some clothes on so you don't redefine the term *bedtime burglar*," Henry quipped.

* * *

Kristin spent the rest of her day pondering Henry's theory about Alma. It made perfect sense to her. *Who would most benefit from my dismissal?* The idea that someone would stoop to the lowest of low for a job infuriated her. Of all the public humiliations she had suffered throughout her days on earth, this was the worst. The only saving grace was that no one in Perrinsville knew her, so her family didn't have to tolerate any unjust ramifications.

As much as she appreciated Henry's comforting assistance, her predisposition about his occupational status and maturity level cast a shadow of doubt about his ability to expose Alma. Kristin re-examined his warning about Fred and didn't see any element of danger in employing his services. He was the only direct pipeline to her nemesis other than Bakewell, who was out of the question at this point. Aware of the phys ed teacher's continued interest in pursuing a romance with her, she made the crafty decision to be her own detective and exploit his vulnerability for answers—without entering the danger zone.

When her cell phone rang that evening, she took a deep breath before getting into the character of a damsel in distress that appealed to his massive ego.

"Hello?"

"Hey, babe—it's me."

"Oh, Fred, I'm so glad you called."

"Are you okay?"

"I'm better now that *you've* called," she hammed. "I can't thank you enough for coming to my rescue this morning."

"Well, I couldn't stand by and watch you be falsely accused of something I know isn't true."

"Then you don't believe the story in the paper about me?"

"Of course not."

"Why? Everybody else does."

"Because I think I know you better."

"But you don't know me at all."

"Well, I'm a good judge of people, particularly when it comes to the weaker sex."

Kristin bit her tongue! Enraged by the admitted chauvinistic opinion of women, she was tempted to slam the phone in his ear. However, she restrained her gut reaction to terminate the call and resumed her role play.

"After the way our date ended and the way I wrote you off afterward…you want to save me?"

"Yes, I do. I know I came on strongly like an insensitive brute."

That's for sure, she thought with a smirk.

"But that doesn't mean I'm incapable of understanding your moral fiber."

"Then you know I can't possibly be the score that the paper said I am."

"I'll be more than happy to use Hurst as a punching bag to defend your honor."

"Oh, please don't. That will just give him another story to print."

"Well, he can't get away with this."

"I appreciate your support, but I'm not a vengeful person."

"I know," he said in a low tone.

"I just want to heal. I need time to really process how I'm going to prove my innocence."

"Let me help you," he begged.

"I need to know how this happened and why. Doesn't it seem strange to you that someone from my past would call the *Gazette* to plant a fake story to hurt me?"

"Well, I know a thing or two about jilted lovers. Never underestimate their vindictiveness."

"Yes, but the one I suspect of being the source goes way back. He should be well over me by now."

"Not necessarily," Fred confessed in a weakness of truth. "You have a knack for making a lasting impression on us men."

She rolled her eyes and shook her head. *Time to really start playing him like a fiddle.* "I'm touched by your flattery."

"I mean it. Can I see you again?"

"Oh, I don't think that would be wise."

"Why not?"

"Now that I have this naughty reputation, if people see us together, what would they say?"

"I don't care."

"Think of the publicity."

"That's nothing new to me."

"I can't let you take the risk."

"Hey, I like to live dangerously," he half-joked.

"Okay, but don't say I didn't warn you."

"Meet me for a cup of coffee?"

"All right…when?"

"How about in an hour?"

She started to fumble over the swiftness of his timing. "Oh…ah…that's a bit too soon…I mean, I'm still in shock and need at least a day to wrap my head around this. Does that make sense?"

"Yeah, I get it. Tomorrow night then?"

"Okay. But promise me: no funny business."

"I promise. I'll be a perfect gentleman."

"See you tomorrow," she said sweetly.

Click.

Kristin flopped on her sofa hoping she hadn't just opened Pandora's box.

Chapter 12

After a sleepless night wrestling with her conscience, Kristin felt morally obligated to disclose her plan of action to Henry. If anybody would back her decision, she figured it would be him. Never one to rely on the advice of others, she took pride in her gumshoe duty to flush out the corruption behind her quagmire. Had it not been for Henry's revelation yesterday, she'd still be spinning her wheels in self-pity.

Making an allowance for Henry to get home from school, she waited until late afternoon to head over to his house. Eying his dilapidated van on the driveway from afar, Kristin gently wheeled her luxury sedan along the curb in front of his ecologically challenged habitation. With a headshake out of the car and the clip-clop of her autumn-laced boots, she trotted to his front door before anything that might be living in his shrubs could strike her. Kristin pressed the doorbell button that appeared to be in need of repair, wondering if it actually worked. Every second that passed without an answer seemed like an eternity, adding to her paranoia of someone catching her on his front porch. Especially since she was dressed for a date with Fred.

As much as she truly admired Henry, her obsession about appearances compelled her to keep any hint of a personal association with him a secret. He couldn't answer the door fast enough for her—particularly with the passing of every car going down the street at a snail's pace in broad daylight. The *Gazette's* false report made her a laughingstock. She didn't want to be mocked further by someone spotting 'Homerun Sharp' at the house of the town jester, Henry Hubbard. She gave the button one more try with her manicured thumb before clenching it into a fist to forcibly pound on the door.

Before her sensitive knuckles could make contact with the durable wooden door, the rough-handed man opened it with a warm smile.

"Hey, Sharpie!"

"Hi. What took you so long?"

"I was in the basement and got here as fast as I could."

"I wasn't sure if your doorbell worked or not. It looks like it's broken."

"Well, looks can be deceiving—kinda like me," he said with a wink.

She giggled for a second. "May I come in?"

"Hurry, before anyone sees you."

His tongue-in-cheek comment screamed at her. His perception about her vanity triggered remorse about her stereotyping of him. He was every bit as intelligent as she was, and she knew it, yet she just couldn't get past his social disposition. *If only,* she brooded to herself upon entering his man-cave funhouse.

"So, to what do I owe the pleasure of your good company?" he asked, shutting the door.

"I thought a lot about what you said regarding exposing Alma, and I want to help."

"Don't worry about it."

"I'm sorry, but I can't."

"Yes, you can, I'm working on it."

"So am I."

"*What?*"

"I'm working on it too. That's what I came to tell you."

"What do you mean?"

"While you're doing whatever you're planning, I'm going to work on Fred."

Henry shivered from those fingernails down a chalkboard again.

"If anybody can lead us to Alma's vulnerabilities, it's Fred," she continued.

"*No*—he can't!"

"I don't understand?"

"I told you yesterday not to go there with him."

"And I didn't take what you said lightly, either, but considering our options—"

"There are no options with him," he interjected. "Just trust me."

"I do…but I fail to see why we can't get to Alma through Fred?"

"Because, he's—" Henry stopped cold before blowing the whistle on his conspiracy theory.

Kristin's antenna went up. "He's what?"

Henry glanced at the floor. "He's more trouble than he's worth."

"I know you don't like him—"

"*Oh gee*…it's déjà vu."

"What is?"

"This conversation. Didn't we have it the last time you were here?"

"We argued about Fred, yes."

"And here we go again."

"Please understand: I just can't sit by idly. It's my life at stake."

"I'm not asking you to sit by idly. I'm asking you to put your trust in me to clear your name."

"How long is that going to take?"

"I don't know, but I've got a good plan in motion."

"What is it?"

"Sorry…the less you know, the better. Just enjoy your time off."

"I don't know how to enjoy time off that's uncertain. I need to do something."

"Then start by going after Hurst the Worst at the paper. Just stay away from Fast Freddie."

"I don't know Hurst, and I doubt he'll tell me anything. Besides, I already agreed to meet Fred."

"Ah, nooo," he groaned.

"It's just coffee."

"Don't expect him to spill the beans."

"Ha-ha…it's not what you think. I'm going to set a trap."

"Be careful you don't fall into *his* trap first."

"I already warned him about shenanigans."

"Nothing I say is going to stop you, is it?"

"I'm a very headstrong Type A personality," she tooted her horn.

"Yeah…I know."

"Then we don't need to keep bickering about it. My mind's made up."

"You know what the real kicker to this is?"

"What?"

"*He's* the one benefitting from this."

"It's just business. I'm not going to let him manipulate me. I'm going to manipulate him to the truth."

"I hope you know what you're doing."

"I guess it's my turn to tell you to trust *me*."

"If I expose Tater Tots first, will you drop it with Freddie?"

"Like a bad habit."

"Good."

"Well, I best be going…I have to meet…"

"I know"—Henry covered his ears—"I don't wanna hear it again."

"Can we make a pact that we'll keep each other up to date on our progression?"

"If it means I have to hear about your dates with Freddie, then I don't wanna know anything."

"Please don't be jealous—there's no reason to be."

"That's not how I see it."

"There's nothing for you to be worried about."

"You're unbelievably naive for a PhD."

Kristin folded her arms. "Huh, that's a little insulting for you to say."

"You know, Sharpie, we may have opposite addresses in the social registry, but we're both members of the same exclusive club. I know you much better than you're willing to admit."

"Maybe…maybe not…"

"No matter how hard you try to keep your cards close to the vest, you don't have much of a poker face—at least not to me."

"I need to go. I've got a hand to play tonight," she said to reciprocate his pun.

"With a dealer who thinks he's got an ace up his sleeve." He one-upped her.

"Okay, that's enough." She stepped to the door. "If I turn up anything, I'll let you know."

"Thanks for stopping by."

Kristin left Henry's house with a feeling of uncertainty. She had been so convinced he would understand and support her strategy—after all, he was the one who planted the seeds just yesterday. Stunned by Henry's obvious insecurity, despite her genuine assurances, Kristin became embittered by his mistrust and started to equate him with all the other men who'd come and gone in her life.

On the flipside of the door, Henry moaned. *Why did you do it, Sharpie? You're about to ignite an inferno that will burn you beyond recognition!*

* * *

Home alone in his haven of gadgetry, Eugene Maloney was parked in front of the large flat screen of his desktop computer. Like his good friend Henry, he had a pack rat mindset, but instead of hording toys, he had every kind of electronic gizmo imaginable. His meager residence was littered with old televisions, radios, speakers, cameras, phones, VCRs, CD and DVD players, computers, power strips, surge protectors, cables, cords, and endless other doodads—enough of an inventory for an electronics repair business.

The accumulation of his hodgepodge stockpile could be attributed to his compulsive habit of garbage picking. The old cliché of one man's trash is another man's treasure epitomized his gold standard of living—nothing is disposable, and everything is fixable. The only problem for him was that he accumulated much more than he could possibly repair—so much to do and so little time to get it done, even for a single fella with no social life.

Tonight, like most nights, Eugene surfed the net in solitude…at least until his phone started to explode with calls from Henry. After ignoring the first few calls, due to his intent focus on a new app, he finally picked up his cell, thinking it could be an emergency.

"*Whaaat?*" he half-joked to downplay the seriousness.

"Took you long enough, Baloney," Henry bantered.

"I was trying to set up a new profile for—"

"Looking for love online again?"

"Not exactly—no."

"Whatever it is, it needs to wait."

"What's so earthshaking that you couldn't wait for me to call you back?"

"Well, Houston…we got a problem."

"What may that be?"

"Our jewel is consorting with the enemy."

"Speak English."

"Sharpie's pretending to buy into Fast Freddie's sympathy routine."

"Why would she do that?"

"I dropped a bug in her ear about Tater Tot's involvement in that phony story, and now she wants to help play Sherlock Holmes."

"What's Freddie's sympathy bit got to do with anything?"

"She thinks she can get some info out of him about Tater Tots because of their history."

"That's good. Why are you so worried?"

"Because I'm convinced he's in cahoots with Tater Tots—that's why."

"Oh…I see…and here I thought you just sounded like a jealous man."

"That too," Henry said under his breath.

"Oh…so you do have feelings for her?"

"I would never tell anyone else, but yes—I really *like* her."

"Do you love her?"

"I'm not sure. I don't think I truly know what love is—at least not this kind of love."

"What a shocker: the man no one ever thought had a romantic bone in his body actually does. Now there's a news headline for the *Gazette!*"

"Please, just keep it to yourself."

"Don't worry, I won't post it on the net."

"Cool. Got anything on our target?"

"Let me check…I'm going to put you on speaker."

Maloney fingered the speaker icon on his phone and set it down by his keyboard. With a few clicks of the mouse, he accessed the keystroke logger he planted in Alma's keyboard. Visually scanning through all her activity, he looked for key words that would connect her to the *Gazette*, and now, anything that would tie her to Fred.

"Still there?" he asked Henry.

"Yeah…did you find anything?"

"Nope—nada."

"Ugh."

"Be patient, it's only the first day. This kind of a thing is going to take some time."

"We don't have much time," Henry stressed. "Every day that's wasted is another day Fast Freddie gets with my lady."

"Well, I still have her phone calls from today recorded. I'll listen to them later tonight."

"And if there's nothing there?"

"Well, I don't expect her to make a full confession out of the blue to anyone. That's why she's under surveillance—at your request, I might add."

"Would you be open to another request to speed things up?"

"It depends on what it is."

"We need her to think she's about to be exposed in order to force her to expose herself—make sense?"

"You want to set a trap."

"Yep…and I know just the right bait to use."

Chapter 13

U nder the fiery sky of autumn's dusk, Kristin took a deep breath in the cool breeze outside Perrinsville Perk. She was torn about her self-dispatched mission to unmask Alma Tater by stroking the ego of Fred Pace. If she *had* to cozy up to someone she'd rather avoid, he was at least easy on the eyes. She'd never been challenged with having to pump someone for information before, so this moment of truth proved to be a brainteaser beyond the safe space of her textbook library.

Kristin entered the busy coffee shop to the noticeable stares and whispers of the patrons and baristas. She halted a few feet from the door to scan the crowd, hoping to spot Fred before absorbing the full import of the bias against her presence. A large tanned hand stuck out, beckoning her to the rear corner. Recognizing Fred's signal, she nervously tiptoed through the crowded room to meet her point of contact. As she neared the small circular table, Fred's muscular physique greeted her with a friendly hug.

"Glad you came to see me, babe," he simpered.

Despite her conflicted attitude toward him, her ears tingled from the nickname "babe" vibrating from his thunderous vocal cords. Her delicate body felt like putty in his strong arms. She hated the way their previous date had ended, because he'd proved to be just another shallow Hal in a long line of romantic malfunctions. No amount of effort on his part could bring them to the emotionally charged intellectual stimulation she yearned for in matrimony. But for now, the firmness of his Herculean torso presented a level of physical safety she believed was lacking in the man she denied as her natural soulmate—Henry.

"I'm glad you're not afraid to be seen with me," she said, pulling away from him.

"I won't let anyone hurt you."

"I want to sit down. People are starting to stare."

"Let them. I'm not ashamed."

Kristin tugged at the wooden chair across from Fred. She slung her purse over the top corner of the backrest, then seated herself. The gym teacher soaked up her tight-jeaned leg cross before seating himself. He then inspected the rest of her fall attire before launching into his normal impulsive behavior.

"Love the form-fitting sweater and jeans with the boots…"

Guarding herself against any further flattery to stay on message, she waved her hand. "Um…can you get me a coffee, please?"

"Sure. What'll you have?"

"Whatever you're having is fine. I just don't want to draw any more attention to myself."

"Okay, I'll be right back." Fred got up and went to the front counter to order their drinks.

In the minutes of his absence, the PhD did her best to keep a low profile, aware that she was under a microscope. Kristin reactively dug into her purse to retrieve her cell phone. While scrolling through her newsfeed, she sensed the presence of someone looming over her. Tilting up, she discovered a creepy guy in her space.

"Can I help you," she asked cautiously.

"Sure can," he puckered with a toothpick between his chapped lips, "I'm a *homerun* hitter."

"Good for you," she responded in disgust.

"Wanna load the bases with me?"

"Ew—get away from me!"

"Aw, c'mon, honey, I'm a real power hitter—"

"Who's about to ground out!" Fred intervened with two piping-hot coffees in his hands.

"Look, Mighty Joe Young," the pervert condescended, "can't you see I'm trying to get a date here? Go pump some iron."

The phys ed coach's eyes narrowed. "Good idea." He set the coffee cups on the table, then manhandled the masher by the back of the collar and belt, sweeping him off the floor. "I'll start with *you!*"

"Put me down!" the man cried.

Kristin was aghast yet impressed.

"Gangway!" Fred shouted to the patrons. "Somebody get the door!"

As people cleared a pathway for the Pace express to plow through, a customer swung the door open for Fred to eject the reprobate like a barroom bouncer. Dismissing all the gasps on the way back to his table, Fred pretended to be shocked by the lewd behavior he was responsible for manufacturing.

"You okay?" he asked Kristin, returning to his seat.

With her palms wrapped around her cup, she gazed at him with a lump in her throat. "No one has ever defended me like that!"

"Well, I couldn't let that punk get away with disrespecting you."

"I'm truly moved," she confessed, nearly forgetting the real reason for their meeting.

"I know I started off on the wrong foot, but I care for you, and I'll do anything for you."

"I can see that."

"You do?"

"Um hmm...between confronting Bob Bakewell yesterday and this guy today, I believe you."

Fred peeled her right hand off her mug to caress it. She didn't resist, playing right into his hand—*or was she?*

"I really need to get to the bottom of that malicious story in the *Gazette*, or there will be more guys making disgusting passes at me."

"Let me know what I can do to help," he affirmed disingenuously.

"Well, you know Alma Tater probably better than anybody—"

"Used to know," he inserted. "Me and her were a long time ago. Bob's got her number these days."

"I can't go to him with my suspicions."

"Suspicions?"

"Yes. Someone set me up."

"I agree. The guy who leaked the story to Hurst is the perpetrator."

"I wish I could believe that, but I don't."

"Why not?"

"Because the details are grossly exaggerated."

"What do you mean?"

"There was enough truth for me to figure out where the story came from, and the guy I was seeing wouldn't have made that many mistakes in his recollection."

"*Really?*"

"Yes."

"I don't understand."

"I honestly don't want to rehash what's passed, but the guy I knew wouldn't have lied about me. He's bitter, yes, but he'd rather ruin me with truth, not lies. Besides, I have no idea how he would've found me."

"Sooo…you think Alma is the culprit?"

"Yes, I do."

Fred yanked his hand away to drink his coffee. Kristin made a mental note about the timing of his sudden hand jerk.

"You look a little surprised," she continued.

"I am. Why Alma?"

"Who profited most from my suspension?"

"Could be a coincidence?"

"I don't think so." She paused for a moment to taste her beverage before it got cold. "You don't know this, but she threatened me in the ladies' room on Parent-Teacher night."

"She did?"

"Yep. She made it very clear to me the principal job was supposed to be hers and that I was on notice to watch my back."

"I'm so sorry that happened."

"There's nothing for you to apologize for. I just need to find out how she set me up. I can't go to Bob after the way he treated me."

Fred shifted full throttle into liar mode. "Well, I don't know what I can do. Alma would never consider talking to me about anything—even if I tried to be sly about it."

"Maybe you can tell me what you know about her? Anything that comes to mind may help me figure out her MO."

"But it's ancient history."

"People don't change…at least not that much. Your past with her may be more revealing than you know."

"Okay…"

Just as Fred was about to leap into his *revised* history with Alma, a married couple approached their table.

"Aren't *you* that disgraced principal?" the woman fired in accusation.

Dr. Sharp's heart pounded to the surface of her chest.

"My wife is talking to you."

"I heard her," Kristin responded gingerly.

"I can't believe the school board was duped into hiring an alley cat like you to supervise our children," the wife continued.

"Please mind your own business. You don't know what you're talking about," Kristin pleaded.

The husband ripped into her. "We read the paper, missy!"

Fred rose to his feet, towering over the egregious man. "Then you know how much of a tabloid that scandal rag is!"

Once again, Kristin marveled at Fred's sturdy "illusion" of protecting her integrity from anyone and everyone.

"Sorry, Mr. Pace," the married man retorted. "We have a right as parents to be concerned about what our kids are being exposed to."

"As a teacher, I think of all the children there as *my* kids. I'm just as concerned as you are about the leadership of the school."

"Then how could you be here with this woman?" the wife asked.

"I don't believe the slander…"

"Libel," Kristin corrected.

"Yeah, the libel printed in that worthless paper. Dr. Sharp is innocent, and I'm going to help her prove it."

The marrieds swapped skeptical glances with each other.

"So if you're done defaming her, please leave us alone," Fred requested.

The couple shrugged on their way out. Fred sat down and took hold of Kristin's hands.

"Sorry you had to endure that."

"Are you my hero?"

"Hope to be."

"I think I've had enough excitement for one evening." She pulled her hands from his manly grip to gather her purse. "Thank you for the coffee. I'm going home now."

Seeming a bit jilted, Fred made an appeal for their evening to continue. "Wait, the night's just getting started, we can go somewhere else."

"Not tonight."

"Don't you want to hear my stories about Alma? I was ready to tell you before we were so rudely interrupted."

"I know." She stood and pushed in her chair. "Let's do it some other time."

"How about tomorrow?"

"I need to think about it."

"If you're worried about a public scene, I could come over to your place?"

"I'm not for that."

"My place?"

His pushiness scared her. "Slow down, Fast Freddie—you promised."

He bowed his head in defeat. "Yeah, you're right. Can I walk you to your car?"

Fearing he might try something outside the shop under the darkened sky, Kristin declined with a headshake. "Goodnight." She departed for the door.

"I'll call tomorrow to check on you," he shouted.

Without looking back, she waved bye-bye, leaving Fast Freddie in the lurch.

Chapter 14

"Attention all students, faculty, and staff,"—Mizz Tater's voice blared over the school's PA system—"there will be an assembly in the auditorium in ten minutes. Everyone's attendance is mandatory—no excuses."

Kids and teachers in all the classrooms appeared to be stunned by the unexpected announcement. The noneducational staff also looked strangely at one another on their way to the theater, as if they'd been summoned to a court of law. Henry could only surmise impending gloom and doom, particularly since he hadn't been instructed to set anything up for the event. He arrived in the packed playhouse to the sight of an isolated podium at center stage.

Intense curiosity mounted as everyone awaited their fearless leader's arrival. The noise level progressed to the height of a coliseum in ancient Rome. All the nonsensical chatter could be attributed to everyone's own psychic intuition of bad news on the horizon. Even Fast Freddie exhibited an air of discomfort in being there. Henry kept a close eye on him, feeling that whatever unpleasantness lay ahead, Fred had to be tied up in it one way or another.

Once Alma took to the stage with a notebook, she waved her arms to silence the crowd. Having a captive audience at her disposal emboldened her forthcoming abrasiveness. She toggled the On switch to the microphone and released an earsplitting pitch of feedback that seemed to last forever. After fooling with the microphone to quiet the tone, she commenced with her political agenda.

"Effective today, Perrinsville Elementary is going to break new ground. Having spent most of my life in our educational system, I have witnessed many institutional changes over the years that I don't believe are in the best interests of our students' curriculum."

Uh-oh, here we go, Henry thought from the back row.

"We must exercise strong discipline in every aspect of our lives from the moment we arrive at school until the bell rings at the end of the day. In fact, I would encourage everyone to apply that same mindset even when they're not in school."

Great—now she's gonna tell us how to live our lives, Henry conceived.

"So, what does this mean? It means that we are going to crack down on all the nonacademic activities. Our main focus and goal is to achieve the highest test scores…not just in the state, but across America."

The entire audience sat open-mouthed at the prospect of how this grand illusion of hers would be implemented.

"Achieving this longstanding dream of mine to become the educational envy of the nation will require strict adherence to the following: replacing morning and afternoon recess periods with increased classroom study time. No more morning football and gymnastics on the grounds before the morning bell. From now on, when students arrive, they will be expected to form lines by grade that the safety patrol *will* enforce. There will be no talking among the ranks, so you can mentally prepare yourself for the challenges of the day."

Henry clenched his teeth. *Is she kidding?*

"There will be a dress code that includes appropriate hairstyles, which I will send home with all of you."

This sounds more like a prison camp than a small-town elementary school!

"I'm going to piggyback on the lunchtime Quiet Time policy of my predecessor by declaring quiet time for the entire lunch period. Students are to be respectful of their teachers and school professionals. Any sign of disrespect, such as addressing them by something other than their proper name, will result in a weekend detention program."

One of the many horrified teachers stood up in protest. "This is ridiculous! We may as well just turn our fine school into a military academy!"

"Yeah," heckled another teacher. "This is crazy!"

Grumblings from the students and faculty erupted. Henry kept his watch on Fred. Instead of joining the growing revolt, the phys ed instructor slumped with a sagging face. It was obvious to the janitor that Alma's partner in crime exhibited buyer's remorse. Henry still hadn't figured out how Freddie factored into Kristin's demise, but he sure looked like a man who'd been double-crossed. No one had immunity from Tater's dictatorial rule.

"How long is this reign of terror going to last?" the first teacher exclaimed.

"Till I say otherwise," Alma mandated. "There's a new sheriff in town, and it's *me*."

Henry jumped out of his seat to set the record straight. "And you're gonna ride off into the sunset soon."

Alma smirked, as if to say, *Not in this lifetime.* "The previous tenant—that would be Dr. Sharp—has moved on to pursue other interests."

"How do you know that?" Henry threw back at her.

"Would you like to come to my office for a consultation?"

Henry's eyes narrowed as it was clear to him, and everyone else, that Alma was riding high on her power trip.

"That same invitation is extended to anyone else, teacher or student, in need of counseling." She scanned the long faces occupying the auditorium seats. "This is going to be the *new normal* around here, and you'll have to learn to like it. It sounds painful now, but when we get ourselves focused and persevere in our hard work, we'll become the benchmark in elementary academics and conduct. Now, let's all get back to class and go to work!"

Acting as though she'd won the crowd with an inspiring inaugural address, Alma closed her binder and exited the stage with her head in the clouds. The attendees arose from their seats and looked down at the floor; leaving the room like a team that just lost the Super Bowl. At that point, Henry was met by Maloney.

"What was *that?*"

"Tater Tot's revenge," Henry insinuated.

"I'm waiting for the bait you promised."

"Can you come to my shop at lunch?"

"Yeah."

"See ya then."

***

In her fuzzy pink robe and slippers, Kristin savored the tasty vegetarian omelet she had fixed herself for breakfast and gazed at the morning sunshine spilling through the windows. The pleasant aroma of hazelnut from the gourmet coffee next to her plate on the table added to the serenity of her quiet meal. It was just after nine o'clock, and she had taken complete advantage of sleeping in later than normal. Without a job, she didn't feel the need to be up any earlier nor to get dressed anytime soon.

Thoughts about last night's pseudo-date with Fred began to creep back into her mind as she chewed on small bites of her egg mix. The more she replayed them, the more conflicted she became—it was strange to her. Kristin couldn't decipher if she was coming or going with him. But what she did understand was a need for answers. Guilt in leading him on to get those answers upset her stomach. Dropping her fork onto the plate of half-eaten food, she clutched the coffee mug to blow off the steam to cool her java.

In the midst of her taster's choice, the ringtone from her cell phone went off on the countertop near the sink. She got up to look at the caller ID on the screen. It was Henry. Still miffed by his distrust of her proactivity to expose Alma Tater, she hesitated answering. Assuming he would leave a voice message, she returned to the table. No sooner did she sit down than the phone rang again. Thinking he would likely keep calling again and again, she reluctantly answered.

"Hello?"

"Hey, Sharpie."

"Hi, there."

"Before I go any further, let me apologize for bickering with you yesterday. I know you're doing what you feel is right. I'm sorry."

The calm sincerity in his voice soothed her soul in a way she couldn't rationally explain. "That's okay. I'm the one who should be sorry. I know you have my best interest at heart."

"You know I do. That's why I called."

"Okay."

"As much as it pains me knowing you went out with Fast Freddie, I wanted to ask how it went."

"Interestingly weird."

"How so?"

"I was stared at the whole time by everyone in the place. I felt completely naked."

"Aw, no..."

"Then I was hit on by a sicko—"

"Who probably undressed you with his eyes." Henry blurted.

"Yuck!"

"What else?"

"I was berated by a rude pair of misguided parents."

"What did Freddie do?"

"He defended me."

"Of course, he did."

"*What?*"

"Sorry—just my jealousy again."

"Please be careful."

"What else happened…with Freddie that is?"

"I let him know that I think Alma is somehow responsible for what happened."

"How did he react?"

"When he was holding my hand and I mentioned Alma, he pulled his hand away suddenly and tried to cover by drinking his coffee."

"He *knows* something."

The excitement in Henry's voice brought a picture of his beaming face to Kristin's mind.

"I think so, too, but I couldn't stand the awkwardness of being the center of attention there. I *had* to leave."

"I understand."

"Then he started to get pushy again when I got up to go."

"He never gets a clue."

"Well said; I couldn't agree more."

"Glad we reached common ground on that dreary topic."

"I don't know if I'll be ready to see him again."

"Don't worry; I'll take it from here. You didn't mention me at all, did you?"

"No."

"Good. Please keep it that way."

"Will do."

"Oh, by the way, Commandant Tater Tots—"

"*Commandant?*"

"Yep. You missed a real beauty this morning."

"What happened?"

"Tater's getting her long-awaited revenge on the town by turning the school into a concentration camp of higher learning."

"There's a real pun if I've ever heard one."

"I call 'em as I see 'em."

"There's never an element of phoniness with you," Kristin acknowledged. "So, what went down?"

"Let's just say, she took her first step out the door. You'll be welcomed back with open arms."

She gleamed. "I hope so."

"Trust me."

"*I do.*"

"Just stay away from Freddie in the meantime."

"*Henry*—what did we just talk about?"

"I'm not saying it out of jealousy this time. The less he knows the better."

"I'm not sure I understand why?"

"This is where blind faith comes in. You said you trust me—"

"Yes."

"Just do whatever it takes to avoid him till you hear back from me."

"How long will that be?"

"Within the coming days—gotta go."

"B-bye."

* * *

Shortly after the lunch bell rang, Eugene stepped into Henry's quarters to find him busy at his workbench soldering the front axle of a toy truck.

"What happened here?" Maloney inquired.

Henry flipped up his magnifying visor and rested the solder gun on its cradle. "Oh, just a cheap truck that was poorly made."

"Good thing no one was driving it," Maloney kidded, pointing to the repaired axle.

"Yeah, no seat belt and no insurance—*eek!*"

"So, what's your plan of action for Tater?"

Henry removed his visor, and slid off the stool to close the door of his workshop. "We're going to smoke her and Fast Freddie out."

"I figured that, but how?"

"Can you tap into their emails?"

"Yeah, but that would be very unethical and illegal."

"Okay…then can you create a fake email that looks enough like their real email addresses, just enough so they won't notice?"

"I think so."

"Good. I'd like you to create one for each of them that we'll send to their real emails, so they think they're communicating with each other."

Eugene's eyes widened. "Very sneaky…and I love it!"

"I want to generate enough panic between them so they agree to meet."

"A sting operation?"

"Elementary, my dear Baloney."

"And what happens when they *do* meet?"

"We get them to confess on tape."

"On tape?"

"Yeah…I'm sure you've got enough electronic doohickeys to rig a hidden camera and microphone to record everything they say."

"I sure do."

"How soon can you scrounge everything together?"

"I'll start tonight."

"Call me when your camera equipment is ready. I'm going to install it in one of the storage rooms—their designated meeting place."

"Not to throw a wrench into your plan, but why would they meet in the storage room when they could talk on the phone or meet somewhere later?" Maloney asked skeptically.

"Because they'll be so concerned with being seen together or overheard in their offices. The storage room is secluded enough to where no one will see or hear them. We'll send them there at different times, making sure they don't start talking until they're both in the room together."

"That sounds good in theory, but how are you going to guarantee this goes down according to plan?"

"Because I know them well enough to push their hot buttons," Henry boasted. "Once they take the bait, they'll want to confront each other immediately. Patience isn't a virtue for either of them."

"All right, I trust your judgment."

"Make sure to let me know when you've created the fake addresses. I'll need access to them."

"You got it."

"Once I send the first note, it's gonna be like dominoes—they'll fall fast and hard."

Chapter 15

Early the next morning, Eugene dropped off the equipment for Henry in a large corrugated box, along with a paper containing the phony email accounts and their passwords. The janitor waited till after hours to hook up the hidden camera system in the storage room. A wireless live feed would transmit the "reality show" to a closed-circuit TV and recorder stationed on his workbench. By sundown, the trap was tested and ready for its unsuspecting prey to step in it the next day. Henry spent the remainder of the evening completing his morning duties in order to be free for the Friday fireworks.

It was a relaxed morning at Perrinsville Elementary School, despite Alma Tater's para-militant policies, which had been instituted two days ago. Henry stood close to the main office with a broom to monitor the arrivals of his nemeses. Fred was the first to blow by him without any kind of a hello. Janet politely engaged in small talk with him until their boss arrived to scold them—*Back to work!*

As Janet returned to her desk, Henry pretended to sweep the floor he'd already cleaned last night. His purpose was to wait until Alma finished with the morning announcements over the PA system. He wanted to make sure she retreated to her perch before launching the hysteria. Discreetly peeking into the executive suite, he watched the acting principal resume her duties. With a broom in his hand, he whisked down the hall and past the gym to confirm that Fred was at his desk, since he had no first period class.

Behind a locked door in his workshop, Henry composed an email message to Alma from Fred on the laptop he had brought from home. His fingers pecked away feverishly on the keyboard next to the television equipment atop his workstation.

Alma,

My coffee date with Kristin went sour—she's onto us. I need to speak with you ASAP! Don't call me. Meet me.

Fred

He then sent another email to Fred from Alma.

Fred,

What is this I hear that Sharp suspects me of planting that story in the paper? I want to talk to you. Be smart and don't call me; just meet me.

Principal Tater

Relying heavily on their radically impulsive personalities, Henry didn't have to wait long for either of them to respond. Alma went first:

You idiot! How did that happen? Why are you emailing me? Our business is done!

Henry replied as "Fred."

I don't want anything going over email or to be overheard on the phone. It's too important and can't wait till later.

Alma fired back—*Why?*

The longer we wait to talk, the more time she has to expose us. We need to stop her now.

Just as he hit the send button, Fred's response to "Alma" flashed on his other browser screen.

Where did you hear that? I was very careful and didn't say anything. You're just being paranoid.

Henry responded quickly as "Alma."

You should know better than to call me paranoid when you do sloppy work. You get way too comfortable with yourself, and it will be to OUR detriment. I'm not going to play email or phone games, this must be dealt with face to face.

Fred typed back quickly—*I'll call you later.*

No, you idiot. I will not take any of your calls. We must talk without being overheard.

Fred reaffirmed his position—*That's why I'll call you later tonight.*

Caught between two stubborn characters, Henry's pulse rate increased. "Aw c'mon Freddie…you're not gonna make it easy for me, are you," he said to himself. In his best Tater mode, he sought to end the chain.

I said NO!!!!! Meet me in the storeroom near the auditorium at 9:30. Do not be late. I will be there a few minutes later so no one sees us together. If you are not there, I will expose YOU before your Barbie princess does.

Without hesitation, Fred agreed—*OK.*

Looping back to Alma, Henry scanned her response.

I'm much too busy for this nonsense. Don't blame me if you're in trouble… I won't save you.

"I'm gonna have to play hardball with *you* too," Henry whispered to the computer screen. In his best Fred impersonation, he wrote back.

She called you out by name to me over coffee. She knows!

Alma responded—*I'll deny it.*

Your denials won't be believed. She knows the guy in the story didn't source it. I'm telling you she knows it was you. Please don't force my hand. Let's talk now before she goes to the press to refute the story, and they decide to investigate us.

Fine!—Alma shot back—*When and where?*

I'll be in the storage room by the auditorium at 9:30. Come a few minutes later so no one sees us meeting up.

There was no response from Alma, which made Henry a bit apprehensive. Yet, he had to rely on his own instincts about them.

Glancing at the clock, he saw that it was almost show time. Logging out of his computer, and closing the screen lid, he turned to the TV screen. Henry switched on the monitor to view an empty storage room. He withdrew a pair of headphones from Eugene's corrugated box to plug into the recorder, as the volume on the TV needed to be muted—a precautionary measure should anyone be outside his door to eavesdrop on the school's amateur soap opera.

In the minutes leading up to Fred's arrival, Henry's nervous perspiration began to soak the armpits of his loosely buttoned flannel, right through his undershirt. If the plan failed, there would certainly be a relentless pursuit of investigations leading right to his doorstep. Getting fired didn't bother him as much as the thought of Maloney's demise and even more the vicious retaliation against Kristin—*they'll destroy her.* The operation was a big gamble, and the betting odds were fifty-fifty.

With that thought in mind, the first half of the dynamic duo entered the storage room right on cue. Judging by Fred's facial tics, it was obvious that he did not want to be there. Fred lived up to his surname by pacing back and forth with his hands in the pockets of his shorts. The visual nauseated Henry. He couldn't wait for Alma to get there. Every sound coming through the speaker of his headphones deepened the suspense of her entry, not to mention the agonizing thought of someone knocking on his own door, which was never locked during school hours.

"Let's go, Tater Tots…we haven't got all day," Henry said under his breath. Several minutes passed, and Fred seemed to be getting suspicious. Henry heard, "I'm out of here," as Fred reached for the doorknob, which started to turn before his hand touched the stainless steel. Alma flung the door open like an angry tigress.

"I'm here," she said.

As the hydraulic door swayed shut, Henry pressed the record button on the digital recorder.

"Let's get this over with," she roared.

"Yes, let's do that," he retorted.

"How does she know?"

"She's not dumb, Alma. Kristin figured out where the story came from and that the guy wouldn't know where to find her, let alone tell such a twisted version of it."

"That's not my problem. Changing the details of the story was your department."

"And I did it flawlessly. Hurst had no idea he was talking to *me* on the phone."

"You're sure about that?"

"Positive! I used a burner phone that can't be traced and disguised my voice."

Henry ground his teeth at Fred's stunning admission coming through his headphones loud and clear.

"Then why am I a suspect?" Alma asked.

"She told me about the confrontation you had with her in the bathroom."

"So what?"

"You have no idea how much of a turnoff your bitterness is—"

"I don't care. Just tell me why I'm a suspect."

"She knows you profited from her suspension, so it wasn't hard to figure out."

"All I'm hearing is speculation—where's your proof?"

"She told me to my face. Kristin wants me to help her expose you by telling her anything and everything I know about you."

"Well, you just stick to the plan and throw her off the scent. Otherwise, you'll have to start looking for love in other places."

"I don't know if I can..."

Alma went for his jugular. "This was *your* scam!"

Fred lowered his head like a wounded puppy.

Showing no mercy, she mimicked him. "Kristin's the kind of girl a guy wants to take home to the family."

"Shut up!"

"You best get your lovesick heart in check because I'm not going down for you," she threatened.

"If I go down, so do you."

Alma stepped forward to get right in his face. "Is that a threat?"

"I never could've done it without you getting her résumé from Bob's office."

"You can't prove it. I'll deny everything. My word carries more weight than yours ever will."

"You're heartless."

"No—I'm winning! And I'm just getting warmed up."

"What's that supposed to mean? You got the job you always wanted."

"Yes, but now I have a bigger mission to accomplish."

"Like what?"

"Seeing you squirm made me realize that I shouldn't have to settle for being the principal of this school."

"What are you plotting now?"

"As soon as my policies culminate, I'm going before the school board to unseat Bobby boy."

"You've lost your mind, sister."

"No more than you, brother. You dumped me all those years ago, and my life's been crap. Bob strung me along after you, and my life is still crap. You're a washed-up athlete on thin ice with the district, so that's one down and one to go."

"You're gunning for Bob?"

"And I can count on you not to utter a word, or I'll see to it that your little Miss Prissy finds out what you did to her, so you could pick up the pieces." She giggled for a second. "You know what's funny about that? It'll be *your* pieces that need picking up, and she won't want to touch them."

Alma's "flexed muscles" had the gym teacher's back to the wall—powerless to defend himself.

As a spectator, Henry almost felt sorry for Fred. Yet, he couldn't contain his good fortune, as the odds paid off better than a Vegas casino. He had more than enough to clear Kristin, and he'd just uncovered Alma Tater's coup to overthrow the superintendent. He had struck gold and couldn't wait to rescue the woman entangled by this elaborate web of deceit.

"This meeting is over. I don't ever want to hear from you again," Alma demanded. "No more emails."

Fred snarled. "Same to you."

"Don't you dare leave until I'm long gone."

"I wouldn't want to be seen with you anyway."

Alma opened the door to exit. At this moment, Henry stopped the recorder and pulled out the video card. As soon as he had removed his headphones, he sprinted out of his shop and down the hall. On his hurried trek to the computer lab, he nearly steamrolled Alma on her way back to the main office.

"Hey, slow down, Hubbard! No running!" she hollered.

"Sorry...I have an urgent mess to clean up," he yelled, rounding the corner.

Alma carried on without a second thought or care about him. As long as she didn't have to look at him, she was fine. To her, Henry Hubbard was nothing more than a conversation piece.

Reaching the entry to the computer lab, Henry disrupted Eugene's class with exaggerated throat clearings. "Ahem..."

"Henry," "Hi, Henry," the kids randomly acknowledged.

"Please continue to work on your web searches for the next few minutes," Eugene instructed the class before stepping outside to converse with the gleeful janitor, bursting at the seams.

"I got it!" Henry squealed.

"You did?"

"It's a godsend."

Maloney clenched his fist and jerked his arm. "Cha-ching!"

"Look, I need to come to your house tonight to make a few copies."

"I'll be there. Can't wait to see it."

Being in earshot of what was just said as he strutted by, Fred stopped to bully them. "Planning to copy a dirty movie?"

"Shh! Seriously, Fred? I've got a room full of kids," Eugene pointed out.

"They didn't hear anything; you're overreacting," Fred replied pompously.

Henry intervened with raised eyebrows. "I'd say your immediate presumption that two single men you believe to be beneath you have to find gratification in obscene media is overreacting."

"One of these days, Henry, I'm going to stuff you back inside the same locker I did when we were kids here."

"Me got big muscles—me break bones," Henry mocked.

Fred tightened his red face. "Maybe that day is now." He double-fisted Henry's flannel shirt.

"Kids are watching," Eugene interrupted.

Fred peered into the room to see the captivated class gawking at him above their monitors. To his chagrin, he was forced to release Henry with a fake smile.

"Get back to your assignment," Maloney instructed his students.

"Go shoot some hoops before it's game over," Henry wisecracked to his adversary.

"We're not done yet," Fred growled.

"For once, I agree with you. We'll settle this score later."

"You *really* want to?"

"Count on it."

The phys ed teacher shrugged in disbelief before moving along to the gym.

"That was close, Henry," Eugene sighed.

"He's just full of hot air. After what I saw of him with Tater Tots, he's just a big bad wolf huffin' 'n' puffin'. He thinks I'm the pig in the straw house, but what he doesn't know is I'm more than the pig who built the brick house—*I am* the brick house."

Chapter 16

On what was just another uneventful Saturday morning for the town of Perrinsville, Kristin began to feel the confines of isolation in the magnificence of her home. Her blind trust in Henry's plan kept her from any sense of normalcy for fear of running into Fred. His relentless pursuit of her since their parting at the coffee shop earlier that week propelled the definition of tenacity into borderline stalking.

Her phone constantly buzzed with voice messages and texts from the overzealous gym teacher. Any sudden noise from outside grazing her ears sent her to the nearest window to investigate, especially at night. Car-door slams were particularly jarring. She debated whether or not to set foot outside the door, worried he might jump out of the bushes. The fact that Fred could be an accomplice in Alma's trickery, as well as Henry's warning to avoid him, added to Kristin's paranoia. She had nothing to do but stew about her predicament, every hour of the day spent in a self-imposed quarantine.

Conventional wisdom gave her the freedom to roam about town during school hours while the man with the deep tan was at work. Yet, her past experience with Clifton Spencer forced Kristin to err on the side of caution—Fred might be desperate enough to call in sick, just to catch her off guard. The drama of daytime serials seemed surreal compared to the new storyline developing in her own little world.

Henry's expected lifeline needed to come *fast!*

Kristin's restless heart couldn't be contained any longer as she lay in bed staring at the ceiling. She wanted a progress report, and she wanted it *now.* Taking hold of the cell phone, she pushed the buttons militantly to the cleanup man's number, then anxiously awaited his pickup.

"Good morning, Sharpie!" Henry answered with a perky smile. "What's up?"

She got right to the point. "Besides my blood pressure, I'm dying for some news."

"Funny you should say that—"

"Why?" she interjected.

"Make sure to get a copy of tomorrow's *Gazette.* There'll be a heck of a headline that's gonna rock this town."

Kristin gulped.

"Hey, that kinda reminds me of an eighties song," he joked. "Great decade for music."

"You're killing me with suspense. What's going to be in the paper tomorrow?"

"Let's just say, Hurst the Worst is going to eat his words."

"Oh, brother, you're talking in riddles—speak plainly, please."

"Okay. In plain terms, the paper is going to print a *huge* retraction about their unfounded story on you."

"That's wonderful!" she sighed. "What's it going to say?"

"Well, if I tell you, then it will ruin my surprise."

"I don't follow."

"And I don't want you to—at least not now. I want you to be just as surprised as the rest of the town. Only for *you* it will be a well-deserved surprise—make sense to you?"

"I think so."

"You said you trust me, Sharpie."

"Yes, I did say that."

"So, fasten your seat belt and put your crash helmet on."

"Oh, now you're sounding like a fortune-teller."

"Yes, I am, and your future, or should I say, your very near future looks bright."

"Then tell me…ahem, oh, great one…am I getting my job back?"

"I guarantee it!"

"Now you're sounding like a used car salesman."

"And I'll give you a far better deal."

Kristin couldn't help but laugh at his comedic comebacks to anything and everything she threw at him. But what was more mesmerizing to her was the innate candor embedded in his humor. She liked it—a lot! Their chemistry was undeniable, and she knew it. Kristin also knew that Fred could never match wits with Henry. If only she could put Henry's personality into Fred's body, then she'd have the man of her dreams.

"Ah, speaking of deals, my good man, did you catch the perpetrator?"

"Caught on tape."

"Alma?"

"Affirmative."

"What about Fred?"

"What about him?"

"Was he involved?"

"Have you spoken to him since we last talked?"

"No. I did what you told me to, but it's been really difficult."

"Let me guess, your phone's gone batty?"

"More than you know. I've been afraid to leave my house thinking he's somewhere outside."

"Good. Stay on track…at least till tomorrow."

"So, he was involved?" she asked nervously.

"As much as I love talking with you—and I do—I think it's better we not continue this conversation until Monday when I see you back at work."

"You're sure about that?"

"I know this town and the people in it far better than I'll ever get credit for."

She sensed a ray of hope in his omen. "I trust you, Henry."

"You've got a big day tomorrow. Just keep your cool, and I'll see you back at school."

"Thank you."

"Ciao."

Tossing the phone on her bed, Kristin bounced up with excitement at the promise of reclaiming her life. As she stretched her arms beyond the cuffs of her night shirt, she heard a humming in the ruffled comforter. Kristin turned on her bare heels to retrieve the phone. Fred Pace—*again!*

* * *

Earlier that morning, just before dawn, Brice Hurst was awakened by a loud knock on his front door. Taking the necessary precaution of fetching the baseball bat underneath his bed, he headed for the door in his underwear. His thirst for gossip to publish had placed him on the town's public enemies list more times than he could count throughout the years. He'd been in the newspaper game all his adult life. Hurst once thrived on honest reporting until it became boring. He envied the loyal readership of the tabloids, despite their questionable stories based on the testimonies of questionable sources.

Once Hurst became editor of the publication he had slaved at for more than twenty years, he subjugated the pages of the *Perrinsville Gazette* with as many sensationalized stories as he could "legally" fabricate. Most people knew nothing newsworthy happened in their stagnant community, so they welcomed the yellow journalism standard of Joseph Pulitzer to spice up their lackluster lives. With circulation fading due to the popularity of online news, Hurst often exploited the pillars of Perrinsville through gross distortions difficult for them to deny. This practice put a target on his back.

Upon opening his front door to a darkened porch, he noticed a mysterious padded envelope on his welcome mat. Hurst scooped up the small package and surveyed the porch before closing the door. He then turned on the lamp by his couch. The blank pouch could be just about anything. He examined it carefully under the light to make sure there wasn't any strange powder or other substance on its exterior. It appeared safe to open. Sitting down on his comfortable sofa, he tore open the package. Inside the bubble wrap was a memory stick and an anonymous typewritten note that read, *Dr. Kristin Sharp deserves a major league apology.*

Curious as ever about what could be on the memory stick, Hurst scooted to his musty-smelling home office in the spare bedroom. Among many stacks of old newspapers and manila folders galore on a desk fit for the president of a large corporation was a dusty computer with a keyboard, spotless from recent use. He plugged the stick into his hard drive and wheeled himself in the chair to the desk. *Let's see what we got here*, he thought, while opening the video file. And within seconds, the incriminating video of Alma Tater and Fred Pace played for the prying eyes of the town's gossiper-in-chief.

"Wow…I don't believe it…get out of here…incredible…" he muttered every now and then throughout the video. By the time it concluded, the veteran news hack, now suffering from extreme anger, pounded his fist on the desk so hard that the dust mites ran for cover. He looked at the note with wonder. *Who? What? Where? When? And how did this tape come into existence?* The journalistic question he didn't need to ask was *why*—the answer to that was in his hand. *And rightfully so,* he thought—especially since they played him for a fool.

Swiveling to clear a pile of papers covering his desk phone, he made a call to the press room at the *Gazette*. "I want you to clear the front page of tomorrow's edition," he told the person on the other end of the phone. "I have the biggest, most shocking exposé in the history of this paper to plaster across the front page!"

Chapter 17

T he big Sunday morning edition of the *Perrinsville Gazette* shook the town like a major earthquake. "SHARP VINDICATION" in gigantic capital letters stretched across the top of the front page, with a photo from the surveillance video of Fred and Alma below the banner. The scathing article completely exposed the fraud perpetrated on the school district, as well as the entire community, through transcribed excerpts from the tape and biographical details of the conspirators' personal histories, and Hurst's admitted embarrassment of being duped by them.

Henry made sure to get a copy hot off the press at the paper's first newsstand outside their building just before sunrise. Hopping back in his van, he flicked on the overhead light to read the investigative piece he uncovered. As pleased as he was about the scandal being made public, it was more important to him that the journal apologized for the damaging pain it had caused Kristin. The further he read, the more obvious it became that Hurst was more interested in the muckraking aspect of the event than the defamation acquittal suggested in the headline. It wasn't till the very end of the report that he read the words he hoped would've led the piece.

The Gazette is deeply sorry for the libel against Dr. Kristin Sharp. We would like to respectfully thank the mysterious party responsible for doing the job we should've done ourselves.

Not exactly the kind of exoneration he sought, but understanding the type of man Hurst was, Henry accepted the weak apology, secure in the knowledge of its good outcome. Folding the paper back up, he started his jalopy to personally, and anonymously, deliver a copy to the person this story mattered to most—Kristin! The sun was about to light up the sky, so he had to hurry to avoid being spotted. Arriving near her house, he made sure to park far enough away that his vehicle wouldn't be seen when she opened her blinds to greet the new day. This was the second morning in a row he had to act like a cat burglar, minus the heist.

By the time he had made it back home, he was fighting the temptation to give Kristin a wakeup call. Henry so wished he could be there to witness her response to the paper's headline. Yet, he painted himself into a corner, powerless to contact her until the plan's chain reaction reached its conclusion. There was no way for him to estimate the time frame of Bakewell's actions in firing Fred and Alma, which he surely would do prior to reinstating Kristin. Henry's gut told him it would be today; he just didn't know *when.* And while his heart began to pound with anxiety, he needed to allow her the time and space to absorb what would surely be the talk of the town.

* * *

Kristin had suffered from insomnia due to her conversation with Henry early the previous morning. His assurance of today's projected events had weighed heavily on her mind since hanging up with him. She knew only that it would be big news, based on the little information given to her. Looking at the clock, she decided it was time to roll out of bed, get dressed, and head for the nearest newsstand. Like a new recruit in basic training answering the call of "Reveille," she got ready on the double and rushed out the door, only to be halted at the threshold by the communique touching her feet.

There they were, the two jaw-dropping words leaping off the paper. Kristin screamed with delight, as if she were a little girl on Christmas morning discovering that long awaited present underneath the tree from Santa Claus. It was the miracle she wanted, courtesy of jolly old Saint Henry himself. Bending at the knees, she squatted to retrieve the paper from the porch before breaking into a happy dance. Pivoting back inside and flinging the door shut, she collected her thoughts to focus on the news clutched in her hands.

Mumbling the written words on the page as she stepped toward the sofa to sit, Kristin cut her victory lap short after her wide-eyed discovery of the principal offender in her destruction. Dr. Sharp's controlled hands went haywire with anger, crinkling the paper into a ball for the kitchen trash can. The heel of her boot nearly left a permanent scratch on the floor from her reflexive foot stomp. Though her justifiable tantrum lasted only a few seconds, she knew the lingering wounds of her injury from yet another man who betrayed her trust needed the kind of therapeutic cure only found in the unlikeliest of professionals—*Calling Dr. Hubbard.*

* * *

Immersed in her own sphere of power, Alma sat at her home computer ready to plot her next incremental move toward usurping the school board's leadership. The occasional email from angry parents in her accessible school in-box was not out of the ordinary, same deal regarding unpleasant phone messages. She routinely deleted them without a care in the world. After all, she knew why kids called her "Mizz Tater Tots," and as far as she was concerned, Mr. Strickland, the fictitious principal in the *Back to the Future* movies, got it right by calling them out as "slackers!"

However, this morning's email attack bombarded her as if it had been infected by a malware virus. Her cell phone also went berserk. Every few seconds there was either another new email notification or phone number on her caller ID. Curiosity about the electronic helter-skelter compelled Alma to react to the influx of communications inundating her devices. Shock and awe overwhelmed Mizz Tater as she scanned the unprecedented volume of requests for her to resign immediately. Her first response mandated that she terminate the messages without examination. Short subject lines, like "Resign," "Traitor," "Fraud," and "Scammer" panicked Alma about the truth revealed in each of the messages.

Confidence in her tactical maneuver now turned to fear, as Mizz Tater realized she had been exposed. And there could only be one logical explanation—Fred! *He double-crossed me*, she seethed. In the heat of the moment, she reached for the phone to give him a piece of her mind. But before Alma could dial his number, the phone rang again, with the name Bob Bakewell appearing on the ID. There was no way to avoid *him* of all people. Mizz Tater knew if she didn't take his call now, he'd be at her door in a matter of minutes. "Hello?"

* * *

Waking up from his long night of beauty rest, Fred fumbled out of bed with only one thought on his mind—Kristin. It had been days since he had seen her in the coffeehouse, and her silence since then was deafening to him. He had always gotten his way with women, including those who later complained about him. Thinking of himself as a Mr. Universe to the female population he was taken aback by the dainty out-of-towner whose *no* really did mean "NO" and not "yes," as imprinted on the frontal lobe of his brain. Fred didn't know how to cope with her willpower, which only inflamed his passion of pursuit to no end.

Draped in his terry-cloth bathrobe, he wrestled with his next move in an attempt to contact her. Not yet ready to let the daylight into his gloomy apartment, he found solace in the dark as it bore a reflection of what lurked beneath the surface of his bronzed tan. His devious heart ached from the sins he refused to repent from in the name of love. Turning to one of the many protein shakes in his fridge in order to spike his sluggish energy level, Fred's ears wiggled from the special ringtone on his phone assigned to Kristin. Responding like a canine to a dog whistle, he vigorously charged for the phone before it went to voice mail. And to prevent his desperate desire from showing through the phone, Fred took a deep breath for an air of confidence.

"Hey, babe."

"Did you read this morning's *Gazette*?" she grilled.

"Nope, not after the story they printed about you."

"Don't you mean the story *you* planted about me?"

A shiver ran up his spine, breaking his firm body into a cold sweat. "Ah…what are you getting at?"

"Don't play dumb jock with me, *Fast Freddie*."

"Why did you call me that?"

"Because *you're always on the move*."

"I'm not sure I understand, but whatever's got you so mad, I want to help."

"You must be joking."

"I don't get it."

"Your secret meeting with Tater Tots is out of the closet—the jig is up. It's all over town how the two of you conspired to set me up."

Fred's trembling hand dropped the phone onto the carpeted floor, which was in desperate need of a vacuuming. With tears of sorrow dripping from his glassy eyes, he fell to his knees, aware that his chickens had come home to roost. He scooped up the phone with a shaky hand while his body crouched like a little boy being scolded by the principal.

Kristin's angry tone continued to pipe through phone. "It was all caught on tape, so there's no denying it."

"What tape?"

"The video tape of you and Alma in the storage closet at school."

"That's impossible."

"If it's impossible, how would I know you were in the closet with her? Tell me that?"

"It's not what it appears to be—I can explain."

"Go ahead, this ought to be rich."

"Well…you see…I remembered your suspicions about Alma, so I tried to trap her into a confession."

"Did your con include Clifton Spencer?"

"Who's that?" he fudged.

"Don't you know?"

"Ah…should I?"

"He's the guy who supposedly made up all the wild accusations about me to the paper."

"Well, there you go. Maybe he worked with Alma to plant that story."

"Not true."

"Huh?"

"You see, I called him after I read about your involvement."

Fred's dark tanned skin turned ghostly white.

"He wasn't very hard for me to find," she continued. "As soon as he heard my voice, he melted like candlewax. Despite what he told you—and yes, he said he spoke to *you*—he's still very much in love with me. It didn't take a lot of pressure to get the truth out of him."

There was dead silence from the boastful man who was typically never at a loss for words.

"Fred? Are you still there?"

"Yeah…" he whimpered.

"So stop with the lies. You're every bit as guilty as your ex, and in my book, you're by far more manipulatively deceitful than she could ever be."

"I'm so, so, so sorry…"

"Your sorrow isn't enough. You masterminded this entire artifice."

"Art-a-what?"

"Deception! You pretended to be my friend and pledged to help me just to string me along, hoping I'd fall madly in love with you and live happily ever after with a scandal attached to my name."

"I understand you're mad at me, and you have every right to be."

"That's the first intelligent sentence constructed by your limited cranial capacity."

Fred was clearly no match for her *sharp* tongue. "Can we just talk this over in a few days when the dust settles?"

"No Freddie, we can't."

"But I love you!" he blurted out loudly.

"People do all kinds of crazy things for love. And I'm discovering that I kind of *like* a little craziness, as long as it's fun crazy—not delusional crazy!"

"So, what are you saying?"

"*Goodbye, Fred*—that's what I'm saying."

"Permanently?"

"Yes—goodbye."

The click of her hanging up would forever echo in Fred's eardrum. In a fit of rage, he hurled the phone clear across the room like a shortstop catching a ground ball to throw out a batter at first base for the final out—game over!

* * *

It had been an exhausting morning for Kristin. Her emotions twisted and turned more than a corkscrew roller-coaster ride, sucking the air out of her lungs. By the time late morning church services had ended, her weary body was ready for a nap. She wanted to call Henry really badly, but his promise of her getting reinstated had yet to be fulfilled. Trusting him prevented her from making that call. He had affirmed that he would see her back at school, so she needed to exercise a fair amount of patience. Even though the morning had been jam-packed with news, the day was still young, and the big reward had yet to surface.

Kicking her boots off at the foot of her couch, she prepared to lie down for that well-deserved snooze by fluffing one of the pillows. Just as she sat down to remove her thick glasses and unclip her hair, the doorbell rang. Composing herself, she ran to the door to look through the peephole. Bob Bakewell stood alone, in his Sunday best, overshadowed by remorse. She eagerly opened the door to welcome his visit.

"Bob!"

"Hello, Kristin. May I come in?"

"Yes, please."

She graciously closed the door behind him. "Can I get you anything? Coffee? Tea?"

"No, thank you. I'm the one who needs to make an offer to you."

"Would you like to sit down?"

"What I need to say, I'd rather do standing."

"Is it about the exposé in today's paper?"

"Yes, and let me say how deeply sorry I am for all the trouble I caused you."

"Given the seriousness of the charge…"

He abruptly waved his hand. "Those blasted words will haunt me till kingdom come. I was sooo wrong in the way I overreacted and mishandled the entire situation."

"I'm sure you were just following protocol."

"That's where I went wrong. We are a small community here, and despite all the stereotypes of a town like ours, I could've bent the rules to afford you the presumption of innocence pending proof of guilt, instead of the other way around." He bowed his head in shame. "Can you forgive me?"

"With open arms." She gave him a heartfelt hug, as he had earned back all the respect she held for him.

"I should've seen this coming a mile away. Alma's been auditioning for that job as long as I've known her. I always assumed that would be her ultimate goal…I had no idea she was also planning to take me out."

"Evil is never satisfied, but it will always be defeated by truth."

"Amen to that. I fired Alma and Fred and would very much like to have you reclaim your rightful position."

"What about Alma's personal items?"

"Henry should be boxing up her stuff now, as well as Fred's trinkets, for home delivery today. They're not allowed back on the school grounds, and I'm going to meet with the board to consider whether or not to press charges. You're welcome to be a part of that discussion."

"I'll abide by whatever additional punishment you decide for them. I have a feeling neither of them will ever work in education again, and maybe that's punishment enough."

"You have a very forgiving heart. I commend you."

"Thank you."

"So, can I assume that you'll report back tomorrow?"

"Bright and early!" She shone like the morning sun.

Chapter 18

"Welcome back, Dr. Sharp!" Janet Goode cheered when Kristin walked through the administrative office door Monday morning in a forest-green pantsuit. To Janet, it was as if a soldier had come to liberate them from the bondage of tyranny. Tears of joy trickled from her eyes as she ran toward her beloved supervisor with arms wide open. Kristin set down her unpacked box of personal belongings and her travel mug to prepare for Janet's wholehearted embrace. She then slid the shoulder strap of her briefcase to free her arms.

"You're truly a vision of grace," Janet cried.

"Thank you. It's great to be back."

"I—or should I say, *we*—all missed you *so* much."

"I was only gone a week."

"Yes, but it seemed like a lifetime around here. It was utterly miserable."

"Well, have no fear. I'm back to stay, and nothing's going to make me leave ever again."

Janet shimmered with hope.

"At least not until *I'm* darn good and ready to go," Kristin kidded.

"When will you be darn good and ready?"

"When I'm old enough to retire." She winked.

The secretary stepped aside for the principal to proceed to her office.

"Please go and take your rightful place. I'll get your stuff here."

"That's very good of you."

"That's why I'm Goody Two-shoes around here."

Kristin chuckled, heading into her office with Janet close behind, carrying all her things like an experienced bellhop. The dead-feeling suite was suddenly brought to life by the woman in green, whose presence restored the integrity of the decisions made from the executive desk. Reclaiming her chair as Janet placed her items on the desk, Kristin remembered the demonization she had experienced the last time she sat there.

"I'll be getting back to my work," Janet said, interrupting Kristin's flashback.

"Oh, yes…thanks for the delivery."

The reinstated principal began to unbox her stuff one piece at a time. Within a few seconds of her unpacking, a friendly voice captured her attention.

"Be careful…there's breakables in there."

Her eyes peered over the top of her horn-rims.

"I should know, I packed them myself."

Releasing the biggest, most jubilant smile of her entire existence, Kristin ran from behind the desk to throw herself at the ragged-looking man responsible for giving her life back to her.

"Get in here, *you!*" she decreed. "Shut the door."

Henry obeyed with his usual slouchy body language saying, *Yes ma'am, but what's all the hubbub about?*

Wrapping her arms around him, she impulsively planted a kiss on his lips. The kind of kiss that conveyed more than just gratitude, it unveiled the suppressed feelings she had been saving up for that special man who would someday sweep her off her feet.

"Wow, Sharpie, what did I do to deserve that?" he asked as if *he* didn't already know, which had heavily influenced his blatant decision to sport a Superman T-shirt under his open flannel button-down.

She lightly fingered the *S* on his shirt. "You came to my rescue—*Superman!*"

Assuming all the modesty of Clark Kent, he blushed. "Oh, I could never be like *him.*"

"Well, you proved to be *my* superhero."

She pressed her tender lips against his prickly whiskers once again. For as brief as the kiss lasted, Henry clung to every second of its moistness. It reflected the purity and innocence he saw in her and added to the exhilaration of his first real kiss. Their temporary lapse in time ended upon the realization of their surroundings. This wasn't the time or place to explore their unfolding chemistry—they certainly didn't want another scandalous headline.

Kristin pulled back. "Forgive me if I got a little carried away."

"No worries. There's nothing to forgive."

She returned to her desk. "Please sit down. I can't thank you enough."

"I think you just did," he responded with a smile, taking a seat in front of her desk.

She leaned forward with a curious look in her eye. "How did you get them on tape?"

"I had a little help from Baloney Maloney in getting the equipment to set the trap."

"I'll have to thank him."

Henry's jealously flared up. "Not the way you thanked me, I hope."

"Of course not, but if he helped out, I at least owe him my acknowledgment."

"I think he'll be fine just knowing you're back and he can breathe freely again."

"Okay, if you say so."

"The only people who know I'm responsible for the sting are the three of us. Let's not let it go any further."

"Doesn't the newspaper know?"

"Hurst the Worst is clueless. He published that malicious story Fast Freddie concocted on anonymity, so I figured he could retract it on anonymity. He has no idea who dropped off the unmarked package at his house, so he can claim plausible deniability if there's any kind of backlash…as doubtful as that is."

"The press has a duty to protect the identity of their sources."

"Maybe in the big cities, but not here. Hurst would cave under the slightest bit of pressure. He's not the muckraker he used to be by a long shot. It's for his own protection that he doesn't know."

"That's very commendable of you."

"I just wanted justice to be done by you getting your job back and things around here to be the old normal again. I could've easily destroyed them by sending that tape to the TV news, a ton of social media platforms, and direct email to the state's department of education…but if I did, I'd be just as bad as *them*—right?"

She nodded, admiring the humility in his wisdom.

"As much as I hate what was done to you, I thought it fitting for the guilty to suffer the same embarrassing consequences they inflicted upon you."

"Hopefully, they learned their lesson."

"I'm sure neither of them is going to risk showing their faces in public anytime soon. If you thought the shunning you got was bad—wahoo—wait till you see how they're going to be treated. And believe me, they *know* it. They're going to be living like hermits, eating a lot of humble pie."

Kristin praised him for his wordplay analogy. "You really have a wit about you—an important quality I've always wanted in a man."

"Then what made you want to date Fast Freddie? Besides his athletic looks."

She rested her chin in her hands. "That really makes me appear superficial, doesn't it?"

"I tried to warn you about him."

"Yes, you did. But his appearance was only a delightful bonus."

"Sharpie…c'mon…"

"I think I was more caught up in his flattery of me. My whole life I always felt guys like him were laughing at me. It's just one of many stigmas I've worked hard to overcome, but I've always fallen short, or chickened out, of evicting the voice of doubt living rent-free in my head."

"There's nothing to becoming your *own* self."

"Well, that's easier said than done."

"Not if you have someone to help you."

"And whom might that be?" Kristin asked as if *she* didn't know.

"You only need to look as far as the front end of your desk."

"Are you asking me out?"

"Would you like me to?"

She nodded giddily.

"Okay…wanna go out sometime?"

"Yes! Today—after work."

"Ooh, that doesn't give me any time to come up with a plan."

"We don't need a plan. An early dinner will be fine."

Henry stood up. "Well, I better go tell Goody Two-shoes the good news."

"About us?"

"Oh no. My lips are sealed till you're ready to go public. I know how reserved you are."

"I appreciate that. So what good news are you telling Janet?"

"The irony of Fast Freddie's debacle. He rigged a crisis so he could be the one, as he confessed, 'to pick up the pieces.' And now, as Tater Tots predicted on the tape, he's the one with the pieces on the floor."

"Why is that good news for Janet?"

"She can be the one to pick up *his* pieces."

Kristin raised an eyebrow.

"She's always been gaga for him." He grinned as if he had a crystal ball. "And this is one time he won't be so quick to write her off."

"You *really* do know how to save the day!"

* * *

On her way to get Henry, just before the afternoon bell, Kristin roamed the halls of the school with renewed confidence. She had received a standing ovation at her impromptu assembly to repeal the hostile policies of the disgraced acting principal. Rounding the corner, she heard a strange sound, like popcorn popping, resonating from Henry's workshop. Unsure of whether to be intrigued or concerned, she zipped straight for his chamber with a loud clip-clop from her low-heeled shoes. And to her astonishment, she caught her man of the hour red-handed passing the time away by popping Bubble Wrap at his tool bench.

"Oh my, how quickly the mighty have fallen," she joked.

"Who's fallen? I'm just relieving stress."

"You have no stress."

"How do you know?"

"Because you always look like you don't have a care in the world."

"Well…as a matter of fact, I *don't* have a care in the world."

The impudence of his candor hit her between the eyes. She envied his audaciousness and took the first step to break out of her norm.

"Give me a sheet of that!"

Using the section he gave her out of a shipping box, she started popping bubbles frantically, as if she were in a race to see who could burst the most bubbles in the shortest time.

"Kinda fun, isn't it?" he laughed.

"I can't believe *I'm* doing this at work, of all places."

"It's contagious like a yawn. When you see 'em, you gotta pop 'em."

"But what if someone catches me doing this? What would the students think of me?"

"They'll see you having fun and think you're awesome."

The idea of being thought of as *awesome* prompted a giggle of glee just waiting to escape her shyness.

Shortly thereafter, they arrived at one of Henry's recommended hole-in-the-wall greasy spoons, courtesy of Kristin's black sedan. Even though she was ready to be an "item" with him, she wasn't quite ready to compromise her standard of transportation. The duct-taped seats in his beat-up van didn't compare to the smooth leather in her Lincoln. It was a way of integrating her brand of classiness into their unconventional alliance.

The establishment was nearly bare due to the odd hour of their patronage. Having seated themselves across from each other at a windowed booth, they were met instantly by a spunky waitress in a traditional café-style dress and a waist-tie apron.

"Beating the dinner crowd as usual, Henry?"

"You know it."

The young lady turned to Kristin. "Say, aren't you Dr. Sharp?" she asked, fluttering her pencil.

"Yes, I am."

"I recognized you from your picture in the paper."

"Oh." Kristin's mouth twitched.

"I just want to tell you that I think it's downright disgraceful what some of the people in this town did to you. I'm boiling mad about it."

"It's over now," she expressed with relief. "The villains' gooses are cooked, so there's no reason for you or anyone else to stew over it."

"Nice comeback pun, Sharpie!" Henry approved by offering a handshake.

Kristin returned his gesture, adding a fleeting smile.

"You're a better woman than I am," the waitress admitted. "I never liked Ms. Tater or Mr. Pace when I was in school, so I'm not sorry to see them gone."

"They received poetic justice," Henry articulated.

"Can we drop the subject? It's making me uncomfortable," Kristin begged, opening the menu on the tabletop.

"Of course, where's my manners," the young lady agreed. "What would you like to drink?"

"I'll just have water," Henry said.

The waitress looked to Kristin. "And you?"

"I'd like a lemonade, please."

"No—she'll have a water too," Henry insisted before the waitress could jot the "lemonade" on her pad.

"Okay, two waters," the server confirmed, leaving the table.

"That was a little—abrupt." Kristin appeared peeved.

"You're going to pay over two dollars for that lemonade. It's a rip-off."

"So? I can afford it."

"That's not the point."

"Then what is?"

"You'll see."

"See what?"

"I'll show you."

He spotted the waitress returning with two ice waters, each having a lemon slice on the rim of the glass, along with a couple of plastic straws.

"There you go," the waitress said. "Are you ready to order, or do you need a few more minutes?"

Wondering what Henry was up to weighed more heavily on Kristin's mind than any of the items on the menu. "A few minutes, please."

After the waitress left their table, Henry squeezed the juice from his lemon sliver into his glass—right to the last drop. "The water here always comes with a lemon."

"Is that your point?"

"Nope." He snatched a pack of sugar from the stack next to the napkin dispenser at the end of the booth. "This is."

Tearing open the sugar wrapper, he gently poured the white grains into his glass until the wrapper was empty. Taking the spoon from the set of utensils preplaced on the table, he stirred the sugar in his water till it completely dissolved, then sipped the beverage to quench his thirst.

"Mmm…ah…perfect! Nothing like free homemade lemonade in a restaurant."

Kristin gaped at his shamelessness.

"And that, my dear doctor, is the point."

"That you're too cheap to buy lemonade?"—she lowered her glasses—"I didn't forget the contest in the grocery store, you know."

"Good. Then I don't have to further explain my philosophy on how to get around overpriced items that are a waste of money."

"That's just a matter of opinion."

"No, Sharpie, it's a matter of taste. I challenge you to give it a try."

"Another challenge?"

"One, two, three—go."

Repeating Henry's steps, she quickly mixed the ingredients into her glass with pinpoint accuracy and took her first sample.

"Ooh—that's amazing!"

"Still want that two-dollar lemonade?" he gloated.

"I surrender." She humorously bowed down to him.

He laughed at her fanciful gesture. "So, does this mean you trust my recommendation for dinner, without looking at the menu?"

She shrugged her shoulders. "It depends on what they have?"

"Well, what they *don't* have is organic bread crumbs," he jabbed with smiling eyes.

She playfully kicked his leg under the table, acting as if she'd been offended. He then pretended to be hurt with an exaggerated yelp. In mere seconds, their silliness morphed into a lasting gaze more satisfying than anything served from the kitchen.

Chapter 19

The following afternoon, Perrinsville's newest couple took advantage of the picturesque autumn foliage with a casual stroll through the town's riverfront park. Kristin packed a pair of jeans, a long cardigan sweater, and walking shoes to change into at the office in preparation for their date. Knowing there were only a few hours of daylight after school before the evening sundown, she didn't want to squander any of it by going home to change out of her pantsuit.

While admiring the tranquility of the still water, along with other folks enjoying the peace in the park, Kristin put Henry on the spot with a series of analytical questions she'd begun to ponder or second guess.

"What's the reason why you nicknamed me 'Sharpie'?"

"Why do you ask?" he responded casually.

"Just wondering if it's a term of affection or a tease or just making fun of my surname."

"I guess you might say all of the above."

"How's that?"

"Well, you know how much I love puns. I noticed you like to write with fine-tip markers, and your last name *is* Sharp, so I'll let you figure out where those two fit in the equation. Besides…you know me, I've got a corny nickname for everyone, including myself."

"Hooray for Henry!"

"Hey, you remembered," he said, pleasantly surprised.

"Yes, it was your favorite children's book."

"Read it sometime—it's me."

"I've found a used copy online and ordered it."

Touched by her heartwarming gesture, he leaned in to kiss her soft lips. "And that's for inking a permanent mark on me from the moment I saw you."

"Just like a Sharpie," she added.

"Hence, the affection behind the nickname."

In a reciprocal act of endearment, she pecked his bristled cheek softly. "Why do you think we click so well?"

"Because we don't click with anyone else."

"Is that what you think brought us here together at this place in time?"

"You're getting deep on me."

"I can't help it; it's the academic in me that's always studying why things are the way they are."

"You think too much. Have you ever stopped to really enjoy the simple things in life?"

"Like popping Bubble Wrap?"

"Yes. It was fun, wasn't it?"

She nodded. "It was."

"It's those kinds of things that everybody wants to do but is afraid to do, so that's why I do what I do," Henry bragged.

"I know."

"When I was growing up, grade school was an equal playing field—all us kids were friends. It wasn't until we reached adolescence that things changed."

"Tell me about it," she agreed.

"I have no doubt that your history mirrors mine. When our friends suddenly thought they were grown up, they rejected the likes of us because we didn't fit into their *cliques*. We share a common bond; we were both oddballs, and even though you and I chose different routes of travel, both routes led us to this place in time as kindred spirits." He skipped a beat before probing deep into her eyes. "Does that answer your question?"

Feeling the cut of his laser-beam stare burning holes through the thickness of her glasses, she grasped the seriousness of his magnified intensity.

"Yes...it does," she murmured with a breath of warm air in the cool fall temperature.

"The only difference we share, apart from our socio-economic statuses, is that I'm not trying to hide from my past."

"And you think I am?" Kristin fired back at his insinuation.

"Yeah, I do."

"Like what am I hiding?"

"For starters, you're still hiding your legs because of a nasty name that's totally meaningless now."

"Maybe I'm just not comfortable in my own skin."

"You can always wear tights," he half-joked.

"Not funny—it's not a laughing matter to me."

"I get it. But seriously, after all these years?"

"I have my reasons."

"Like what?"

She suddenly turned away from him. "This is getting a bit too personal."

"I may appear to be very immature on the surface, but I promise I'll never make fun of you...especially about the things you fear."

The compassion in his voice began to ease the worried expression on her face. Kristin fundamentally understood there was no future with Henry without a basis of trust. To validate her implicit trust in him, she'd have to bare it all.

"There's a lot more to 'Bird Legs' than what I previously told you."

"I'm listening."

"It goes back to the nasty girls who were jealous of me. They made fun of my skinniness as a way to belittle me—no pun intended."

"Don't worry, I wasn't going to laugh. I think you already mentioned that's how you got the name."

"Yes, but what I didn't reveal was *why* they stuck me with that awful name."

"Please tell me," he begged.

"I was the *best* cheerleader at my middle school because I could bend like that rubber doll and jump like a pogo stick. I had moves unmatched by the other girls, which gave me the potential to be the most popular cheerleader in school—a status I pursued aggressively. While I was scoring so much attention from the coach, not to mention the guys on the football team, jealousy among my squad began to take shape.

"Starting with the squad captain, they began to shun me by making me self-conscious about my tiny frame. Every Friday from football season through basketball, I had to wear the very short skirt of the uniform to school. My squad mates branded me with that unflattering label because it was impossible to hide. It followed me everywhere—in class, in the halls, and at the games—I couldn't escape it. What started with the girls quickly spread to the boys. They laughed at me all the time, especially the athletes I had huge crushes on all the way through school."

"The Fast Freddie types?"

She nodded with a frown. "I refused to be that vulnerable again. So after I quit cheerleading, which I loved, I couldn't bring myself to wear another skirt or dress or shorts—and forget a bathing suit—outside my house again. It was the genesis of my many self-imposed phobias that impaired my coping skills, particularly with guys. I wasn't called *Strikeout Sharp* for nothing."

"That was sooo long ago, Sharpie. Look at you now: you're a very intelligent—your vocabulary alone says it all—successful woman worthy of respect and admiration from everyone," Henry praised.

"As hard as I've worked to overcome my personal struggles, I just keep failing at them like a remedial student."

"Maybe you just need the right man to believe in the real you."

"He's never arrived..."

Henry narrowed his eyes as if to say, *Are you kidding me? You're looking at him.*

"...until now," she confessed with the utmost respect and sincerity.

"Whew. You had me worried there for a second."

"I'm willing to take a chance with you, Henry. I'm not getting any younger, and I've reached the crescendo of my career. It's time to start living the personal life I've denied myself, before I turn into a spinster."

"The only spinster I know of is in the Beatles' song 'Eleanor Rigby,'" he chuckled.

"I've actually heard that song and it's such a grim lyric."

"Then how about the Turtles' Eleanor that's swell? Have you heard that one?"

"No, but on that 'stupendous' note..." she segued in sarcasm to get back on message. "I'm trying to tell you, quite seriously, that I don't want to pursue a relationship for the sake of being in a relationship. I need to know it's going somewhere. I want to get married and have a family."

"Then we'll have to change our names to Blondie and Dagwood Bumstead."

"And whom might they be?"

"You're kidding?"—Henry mocked, aware that she had no clue—"You've never seen the old Blondie and Dagwood movies or comic strips?"

"No…just how old are they?"

"Ah, the nineteen thirties and forties."

"That's why. I don't watch anything that's not in color," Kristin stated firmly.

"You don't know what you're missing, Sharpie…black and white movies are the best!"

"So, why are we the Bumsteads? Which, by the way, sounds like a typo."

"Blondie was this beautiful and shrewd sweetheart who married a bumbling klutz named Dagwood. Even though he was the butt of everyone's jokes, Blondie loved him—he was her hero—get the picture?" he explained with a dimpled grin.

"Did they have any children?"

"Two: a boy and a girl."

"Dare I ask what their names are?"

"Baby Dumpling and Cookie."

"Oh boy…I think I've had enough pop culture trivia from the twentieth century for today." She tugged his shirt sleeve. "Can we resume our walk?"

"Lead the way."

The pair joined hands as they left the boardwalk for the paved walkway through the scenery of trees turning from green to red, yellow, and orange. It was the perfect time to appreciate the color tour before the leaves would begin dropping in the coming weeks. As they continued their conversation of future plans, they crossed paths with a young mother pushing a baby in a stroller, while her small child peddled a little bike with rickety training wheels. Henry and Kristin could hear the mom yelling at her daughter to quit kicking the pedals. The girl was defiant, kicking them harder, until the chain fell off the sprocket. She crashed on the grass and started to cry.

"I told you not to do that. Now it's broken!" the mother scolded, as she stood by, clutching the stroller in frustration. "You're not going to get a new one."

Those harsh words sent the girl into a loud cryfest. Unable to ignore a child in need, Henry stepped up to lend a helping hand.

"There's nothing with this bike that can't be fixed," he told the little girl to stop her crying. "The chain just fell off, that's all. I'll put it back on."

"That's kind of you, sir," the mother said. "But she doesn't listen, and as far as I'm concerned, it can stay broken."

The girl's face puffed with quivering lips at the thought of losing her bicycle. Kristin identified with the girl's agony and was put off by the mother's insensitivity—a scene very familiar to her.

"What about your daughter's father, can't he fix it?" Kristin asked.

"My husband is never home, and I don't have the time or desire to play mechanic with a brand-new bike my kid continues to abuse," the young mom snapped, causing her baby to cry now. "It's none of your business."

Bending down to cradle her baby boy from the stroller, the lady was forced to cool her jets for the next few minutes. Henry capitalized on her indisposition to put the chain back on the sprocket. He removed a jackknife tool kit from its tattered leather case attached to his belt and concealed by his untucked flannel shirttails.

"This is a simple operation," he whispered to Kristin before unscrewing the chain guard to access the top of the pedal sprocket.

"I told you I didn't want that bike fixed," the mom barked at Henry, as her baby cried his heart out. She gently rubbed her son's back to calm him down. "Shh...shh..."

"Ma'am, I've not walked in your shoes, but I've walked in your daughter's." Henry appealed to her sympathy. "There's no reason to punish her for what we've all done when we were that age."

"Are you telling me how to be a parent?"

"No, I'm telling you what it's like to be a child who doesn't comprehend why Mommy and Daddy would rather do nothing than be helpful in restoring the value of things. Don't let her grow up thinking her stuff is junk."

"Daddy will never fix this, Mommy," the little girl pouted.

With a crying baby in her arms and a sulking daughter at her feet, the mother of two realized deep down that the scraggly man was right. "Fine—go ahead."

By the time the baby fell back asleep and was returned to the stroller, the little girl saw the chain back on her bike.

"Look, Mommy!" She jumped for joy. "That man fixed it!"

"Just in time too," the mother noted.

After Henry reattached the chain guard, he inspected the rest of the bike. "The nuts on the training wheels could use a little tightening."

He swapped out the screwdriver in the miniature set for the wrench. With a few twists of the wrist at each wheel, the bike was as good as new.

"Thank you, mister!" The girl ran to Henry, as he wiped the grease from the chain on his shirttail, to give him a big hug.

"I'd also like to thank you," the mom said gratefully. "I'm sorry for the way I acted to both of you." She then turned her attention to Kristin. "You have a wonderful husband."

Kristin's eyes widened—*Husband?*

"He really made me rethink my priorities."

"Me too," Kristin concurred.

Henry beamed—especially about the husband part.

The youngster saddled herself back on the two-wheeler. "Come on, Mommy; let's go."

"Be careful with those pedals, and listen to your mom," Henry affirmed to the girl.

"Okay," she said prior to departure with her mother and baby brother.

Kristin turned to Henry, bowled over, once again, by his unbelievable kindheartedness. The timing of this event was mind blowing to her. She thought about the difference he had just made in the lives of that family by doing what seemed normal to him—and from the perspective of a child.

"Miracles never stop with you, do they?" she asked.

"What miracles?" he shrugged.

"You just changed that family's values forever."

"I did?" he muttered.

"Why do you do such selfless acts for people?"

"Probably because I know what it's like when you can't get blood from a rock."

"You mean a stone?"

"Rock, stone…whatever."

"You're always off just a little bit. But that's okay—I find it cute." She laughed at Henry's imaginative way of displaying the nature of his true colors.

Chapter 20

The blossoming romance between Kristin and Henry was about to become public. Their afternoon rendezvous that lasted well into the evenings had escaped the radars of the many busybodies roaming the halls of Perrinsville Elementary—including the chieftain, Janet Goode. She had become too preoccupied with comforting Fred to pay attention to her boss's affairs. As far as she was concerned, Kristin's blissfulness was normal for someone who'd been vindicated, and Henry's cheer was, well, Henry being himself.

On Friday, Kristin received a last-minute wedding invitation from Bob Bakewell's secretary, Kathy, whose nuptials were planned for the next day. Kathy's empathy toward Kristin persuaded her to extend the special invite for the event at the town's swankiest hotel, the Mayflower. This being the first social gathering since her arrival in town, Kristin saw it as the most logically opportune moment to unveil her new relationship with finesse. She loved getting dressed up for formal occasions and looked forward to seeing Henry all cleaned up in a suit.

"Do you have appropriate attire?" she asked him over the phone.

"Don't worry, I know what to wear to a wedding," he replied.

Kristin spent much of Saturday afternoon perfecting an updo that would rival the bride. Despite her abstinence from dresses, she felt comfortable in a full-length gown—no risk of leg exposure. She selected an elegantly beaded long-sleeve gown of midnight blue, figuring it would complement whatever color and style her suiter chose to wear.

The unpredictable weather pattern, typical of the upper Midwest in the fall, sent a blast of cold air to chill the evening. Kristin took out her black wool overcoat from the front hall closet, collected her clutch handbag, and departed to pick up Henry at their appointed time. On the way, she tried to imagine how he would look in a dark suit with a clean-shaven face. She pictured them making a grand entrance into the ballroom as if they were a couple to be wedded. In her mind, this would be a dress rehearsal for the day she had always dreamed of but never thought possible.

By the time she drove up Henry's driveway, it was pitch black outside. The only illumination beyond her headlights came from the dim porch light by his front door. No call or horn honk was necessary, as Henry stood idle in the doorway. He rushed his silhouetted figure into her car, greeting her with a quick kiss.

Kristin ran her hand down his smooth cheek. "You shaved!"

"Couldn't go looking like a grub, especially when your hair looks so beautiful."

"Thanks. Yours is neatly groomed too."

"Isn't it amazing how a slicker brush can shake the dog out of a man?" he teased.

She chuckled at his corny reference. "I think there's a subliminal ad in there somewhere."

"I believe there is. I'll have to write that one down."

"Oh, somehow I think you already have it stored in your mental database."

His signature smile glowed in the moonlight, as she shifted gears into reverse and backed down the driveway. On the road to the wedding,

Henry noticed Kristin wasn't wearing pants.

"I thought you didn't do dresses, Sharpie?"

"It's not the kind we discussed before; it's an expensive evening gown down to my feet."

"Kinda hard to see from my angle."

"So, what do you have concealed under that topcoat buttoned all the way up to your neck?" she flirted. "All I can see from *my* angle is the bottom of your slacks."

"You asked me if I had appropriate attire, and I did my best."

"Unbutton your coat and let me see."

He waved his finger playfully. "Ah-ah-ah…no can do. You'll just have to be in suspense until we get there."

"Hmph," she huffed jokingly, expecting to be thoroughly impressed later.

The distance from Henry's house to the Mayflower was relatively short. They made it there in plenty of time to get decent seating. Upon entering the hotel's crowded lobby Kristin's anxiety about Henry's wardrobe had reached its peak—she couldn't wait to see what he had under his overcoat. At the coat-check booth outside the ballroom, Henry helped her out of her wrap like a perfect gentleman.

"So what do you think?" she asked with a lively twirl.

His eyes popped. "You look like a million bucks, Sharpie!"

"I agree. You look fabulous, Miss," the coat clerk asserted.

"Thank you," she replied, feeling on top of the world. Turning to Henry, "Are you going to take your coat off and stay a while?"

"Oh…right." He turned his back to her, and unbuttoned his long coat. "Do me the honor?" he asked, glancing at her over his shoulder.

Wearing a grin from ear to ear, she enthusiastically removed his coat. And like a whirlwind, he faced her in a printed long-sleeve T-shirt of a suit jacket and necktie. His spectacle caused her smile to fall on the floor. She was mortified! The thread in the fabric of their relationship just hit a major snag. She saw his lack of effort to dress properly as cheapening the value of their romance. It made her feel unworthy of male affirmation—yet again! And to make matters worse, she spotted a photographer turning her visible distress into a Kodak moment.

"Please put this back on." She threw his coat back at him with tears in her eyes.

Her sudden change of attitude caught him off guard. "I don't get it… why?"

"Put your coat back on!" she growled with gnashed teeth.

Henry looked at her like a deer in the headlights. "Did I do something wrong?"

"Are you kidding me?"

"No…"

"If I've got to explain this to you, then maybe I made a big mistake." She turned to the coat check, "My coat, please."

The young man returned her seasonal garment. She flung it over her shoulders like a cape and walked briskly out the door—totally humiliated. Henry dashed after her with his coat stuffed under his arm.

"Sharpie…wait…" he yelled, dodging the human traffic along the way.

Catching up with her in the lighted parking lot, he prevented her from opening the car door.

"Wait…please stop," he begged.

"Get away from the door," she ordered.

"Not till you talk to me."

"Your cartoonish shirt did enough talking—let me go."

"At least hear me out…please?"

She hesitated for a minute in contemplation of giving him the time of night. The heat from his quick, short breaths blew the cold from the wind off the skin of her neck. It made her feel his desperation to provide some sort of justification for the joke she deemed as painfully tasteless. It was a decision whether to react from her heart that had just been wounded or her intellect that reminded her of the huge gamble he took to prove her innocence against insurmountable odds. She at least owed him the courtesy to hear his explanation.

"Say what you have to say, Henry," she muttered.

"Can you look at me?"

She pivoted to him in disgust.

"Can you relax the tension in your face? It looks like it hurts."

"I asked you if you had appropriate attire, and you said you knew what to wear, didn't you?"

"Yeah…"

She tugged the bottom of his printed tie to make it snap upon release. "Was this supposed to be a joke?"

"Well, if we don't go back inside, I'll feel pretty silly getting all dressed up for nothing."

Kristin was unamused at his attempt to make light of her mood. "Just what I thought."

"No…what I just said was *supposed* to be a joke."

"I thought you understood me, but you don't…just leave me alone," she pleaded, opening the car door.

Henry pushed it closed. "Not till you tell me why my shirt is such a problem."

"Take a good look at me, I spent all day taking my time to look good for *you.*"

"You're breathtaking!"

"I wanted *us* to look good. I thought this would be the perfect venue to premiere our relationship. I don't want people to think you're a clown."

"But I am a clown, and all those people in that hotel know it. It doesn't bother me."

"Well, it bothers me because I want everyone to think the very best of you."

"Is that really for my benefit? Or yours?"

"Don't insult me."

"I didn't. I'm just trying to get you to be honest with yourself."

"Speaking of honesty, why did you lie to me about your clothes?"

"I didn't lie. I've worn shirts like this to every wedding and formal shindig around here. I've a got bunch of them with different tie patterns," he chuckled.

"I thought you were going to wear a suit."

"I don't own a suit."

"I was hoping to see how handsome you'd look in one. I thought about it all day."

"Suits ain't me—just like uniforms."

"Yes, how could I ever forget your Tony Award–winning striptease?" she remarked sarcastically.

"The untidy man you see every day at school is who *I* am. I don't know if I'm capable of changing that."

"Not even for the right woman?"

"She's never arrived."

"Then I guess it's my turn to say, *until now*—right?"

"We both got our quirks."

"I wouldn't call everything I confessed to you *quirks*."

"Okay…oddities…hang-ups…what term suits you best?"

"Pun intended on the use of suits?"

"I wasn't exactly going for a funny; it just came out that way."

Kristin shook her head with an eye roll.

"The wind out here is cold." Henry quickly put on his wadded-up coat in dire need of pressing. "If I keep my coat on the whole time, will you accompany me back to the wedding?"

"Your coat is totally wrinkled. You'll look worse."

"Is it really that important? Kathy's a sweet girl, and her fiancé, who's probably her husband now, is also a good guy. They invited *you*, not me, and they don't deserve punishment over your bruised ego."

"Whoa…wait a second. Let me get this straight. *I'm* punishing them because *my* ego is bruised?"

"Yeah, you're always concerned about appearances."

"You're darn right I am—it's called etiquette."

"What you confuse for etiquette could easily be mistaken as snooti-ness."

"Not where I come from it isn't."

"Well, I've never been anywhere outside good old Perrinsville, so maybe this is a learning curve for both of us—pun intended this time."

"This is *your* town, Henry. Maybe I just don't belong here."

"That's nonsense. Of course, you do—this is *your* town now."

"All I've gotten in this small blip on the map is embarrassment at warp speed. I don't know anyone here outside school, but everyone here knows about me, or at least think they do."

"I took care of that for you."

"And I'm eternally grateful. But I think the payback is too high a price for me."

"Oh please. You make it sound so transactional. I'm not aiming to collect a debt. *I love you!*"

"I don't know if I'm capable of love."

"Yeah, you are. You just need to give yourself the chance."

"Sorry, Superman; I need to go into deep self-analysis on this one."

"Oh, good grief. You can't keep running away from yourself."

"Maybe not, but I can run away from you." She climbed into her car, started the motor, and rolled down the window. "Please call a cab. I want to be alone."

And just like Greta Garbo, in true Hollywood fashion, she drove away, leaving Henry to wonder if they'd have another tomorrow.

* * *

Sunday proved to be an unwanted day of silence for Kristin and Henry. Neither was willing to make the first move toward reconciling their first major setback as a couple. The obstacles they thought they overcame resurfaced. The importance of appearances was an essential difference Kristin needed to embrace or reject. Henry broke the mold when it came to her off-the-charts different prerequisite, so why was she so bent out of shape when he was being true to himself? That was the underlying question she failed to grasp in the heat of the moment.

Perhaps she really didn't want a man like Henry as much as she thought. The maturity in his choice of wardrobe was that of a juvenile. Although his childlike qualities endeared him to her, she wanted him to be a man. *Is that asking too much?* she pondered restlessly. The connective tissue between them was undeniable but not deep enough to keep her from treading the shallow waters of pretentiousness. Simply put, she became a hot mess of her own devising.

Meanwhile, Henry resisted the temptation to contact her. The last thing he wanted to do was further antagonize her by acting like Fast Freddie—blowing up her phone. As much as it worried him, he knew better than to provoke her with a disingenuous apology. Not that he couldn't understand her feelings about his getup; he just didn't agree with her. He related more to Popeye—*I yam what I yam*—than the likes of James Bond. Acting out of character was not one of his better aptitudes, and he knew it wasn't one of hers either. He just needed the right angle to help mend her private quandary, after he patched things up with her first.

While their ears were deafened to each other, their eyes were blind to the society page in the Sunday edition of the *Perrinsville Gazette*. Among a collage of photos from last night's wedding lay the picture of Kristin and Henry that had been snapped during their awkward exchange at the coat-check booth. A caption beneath the image, which was intended to be lighthearted, read, *Meet the Odd Couple: Felicity and Oscar.* The revelation she thwarted to save face came back to bite her in the "Toast of the Town."

Kristin seemed puzzled upon her arrival at school on Monday morning by the stares and giggles coming from the staff and kids—some of whom rooted, *Hooray for Henry!* Even Miss Goody Two-shoes jumped on the bandwagon with a waggish "Good morning." It was a head-scratching scene that quickly disappeared from her thoughts. She had already lost two nights of sleep trying to decide if she wanted to keep riding the merry-go-round with the institution's master showman. However, now was not the time to keep spinning the wheel, she seriously needed to get back to her other true love—work.

After getting settled at her desk, Kristin started the day with a check of her emails. Much to her surprise, nearly all of them were part of a chain with "Re: Odd Couple" in the subject line. Concerned about the threat of a cyber infection, she reacted accordingly.

"Janet!" she hollered out the door.

"Yes?"

"Call Eugene and tell him I think our computer system has a virus."

"A virus? What kind?"

"I've got a flood of email spam."

"Have you opened any of them?"

"Absolutely not. They all say 'odd couple,' whatever that means."

Janet delightedly retrieved the page from yesterday's *Gazette* she'd kept in her purse on a hunch she'd need it this morning.

"That's not spam," Janet said, coming into Kristin's office.

"It's not?"

"Nope." She handed her the paper. "You made the society page."

Scanning the photos, Kristin was shocked to see the picture of her and Henry. "How did that get in there?"

"There's only one professional photographer in our midst, and he's a part-timer at the *Gazette*."

"That figures…this paper is going to be the death of me."

"Well, I just want to say that I'm happy for you and *Oscar*."

"Who's Oscar?"

"Didn't you read the caption?"

Kristin's eyes bulged. "'Meet the odd couple! Felicity and Oscar!'"

"That's so fitting…I think Felicity is supposed to be the female name for Felix."

"Yes, I get it!"

"Lighten up. It's all in good fun. They do that to everybody."

"So that's what all these emails are about?" Kristin stewed.

"Ah, yeah…we're happy for you and Henry."

"Is that *everyone?*"

"Most of us, that is. I know there's a few scoffers because they think Henry's a buffoon and they think he's beneath someone like you."

"Or they think I must be totally desperate," Kristin worried.

"Who cares what those hypocrites think. I can tell you enough stories about each of them to compose a string of chart-topping songs in country music. Besides, all the kids are thrilled—they love Henry—and so do I. He's like family to me."

Janet's comment packed a powerful punch. Kristin felt like a heel. The complex answer she had tried so hard to find had just broken her superficial glass jaw.

"As far as I'm concerned," Janet continued, "you two are the *real* toast of the town."

"Where's Henry now?"

"I don't know; he didn't come in today."

"I better call him."

"Tell him there's a light out in the cafeteria."

"You can tell him that yourself. I have a more urgent message to

deliver."
    "What's that?"
    "A big huge apology."

Chapter 21

The school day passed by without a sign of Henry. Kristin worried, as it was unlike him to not return her calls. She couldn't say "I'm sorry" enough times in her numerous voice messages. The absence of a response consumed her with thoughts of guilt backed by feelings of remorse. He was right on a number of levels that had been invisible to her until Janet brought them to light in the simplest of terms. Kristin finally admitted to herself that she loved Henry for many of the same reasons the kids did.

Going into her empty home that afternoon was tough. She missed her dates with him. Their parting of the ways at the Mayflower seemed frivolous now. All she could do was lament to the lonesome walls in her home. Unbuttoning the blazer of her pantsuit, she stepped into the bedroom to change. Kristin went to her closet for something casual to brighten her dullness. The dresses and skirts screamed at her—it's time.

Despite the uncertainty of her relationship with the man of her dreams, she believed the day had come to release the womanliness bottled up inside her for so many years—the personality Henry knew she imprisoned. Like a quick-change artist, Kristin stripped off her business attire and slipped into one of her sleeveless knee-hemmed dresses. Stepping in front of the full-length mirror, she modeled the formal burgundy flare in a series of poses. She liked what she saw below the neck—impressed by the garment's contouring of her figure—but what sat on top of her head needed to come down—now.

Sitting at her makeup table, Kristin began to dismantle all the strategic pieces of hair held in place by small clips and bobby pins. She shook her head, allowing the long locks of honey blond to fall freely onto her shoulders, as if she were in a hair commercial. The texture was a little coarse, so she spent a few minutes brushing out all the kinks until it was silky smooth. Only one detail was left to complete her transformation—the glasses.

Extracting the lens case from her table drawer, she stared at the contacts, which had never been worn, and took a deep breath. The thought of touching her eyeballs made her queasy, especially with dirty fingers. Kristin removed her thick glasses before going to the bathroom, with her contacts, to wash her hands. Scrubbing up like a surgeon, she prepped herself for the most delicate part of her procedure. Losing the glasses would be like saying goodbye to a lifelong protector. She had empowered them to be the barrier shielding the window into her soul.

Grimacing during the insertion of each lens, Kristin looked in the mirror to see a liberated woman smiling at her with poise. Oh, how she couldn't wait for the world to see her, especially the man most directly responsible for her makeover.

It was getting close to the dinner hour, and she wasn't about to cook in a dress and heels. Before she could unzip, there was a knock on the door. *Who could that be?* she worried. It might be a delivery requiring a signature, she assumed, or it could be Fred. Either way, she couldn't avoid answering since her car was parked on the driveway, indicating she was home. That meant now was as good a time as any to debut her new appearance to whomever stood on the other side of the door.

"Who is it?" she asked.

"Grocery store," the strange voice replied.

"There must be a mistake; I didn't order groceries."

"No mistake, ma'am; these are for you."

Peeking through the peep hole, she heard the familiar jingle of keys, as the man dropped the grocery bags and ducked out of sight. His split-second reaction caused him to lose his balance on the porch; he tumbled into the bushes.

"Whoa…whoa…whoa…" he yelled.

The sound of the keys and the scream that followed told Kristin exactly who was there. She flung the door wide open to run out as if there'd been a fire.

"Grocery store, hah?" she teased.

Henry's eyes widened like flying saucers. "Va-va-voom, Sharpie!"

"Ta-da…" she flaunted with open arms.

He applauded. "Magnificent!"

"So does that mean I look hot?"

Henry put his hand by his ear. "I think I hear a fire truck coming."

"Would you like to come inside before the fire's extinguished, or would you rather play in the bushes?"

He extended his hand to her. "Can you help me up?"

She knelt down to cup his crusty hand. Their bodies met in a warm hug full of unbridled emotion.

"I love you, Henry—please forgive me."

"I love you, too, Sharpie."

"Where were you all day?"

"I wanted to respect your wish and wasn't ready to see you at school."

"Why didn't you return my calls? I left you a ton of messages."

"I didn't listen to them until an hour ago."

"Why?"

"I figured the calls were to chew me out because of the photo in the paper."

She put her hands on her hips. "I thought you didn't read the paper?"

"I don't, but I knew when our picture was taken we'd be *toast*...of the town that is."

"The odd couple...what did you think of that branding?"

"I was pleasantly surprised."

"Surprised?"

"Yeah, I figured it was gonna be *Beauty and the Beast*."

"Why would you refer to yourself as a beast?"

He comically threw his arms in the air. "Well, look at me."

She studied his scruffiness from head to toe. "A diamond in the rough is more like it."

He also examined her from top to bottom. "And I still stand by calling you beauty."

Kristin rewarded him with a kiss on his sandpapery cheek. "Let's go."

Henry gathered up the grocery bags.

"What's all that for?" she asked, as they stepped inside.

"Would you believe I wanted to show off a hidden talent of mine?"

"What's that? As if I haven't seen a number of them already."

"This is one that you're gonna digest with delight. I'm gonna cook you a gourmet dinner."

"Ooh...I *like* it."

In the kitchen, Henry started to unpack the bags on the center island countertop. "Got a couple of candles to set the mood?"

"Oh, I like where this is going."

"I thought you would. Do you mind setting the table while I get started?"

"Not at all."

"Ah, one more thing..." He rummaged through her cupboards, not finding what he needed. "Where do you keep your cookware?"

"Under the island."

Henry smacked his forehead. "Duh, why didn't I think of that?"

"You're funny."

"Except when it comes to my cooking—that's serious business." She twinkled.

"By the way, as much as I love what you have on—and really I do—I don't expect you to wear a dress in your own house for a dinner with me."

"What if I want to?"

"Wouldn't you rather wear something more comfortable?"

"I am comfortable this way," she said confidently.

"Honestly?"

"Yes, I've waited a long time to come out of my shell—*you* brought this out of me."

"You know, as much as I'd like to take the credit, *you* did it on your own. I just helped show you the way."

"As far as I'm concerned, you earned it."

"Then I guess we're both gonna enjoy a *spicy* dinner," he chuckled.

"You're a goofball," she laughed. "I'll get the candles; you get the stove."

"And we'll spark our flames."

"Good pun."

"You're getting the routine."

As the evening dusk darkened the sky, dinner was served on a tastefully decorated table in the candlelit dining room. Kristin broke out a bottle of red wine to complement the pasta dish Henry had prepared, along with vegetables and sliced bread on the side. The strong aroma rising in the steam from the linguine on the plates overpowered the scented candles, creating the atmosphere of an authentic Italian bistro. The food was every bit as delicious as it smelled. Kristin was thoroughly impressed!

"Oh my!" she blurted with a mouthful of pasta strands dangling from her lips. "You're an awesome cook!"

"Just call me Chef *Hubb-ar-dee*."

His punch line nearly caused her to spit out her food. "You're so cute!"

"And better than anything that comes in a can."

"Where did you learn how to cook like this? Culinary school?"

"What I learned didn't come from a school. I had the best teacher in the world—an Italian grandma on my mom's side."

"Now I know why you say *ciao* sometimes."

"Sì, signorina, it's in my DNA. Anyway, my grandma made everything from scratch; she didn't believe in processed anything. She canned her own tomatoes, made her own pizza dough…good food was numero uno to her. She always sent care packages to us from her cucina: pizza, rigatoni, lasagna with these huge meatballs to die for, and pastina soup—my favorite. Grandma always cooked enough for an army, and we'd have leftovers for a week. Everything on your plate I learned from her."

"You could make a fortune in the restaurant business."

"Maybe…but it's not for me."

"Have you ever thought about it?"

"Nope. I'm having a blast doing what I do every day." He bit into his bread.

"May I ask a personal question?"

"We've come a long way to continue with timid formalities. Ask me anything you want."

"After everything you just said about your grandmother's attitude concerning food, why do you eat so much unhealthy processed food?"

He laughed. "Unlike my *nonna*, that means grandma by the way—"

"I got that."

"Preparing food like this takes a lot of time and prep. I'm a typical bachelor—a simple guy who doesn't need anything fancy. Now *if* I had someone in my life worthy of all this labor intensiveness, *that* would be a different story."

Henry's implication about their future gave Kristin goose bumps.

"And speaking of stories," he continued. "Care to explain *your* frozen stockpile of organic entrées?"

"Touché. When I was growing up, my mother didn't cook. If she couldn't tear open a package and consume the contents, we didn't have it. I didn't like that kind of living, so I didn't eat much, which is probably one of the reasons why I was so skinny. When I moved out on my own, I decided I needed to adopt healthier eating habits."

"With prepackaged frozen meals?"

"Yes," she answered timidly. "I never learned to cook…just like my mother."

"Well, don't let my efforts slaving over a hot stove get cold—dig in. Don't be shy, as my grandma used to say."

"You've cured my shyness."

After finishing their dinner, the happy couple moved into the dimly lit living room to snuggle on the sofa. The bottle of wine sat on the glass coffee table between their half-empty goblets.

"Tonight was perfect Henry. I don't think there's anything else you could've done to make this evening more romantic."

"Well…" he responded with a sly grin.

"Oh no…" she perked up.

"I was thinking of a little music."

"Let me turn on the stereo."

"Nah…I'd rather serenade you." In his best Luciano Pavarotti voice, he sang a few lines of "Santa Lucia."

"What's that? I didn't catch a word of it."

"It's 'Santa Lucia'—it's Italian."

"If you're going to serenade me in Italian, do one that I can understand."

"Okay…" he cleared his throat to change his rendition from Pavarotti to Dean Martin singing about the moon and a big pizza pie.

Kristin joined in on the lyric "that's amore," causing both of them to crack up.

"I should've seen that one coming," she confessed.

"You opened the door and stepped in it."

She kicked up her foot. "With my heels on too."

Henry raised his glass. "You're the toast of the town, Sharpie."

Kristin took her goblet. "*We're* the toast of the town."

"Here's to you, *Felicity.*"

"And to you, *Oscar*—cheers."

Chapter 22

Kristin swooped into school as the beautiful swan in her living fairy tale. With her ugly-duckling feathers behind her, she became an inspiration to her students and colleagues. Around town, she sizzled as the envy of many women and the desire of most men, which posed a baffling question: *What's she doing with Henry?* By her own design, she evolved into a modern-day Blondie Bumstead.

Contrary to her stunning exterior of womanliness, Kristin's internal harmony ascended from the boyish charm of her man. She was completely enamored of his unabashed freedom of expression—a personal trait she had curbed for the sake of what others would think. Through his eyes, she saw the pitfalls of her life's choices, and she desperately wanted a do-over. Every week she marked off on the calendar, revealed another *Henry-ism* manifesting itself inside her.

One of the first indicators was her handling of phone solicitors. Like her mentor, she enjoyed sparring with the callers, driving them insane enough to hang up on her. She didn't limit the pranks to her cell phone; she expanded them to her phone at work. Janet couldn't believe it when Kristin asked to have those annoying calls transferred to her office. The school's biggest busybody got an earful one afternoon when her superior put a telemarketer on speaker.

"Hello, this is Dr. Sharp."

"Hi, I'm Jason with Butch's Burglary Systems—"

"Ooh, I feel safe with him on the case."

"We've cornered the market in security—"

"So you have it all locked up?"

"Excuse me? I don't understand you."

"Well, that's alarming."

Click!

Janet laughed out loud. "Sounds like you've taken a chapter out of the Henry Hubbard playbook!"

"Yep, the one called 'Know How to Own the Phone.'"

Another display of Henry's magic working on Kristin showed up in their choice of dating venues. She didn't have to be dragged into going out for go-cart rides, toy exhibitions, comic cons, arcades, and playgrounds—all places she was sure to be spotted by the children attending her school. The janitor's influence rubbed off on the principal with an engaging simplicity that had been absent from her self-imposed complications. He taught her to have fun *as he knew it*.

But as the November winds started to howl through the emptied trees, so did the gusts of gossip bent on knocking down the couple's euphoria. Disapproving phone calls and emails began to circulate among "concerned" parents who felt the office of the principal was being occupied by a wannabe adolescent.

"She's beginning to set a bad example for our children."

"A school principal should be a role model, not a BFF."

"If she can't act like a mature adult outside school, then she has no business running a school."

"I liked her better when she was a nerd."

Some of the covetous faculty and board members mocked her newfound hotness going to waste on an unambitious caretaker.

"Is it me, or has anyone else noticed her dresses getting shorter? Who's she trying to impress? Oh, that's right…the trash man."

"I've heard about women who like fixer-uppers, but seriously?"

"She gives a whole new meaning to lady and the tramp."

The sudden change in attitude was a crafty attempt to remake Kristin into who the town's people thought she ought to be. No one expected more from Henry, and few cared about him, but their school's leader gallivanting around with the likes of him was a different story.

Rumors quietly spread like a pandemic behind the scenes, throughout the four corners of Perrinsville. For Kristin and Henry, it was business as usual. When Henry's van needed to be serviced for a radiator replacement on special order, Kristin offered him the use of her vehicle, since the only mechanic shop in town didn't provide loaners.

"I can't put you out of a car," Henry insisted.

"Then let me be your personal chauffeur."

"I can't let you do that either."

"Why not?"

"It'll take days for the radiator to come in, and that's too long of an inconvenience to put you through."

"So what are you going to do?"

"Rent a car."

Kristin drove her boyfriend to the car rental and stood by his side during the course of the transaction.

"Okay, that about does it, Mr. Hubbard," the counter clerk said. "Before I give you the keys, we strongly recommend the purchase of our insurance for twenty dollars a day."

"I don't need it. My auto insurance covers rental cars," Henry replied.

"Yeah, but's that's only for liability. What they don't tell you is you're not covered for collision…"

Henry flickered his eyes at Kristin to say, *Watch me do this with a straight face.*

"…so it's really worth the extra twenty a day for peace of mind."

"If I have to buy your insurance, the first thing I'm gonna do after I get in the car is drive it straight into a brick wall…"

Kristin cackled.

The clerk's jaw dropped.

"…that way I'll get my money's worth of coverage. The damage will cost you about four thousand dollars to fix, but I'm only gonna pay twenty."

The clerk glared at Kristin's bubbling face. "He's not serious, is he?"

"Deadly," she affirmed.

"Here's your key, Mr. Hubbard."

Kristin's admiration of Henry's eccentric methods to save a buck or get freebies reached its climax on a Saturday afternoon at the local furniture emporium's annual pizza promotional. Every year, in the weeks before Thanksgiving, Countryside's Discount Furnishings advertised a free pizza gimmick to showcase their pre-holiday seasonal merchandise. Henry never missed the chance to capitalize on their annual communal investment—*Who says there's no free lunch in this town?* He convinced Kristin that he was considering new furniture pieces for his home. She was thrilled and dressed fashionably to accent the style of living she hoped to project in his choice of furnishings.

"Hey, look, Sharpie—free pizza!" Henry touted upon their entry into the store.

"That explains all the balloons outside," she concluded.

They walked toward the semicrowded table to help themselves to a few pizza slices topped with cheese and pepperoni. With paper plates in hand, they browsed through the store, telling every salesperson along the way, "Just looking right now."

"What exactly are you thinking of buying?" Kristin posed to Henry, who was more focused on eating than shopping.

"Ah…not sure…I'll know when I see it."

In the meantime, Kristin eyed many living room and dining room sets she thought would be an improvement over the worn-out rickety pieces in his house. Henry never stayed in one showroom setting long enough to sample the furnishings. After swallowing the last bite of his pizza, he stood on his toes to count the remaining unopened boxes on the food table, way at the opposite end of the store.

"Oh good," he announced. "I want another couple of pieces of pizza. Let's head back."

Kristin handed him her empty plate. "I'm done. I didn't come here to eat."

"Well, I did."

"*What?*"

"Why not? It's food for free, and that's for me."

"I thought you wanted to shop for furniture?"

"Well…I didn't think you'd be open to coming if I told you the real reason I wanted to be here."

His luring her there under false pretenses called for a time-out.

"Then go by yourself," she said, slightly irked. "I'm going to stay here. I want to keep shopping when you get back."

"Okay…going to reload my plate."

As Henry shuffled off, Kristin sat down and crossed her legs on a herringbone-patterned sectional with a "big sale" price tag. A sales lady and a female patron stood a few feet away, and she couldn't help hearing their disturbing conversation.

"There goes that freeloading janitor," the saleswoman griped.

"Has he ever bought anything here?" the customer asked.

"Of course not. He graces our presence this time every year to scam a free meal."

"Why don't you throw him out?"

"Because he can always claim he was going to make a purchase, so there's nothing we can do to stop him."

"Have you heard the latest about him?"

"What's that?"

"He's building a love nest with the principal at my daughter's school," the customer uttered in a snarky tone.

"*Really?*"

"We all thought she was this well-educated high-class woman—"

"With *him?*" The saleswoman pointed in Henry's direction.

"Hard to believe, isn't it?" the customer giggled.

"Well, she can't be *that* bright if that's the best she can do."

"They have no idea how much everyone's laughing behind their backs."

Kristin had all she could stomach from those catty women—their comments made her sick. She stood up to confront them. "She does now!"

Caught with their pants down, the talebearers were tongue-tied.

"You're..." the saleslady mumbled.

"That's right—I'm the lovebird."

"Gosh, we are sooo sorry, Dr. Sharp!" the customer exclaimed.

"No, you're not. You meant every word of it," Kristin lashed out.

"What can we do to make this right?" the saleswoman begged.

"Nothing—you won't ever have to worry about that freeloading janitor ever again because I won't allow him to set foot in here, and for that matter, neither will I." She glared at the other woman, who avoided eye contact. "And as for you, missy, better hope your daughter never finds out what you really think of the man who fixes her toys. She loves him as much as I do, and she'd be heartbroken."

"Oh, please don't tell her. Henry repaired the walls of her doll house last year," the customer pleaded.

"Both Henry and I think a great deal of *our* children at school, too much to expose the hypocrisy of their parents. They'll find that out on their own without any help from us. Good day!"

And like a storm, Kristin blew out of their presence to whisk Henry out the door. With her purse in one hand, she grabbed hold of his arm with her other hand as he stood in the center aisle. The force of her bump almost sent his pizza flying.

"Hey, what's wrong?" he asked worriedly.

"We're getting out of here—now," she commanded.

"I'm not done eating."

"Finish it in the car."

Kristin's tense body language was in lockstep with her fiery temper. The heels of her buckled knee-high boots echoed like a wild horse warning anyone in its path to get out of the way. Henry knew better than to say another word for fear of having to call a taxi. She needed to burn rubber to cool down, and he was just along for the ride.

In her mad dash out the door, Kristin failed to check her surroundings in the parking lot. The store's small delivery truck slammed on its brakes to avoid hitting them; sending the rear end of the vehicle upward. The hard stop didn't seem to faze her, as she ushered Henry to her Lincoln without any backlash from the truck driver. The man behind the wheel of the truck, in dark glasses and a baseball cap, just watched them drive away till the luxury sedan was out of sight.

The trucker's captivity with Kristin's shiny long hair, denim dress, and wool peacoat overshadowed his concern about almost being thrown through the windshield by his hard stop. The only rage causing him to grit his teeth was seeing her loveliness being attached to a guy like Henry instead of him. Another man's fist knocked at the side window to clear the driver's mental fog. Rolling the window down, the trucker turned to the man wearing a business suit with a name tag titled "Manager."

"Yeah?" the driver answered.

"Get going, Freddie. You're late with your deliveries."

The disgraced gym teacher turned delivery driver jammed the shift lever in gear to roll out.

Chapter 23

Henry spent the remainder of his day at Eugene Maloney's house to give Kristin some alone time and sing the blues to his trusted friend. He knew her temperament well enough to keep his distance during her fits of anger. She had nothing much to say during the car ride home, which perplexed him. He racked his brain about the deception at the furniture store but couldn't accept it being the cause of her total one-eighty.

"So, your cheapness finally caught up with you?" Eugene wise-cracked.

"Yes and no…well…I'm not entirely sure."

"Maybe you should've told her straight out that you just wanted to scam a free lunch."

"It's not a scam when they're advertising free stuff," Henry claimed.

"You've been very fortunate to have a class act like her to go along with all your flakiness."

Henry shrugged his shoulders.

"In fact, you're lucky just to have a woman go out with you at all. You've never had a girlfriend before."

"Neither have *you*, my longtime pal."

"I'm working on that as we speak."

"*Oh?*"

"If a bum like you can get a beauty like Dr. Sharp, there's hope for a nerd like me," Eugene rationalized.

"Anyone I know?"

"In due time. The rumor mill will have as much of a field day with mine as they are with yours."

"*What?*"

"You mean you don't know?"

"No, I don't know what you're keeping from me."

"I can't believe neither of you heard."

"C'mon Baloney, spit it out."

"Your courtship is being lampooned all over town. You didn't really think people were going to accept it, did you?"

Henry paused for a moment to let the news digest. "Maybe that's why she muttered in the car about duplicity being a disease around here."

"She must've found out."

"You know, we've been so over the moon, we forgot to land."

"Welcome back to planet Earth."

"Well, I guess this was coming. I expect to be made fun of; it's part of my lifestyle. But not for Sharpie; I thought she had gotten past appearances."

"She's been parading around with you. That's a milestone in and of itself."

"Hee-hee," Henry replied sarcastically.

"You can't expect a woman, no matter how much she loves you, to react to situations as you would."

"She's done a great job with phone solicitors."

"That's for fun. But mass criticism about your competency to administer a school, based on other people's judgment about your love life, isn't so easy for anyone, other than you, to dismiss," the computer whiz explained.

"She was pretty mad."

"Can you blame her?"

The janitor shook his head. "No. Maybe I need to learn to step outside myself now that I have someone else to consider."

"There's a brilliant idea!"

"What is?"

"Stepping outside yourself."

"Are you suggesting I turn into a spendthrift?"

"No, but could you at least try to *look* like one."

"I don't need to put on any falsehoods," Henry proclaimed. "She loves me the way I am."

"I'm sure she does, but look at the big step she took to become a hot dish for you."

"And your glass is only half full. She did it more for herself than for me."

"Fair enough, but I'm sure you were a part of her motivation."

"Kinda sorta…I just helped her bring out what was already there."

"So then let her do the same for you," Eugene proposed.

"What do you mean?"

"Ugh—what do you think I mean?"

"Guess you gotta spell it out, cuz I ain't gettin' it, dude."

"Let her make you over."

"Into what?"

"Someone who *looks* like he doesn't need other people's spare change."

"Oh…so you mean getting dressed up?"

"Yes…and not with fancy T-shirt prints of dress shirts or sweaters." Henry's mouth twisted.

"It means wearing matching socks—without holes."

"For a pocket-protector-wearing bachelor, I'm surprised you're not taking your own advice for this mystery woman of yours—*look at yourself.*"

After an awkward moment of silence, they intuitively bust a gut at the irony of their extreme appearances.

* * *

"I'm so sorry, Henry," Kristin apologized early the next morning, standing on his doorstep holding a bag of bagels and a carrier with two coffees and looking every bit as fresh as the continental breakfast in her hands.

"Is that a peace offering?" he joshed, standing before her like an unmade bed.

"Yes, I've come bearing gifts. May I come in?"

"You know the gate to my pigsty is always open."

She giggled on her way inside his *natural* habitat. After shutting the door, Henry trotted his bare feet to the couch to sweep the accumulation of cut-up coupon fliers, opened junk mail, and torn food wrappers from the cushions and coffee table onto the floor.

"There...now you can sit down."

"Thank you." She sat on the edge of the couch and unpacked the edibles on the coffee table. "Do you like cream cheese on your bagels?"

"Who doesn't?"

"I'll take that as a yes."

"May I?" he asked pointing to one of the coffee cups.

She nodded while preparing the cheese spread on his sliced bagel. "I never should've created a scene in the store yesterday. I embarrassed both of us. Can you forgive me?"

Henry sipped his hot beverage. "There's nothing to forgive, Sharpie."

"I don't understand. I dragged you out of there like a scolded child."

"And that's why there's nothing to forgive."

She handed him half of the bagel while keeping the other half for herself.

"When I was a kid," he continued, "I wanted a pair of gym shoes that were very popular at the time. All the kids at school were sporting them, except me. I bugged my mom till she was blue in the face for them. She finally took me to the shoe store to get 'em. When she saw how overpriced they were, she said in no uncertain terms, 'I'm not paying this ridiculous price for a pair of shoes!' Mom yanked me by the arm and dragged me out of the store, kinda like you did, with me sobbing all the way."

Kristin nearly choked on her bagel, releasing a cough.

"Are you okay?"

She nodded.

"Want some water?"

She shook her head and drank her coffee to wash down the dry crumbs stuck in her throat. "Please finish your story. I want to know where this is going."

"Well, the point of the story is how I didn't understand, at the time, what caused my mom's resentment. You see, I thought it was because she'd had enough of my nagging and it was her way of saying, 'I took you and they're too expensive, so don't ask me again.' But I later learned she did it to cover up the truth. Mom really wanted me to have them, but the price exceeded, not just the value of the shoes, but their worth in my life."

He paused to take a bite of his bagel, then continued while chewing as Kristin listened intently. "You remind me a lot of my mom."

"Should I start calling you Sigmund, as in Freud, with that psycho-analysis?"

"Oh no. I just was trying to be anecdotal. I've learned not to get between you and your temper. I knew I couldn't have upset you that badly."

"I wasn't pleased about your dishonesty for going to the store."

"Now it's my turn to apologize. I won't do it again."

"Trust is a big issue to me." She looked him square in the eye. "I *never* want a reason to mistrust you again—for anything."

"Come here."

She leaned into his open arms for a devoted hug.

"I'll never let you down again—I promise," he pledged.

Raising her lips to him, she sealed their pact with a rewarding kiss.

"I know you have a fiery temper..." Henry started to say.

"Because I've been the subject of malicious hearsay for so long, I just don't know how to contain my anger so easily."

"Yeah, I know."

"Okay, you don't have to be so agreeable."

"You want me to be honest, so I am." He extended his fingers to play with the locks of her hair. "And I'm no different than you when it comes to being the butt of cruel jokes."

"I know that, but it never seems to bother you."

"Sometimes it does—more than you'll ever know. I made the decision long ago to never let it show to anyone, including myself. I've compartmentalized it into a lockbox and thrown away the key."

"Standard operating procedure for the male mind."

"It's all I have...my mom nearly suffered a nervous breakdown from so much worry. I vowed never to let that happen to me, and I won't let it to happen to you either."

"How's that?"

"Baloney Maloney told me yesterday there's a lot of buzzing in your beeswax because of me."

"I had no idea about any of it."

"Neither did I. Goody Two-shoes must be short-circuiting."

"It was beyond shocking what I overheard in the store yesterday when you went back to the food table."

"I'm not gonna let it happen again."

"How?"

"We're gonna take their power away."

"How?"

"It's a big sacrifice for me, but I'm ready for a makeover,"—he checked himself out—"as you can plainly see."

Her face lit up brighter than a spotlight in a darkened theater.

"I think there's a salon downtown that's open on Sundays," he continued.

"Who needs a salon?" she countered with a confident smile. "Got a pair of scissors?"

"Does a maintenance engineer have scissors? That's like asking a teacher for a grade. Of course, I do."

"Why pay an overpriced beautician for something I can do myself."

"You know what you're doing?"

"Time to reveal *my* hidden talent in the kitchen."

Per Kristin's request, Henry supplied her with all the hair and shaving products he could scavenge up, along with a couple of towels. In the kitchen she prepared to wash his hair over the sink.

"Ah, do you mind doing me the courtesy of taking out the dirty dishes *before* I wash your hair?" she contended.

"That would help, wouldn't it?"

"You think?"

As Henry began to pile the dishes and silverware on the counter, Kristin turned her attention to the clutter on his kitchen table, which served as a catchall for an array of household jumble that should be in his cupboards. Clearing a small space, she arranged the hair-care items neatly for easy access. With the sink now emptied, Kristin nearly gagged from the rancid odor of the mucky dish pile. She covered her face like a surgeon with her sweater's turtleneck.

"Ahem…is there something you can do about *that?*" she asked, pointing to the wobbly stacks of plates, bowls, and glasses.

"That bad, huh?"

She nodded urgently.

"Guess I'm so used to it, I've become immune to the stench. I don't have a dishwasher to stash them in, but I'll find something to kill the smell."

He stood still for a minute to think.

"Any day now would be nice," she advised.

"Got it!"

Like something out of a zany cartoon or silent movie, Henry rushed out of the kitchen and returned in a jiffy with a hand-knitted afghan made by his grandmother. The multicolored patterned stitch was carefully tossed over the tops of the piles so nothing broke.

"Outta sight, outta smell," he boasted.

The look on Kristin's face, as she lowered her turtleneck, was one of total confusion. "I don't know whether to laugh or cry."

"Try not to think about it."

"I just hope the weight of the afghan doesn't shift any of the dishes."

"Otherwise we'll have the sound no one wants to hear in a restaurant."

Kristin tittered. "Get your head under the faucet."

Henry complied with her order. She spent the next several minutes running her manicured fingers through his thick hair—cleaning every strand thoroughly. Afterward, he sat on the designated kitchen chair where she covered his wrinkled T-shirt with a bath towel like a bib.

"It's time to let out the beautiful man I see inside you," she whispered, taking hold of the scissors and comb from the table—*snip, snip!*

"How did you learn to cut hair?"

"Kind of like you…I had an aunt who was a beautician, and she taught me a thing or two, just in case I needed an alternate career."

Henry's body turned to gelatin from the tingle of her hands coursing through his hair and again when she lathered his cheeks to sculpt his beard into a goatee—keeping a vestige of his personality intact.

Her approving winks and nods were of great comfort to him along the way. He felt completely at ease feeling her touch and didn't want the experience to end. It was more than a haircut to him; it was a transformative moment he had never experienced before—she was cutting out the hidden jewel that only *she* could find in him.

"This gel looks like it's a hundred years old," she noted, eyeing the thick coating of dust on the sealed bottle.

"It was a secret Santa gift I got a long time ago."

"That's a strange thing to give someone for a work gift."

"Not when the *someone* who gave it wanted to make a public statement."

"And who might that be?"

"Oh, a certain wannabe principal."

"Uh-huh…I wonder *who* that could be," she muttered while opening the bottle. "Let's hope it's not full of glue."

"That'll be one way to keep my hair in place permanently."

"And we'll change your name to Elmer," she giggled, rubbing the sticky gel through his wet hair to create a cool style of masculinity.

Making one final inspection before brushing off the mess of clippings all over his towel smock, she was quite pleased with the outcome and gave him a double thumbs-up. "You are so handsome! I'm going to have a lot of competition."

"The suspense is killing me—mirror!"

Kristin retrieved the handheld mirror she had purposely kept out of his reach until the unveiling was ready.

Taking hold of the mirror, Henry's eyes nearly poked through the glass. "Who's that looking back at me?"

"The man I love."

"I don't even recognize myself."

"Are you not happy?"

"I'm speechless."

"Good or bad?"

"Neither—I'm awesome!"

"Well, do I get a kiss for all my hard work?"

"Absolutely."

Leaping to his feet, he ignored the towel that fell to the floor as they embraced for a kiss. When Kristin pulled away, Henry's wrinkled T-shirt and pajama bottoms came into her full view.

"Ooh…we're not out of the woods yet," she commented, waving her finger up and down his body.

He shivered like a comedian discovering he's in his underwear before a live audience. "Oops…"

"Get dressed, Superman; we're going shopping."

Chapter 24

"I don't know about these clothes you picked out, Sharpie…all the tags say 'dry clean only,'" Henry voiced from the men's fitting room, as Kristin sat patiently outside by the department store's three-way mirror.

"Is that a problem?"

"Well, if I can't throw 'em in the washing machine, they're gonna cost me more to keep clean than what they cost to buy."

"Don't worry about the price tags, I'm paying the bill."

Henry popped his head out of the door. "I can't let you do that."

"Why not?"

"It wouldn't be right."

"These are high-end brands out of your price range."

"I can afford them." He ducked back in the stall.

"You don't need to be prideful."

"Who's being prideful? How do you know I'm not independently wealthy?"

"On a custodian's salary? Besides, I'm well acquainted with your thoughts about the price of things."

"You wanna know why I live like I do?"

"I'm sure you're going to tell me."

"So when I get old and can't work anymore, I'm not stuck eating cat food."

"*Meow*," she laughed.

"Good one. Are you ready for my fashion statement?"

"Shall I cover my eyes?"

"Not a bad idea."

She placed her hands over her eyes. "All right, they're covered."

"Okay…ready or not, here I come."

Emerging from behind the louvered door of the tiny changing room, Henry breezed past Kristin to place himself on the raised platform with his back to the three-way mirror.

"Can I open my eyes now?" she asked anxiously.

He placed his hands in the pockets of the pleated wool-blend slacks like a model in *GQ* magazine. "Only if you can handle it."

"Wheeeet wheeeew!" she wolf-whistled. "Look at you!"

He blushed redder than a tomato.

"Turn around so I can see what's behind you."

He spun around to face the center mirror.

"Very nice!" She smiled from ear to ear. "Just one thing…turn back around."

He pivoted. "What's that?"

"The way you're wearing the shirt is not quite right."

"How so?"

She approached him to unfasten the second button from the top of his black rayon shirt to expose a portion of his bare upper chest. "You don't have to be so closed up. Women like when a man *wears* his confidence."

"Then I should probably roll up my sleeves too."

"Get to work, Superman."

In the spirit of his pet name, he changed in and out of the remaining clothes like Clark Kent in a phone booth. Next came the selection of accessories: belts, shoes, socks, and even a new wristwatch.

"This is gonna be expensive," Henry worried, as they stood in the checkout line with armfuls of garments.

"My offer to pay is still valid," Kristin said comfortingly.

"I've got money—I just hate parting with it."

"Am I not a worthy investment?"

"That's why I'm parting with it."

"Next?" the cashier called out.

After the sticker-shocking transaction, Henry agreed to don one of the outfits before leaving the store. He wanted his girl to have something to enjoy during their long ride back to Perrinsville from the capital city's shopping mall. Only one minor detail needed correcting for the makeover to be complete.

"Please do me a favor," she requested at a glimpse of him in the passenger seat of her car.

"Another one?"

"Quit slouching and sit up straight. Your poor posture will ruin the new you."

He thrust his shoulders back and chest out like an army buck private. "Better?"

She nodded with a gleaming smile. "Uh-huh—good boy. Be sure to stand tall and proud when we get home. I can't wait for everyone to see my…"

"*Sharp* dressed man," he teased. "I guess we're both living ZZ Top songs now—do you know who they are?"

"Actually yes…the guys with the long beards."

"I'm impressed! How did you know?"

"I figured if I'm going to have a life with you, I'd better educate myself about old movies and music or I'll never understand the analogies of your pop culture references."

Henry applauded her with a brief hand clap.

Kristin patted the radio console on her dashboard. "The eighties station on satellite radio just earned it's monthly fee."

Henry laughed. "I told you it was a great decade for music."

"I agree. So, which ZZ Top song am I supposed to be?"

He broke into an air guitar and jammed the opening line of "Legs."

She glanced at him with fluttering eyelashes—flirting at the silliness worn on the sleeve of his shiny new leather jacket.

* * *

"Watch out mister!" shouted a boy in the front schoolyard, as the football torpedoed toward a well-dressed man with a stubbly goatee and dark glasses. Thinking fast, the man stunned everyone with a swift clasp of the ball before it took his head off.

"Great catch!" yelled another boy.

"Ready to go long?" the man asked the boys.

The kids in the game began to scatter.

"Hut! Hut! Hut!" the man commanded. He then bounced the ball off his knee, back into his hands, to throw a centerline pass.

"*Henry?*" asked a first-grade girl nearby, recognizing his famous maneuver.

He slid the shades down the bridge of his nose. "Good morning, Cassie."

"How come you don't look like *you* anymore?"

He knelt down to her level and spoke softly. "Can you keep a secret?"

She nodded.

"I'm pretending to be someone else."

"Who?"

"A grown-up."

"Why?"

"It's an experiment."

"What kind of experiment?"

"To see who really has more fun—kids or grown-ups."

"Kids do!"

He looked around to make sure her loud volume didn't draw attention to their huddle. "Shh! Of course, you do. We both know it, but the grown-ups don't...that's why it's an experiment."

Cassie's eyes brightened. "Oh...I get it."

"Remember, it's a secret—okay?"

"I won't tell anyone about your disguise."

Henry winked at her with a smile. "Good. I'm counting on you."

The morning bell rang, but Henry remained outside as the students assembled to file in the building. He noticed many of the moms who normally drop their children off hadn't left yet. They were sticking around to check out the cool dude in the leather jacket. They were ogling *him!*

Waltzing into the office as if the "Blue Danube" were piping through the PA system, Henry swept Janet out of her chair.

"C'mon, Goody Two-shoes, let's dance." He twirled her around.

"Whoa—look what crawled out of the fur ball!" She stroked the material of his duds. "Very snazzy."

"And they're dry-clean only," he proudly advertised.

"Well, you finally *cleaned* up your act."

"Well, I didn't exactly do it."

"I know—"she pointed to Kristin's closed door—"she texted me earlier, saying I'd be flabbergasted."

"*And?*"

"The gossip about you two is going to have a much different tone."

"Which reminds me...you've been derelict in your duties lately."

"Both of you deserve happiness, and I couldn't bring myself to dampen it. I assumed you'd hear the obnoxious rumors eventually."

"What about your happiness? Any progress with Fast Freddie?"

"One day at a time."

"What's he up to these days?"

"A lot of heavy lifting. That's all I'm allowed to say."

"Keeping it under wraps," Henry chuckled.

Janet quickly changed the conversation. "Ah…Kristin hasn't come in yet."

"I know, she's at a meeting with Cakewell."

"There's a few bulbs out in Miss Krackett's classroom. Try not to tear your new clothes on the job. I'm sure they cost Kristin a pretty penny."

"She didn't buy them—I did."

"*Really?* The cheapest man in the whole world broke his piggy bank? You must be in love."

"I'm not cheap, just very frugal."

"It's *me*, Henry…you're not frugal; you're cheap."

"You know why I'm so cheap?"

"I've heard the pet food analogy before."

"Oh."

"I don't think you have to worry about growing old alone; our principal adores you."

"And I adore her right back."

"Well, if you don't want Miss Krackett to go bonkers, you need to get going."

"Then I better get Miss Krack-a-lackin' Krackett lit up before she blows another fuse," he quipped.

Word about Henry spread like wildfire. He soon got a taste of the same flattery Kristin received following her breakout moment. The scuttlebutt did indeed take on a different attitude. The meanness morphed into praises, particularly from the female staff at the school, who looked for every menial opportunity under the sun to call the janitor—even if they had to fudge their own maintenance requests.

On jersey day, he garnered the attention of a star athlete by sporting an old Perrinsville High football shirt he'd never earned. Yet, to him, valor didn't come from wooing the women who used to belittle him—he didn't have a spiteful bone in his body—it came from the respect of the children, which began to wane. They didn't easily adapt to their new and improved custodial engineer. Henry knew how important it was to Kristin for all the ugly rumors to stop, so he didn't regret the transformation for her sake. But, like the schoolkids, he inherently started to yearn for his old habits again—his manly facade could only be sustained temporarily.

Chapter 25

S now fell early on Thanksgiving Day—not an unusual occurrence for the upper Midwest. Kristin enjoyed having Henry at her house for the festivities. It was more than her first holiday with him; it was her first holiday away from her family back home. She had called her estranged parents that morning for the first time since moving to Perrinsville.

Both of Kristin's folks were emotionally distant, which contributed to their only child's inability to cope with people and problems. Their lack of time with her rebounded, as she gave them very little of her time in return. Thanks to Henry, she had learned to be more forgiving and begun to reestablish a relationship with them. Today's call was a huge step for her—she couldn't wait to brag about her new boyfriend.

Henry roasted the free turkey given to them by the school district and helped Kristin prepare the traditional side dishes: mashed potatoes with gravy, stuffing, and assorted vegetables—way more food than either of them could eat at the dinner table—with a bottle of their favorite red wine and a pitcher of ice water.

"There's gonna be a lotta leftovers, Sharpie."

"Perfect…then I know you'll be eating right for the next week."

"Everything I eat is healthy."

"For your wallet, not your stomach."

"Is that your way of saying, 'Will the real turkey please stand up?'"

"If the drumstick fits…"

Her quick jab caused him to miss his mouth with a fork full of gravy-soaked turkey; the meat slid down his shirt onto his lap. "Wear it—*and I am!*"

They giggled at the flawlessly timed serendipity. Henry tossed the fallen turkey back onto his plate.

"That's what these fine linen napkins are for," Kristin pointed out, "to cover your lap in case of a snafu like that."

"And I can think of another thing they're good for—watch." He wadded his napkin like a cleaning rag to dip into his glass of water. He then proceeded to rub out the stains on his shirt and pleated slacks. "Does it look like they're coming out?"

"You're going to need more than water to get rid of the gravy stains."

"No biggie. I'll just wash my clothes when I get home."

"You can't. They're dry clean only, remember?"

"Duh…that's right. See why I was so worried about buying them?"

"If you didn't miss your mouth, you wouldn't be in this mess."

"There's a janitor gag in there somewhere."

Kristin raised her wine glass. "Happy Thanksgiving!"

"Happy Thanksgiving to you too."

They clinked their goblets and drank the wine.

"I told my parents about you today."

"You did?"

"Uh-huh." She nodded eagerly. "I told them how much I love you and that you're nothing like any man I've ever met."

"I'll bet they were thrilled to hear you're in love with a janitor."

"Ah…maintenance engineer."

"Everyone knows what that means. It doesn't take your PhD to crack the code."

"My father was very impressed by the measures you took to restore my honor, and that meant more to him, and my mother, than what you do for a living."

"Is that because they're blue collar like me?"

"No, my father's a lawyer…a very successful one."

Henry nearly inhaled the food in his mouth before looking at her with a slack jaw.

Kristin continued. "Do you remember when you told the manager in the grocery store about my practice being in slip and fall?"

"Yeah."

"Well, my father is one of the biggest personal injury and medical malpractice attorneys in New England."

Henry dropped his fork to refill his wine glass.

"Are you okay?" she asked.

"Yeah, just a little thirsty. Please…tell me more."

"Building a successful law practice had been an obsession with my father. Personal injury cases made him financially wealthy at the expense of our family. My mother was his first client when he struggled to pay the rent for his tiny office. Her slip-and-fall accident from a grease spot at the fast-food chain where she worked resulted in a broken hip, lower back injuries, and a massive settlement.

"The dividends from the case profited them well beyond their finances—they fell rich in love. Shortly after Mother's hip replacement, they married and then I was born. My mother's chronic pains prevented her from ever working again, which added to the emptiness of their marriage. She found solace in daytime soaps and game shows but couldn't escape the pressures of motherhood. Her self-described 'single' parenting accounted for giving me everything money could buy at the expense of values that couldn't be purchased—at least not with cash or credit cards. I repaid them with a lot of indifference."

"That's quite a story." Henry noticed Kristin's glass was nearly empty. "More wine?"

She nodded with her goblet held out for him to pour the libation. "I think now is the right time to mend the fences, so I invited them here for Christmas."

Henry raised his brows. "That's great."

"And I can't wait for them to meet you."

"It'll be a Christmas to remember," he interjected satirically.

"You really underestimate yourself. I've never seen anyone in all my years in the public school system connect with kids better than you."

"That's because I'm a kid trapped in a man's body," he half-joked.

"And that's just one of the many things I love about you."

By the time they finished their meal, both were too full for dessert. Kristin boxed up a care package of sizable leftovers, including the entire pumpkin pie she had bought. It was getting late, and neither of them wanted to fight the Black Friday shopping crowds the next day. *What to do?*

"Eureka! I got an idea for tomorrow," Henry proclaimed at the doorstep with his coat on.

"What's that?"

"There's a really cool indoor water park about a couple of hours from here, and while everyone is jostling in the stores, we'll probably have the whole place to ourselves."

Kristin broke her eye contact with him. "I don't know about that."

"You don't know about the existence of the park, or you don't know about going?"

"Both."

"You don't like waterslides?"

"I don't like pools."

"Why?"

"They make me nervous."

"Are you afraid of water?"

"Yes," she demurred.

He set his bag of goodies on the floor and extended his thumb to tilt her chin up. "Can I ask why?"

"I never learned to swim. I'm afraid of drowning."

"I don't mean to make light of your fear, but the water's only waist deep there."

She looked back at him with a faint expression.

"Besides," he continued, "I have an ulterior motive."

"What?"

"I kinda wouldn't mind seeing you in a bathing suit."

"I don't do bikinis."

"And I don't do speedos, so there's no show for you either."

The mental image of him prancing around in a speedo livened her deadpan face. "*That* would be a sight to see if it weren't so comical."

"So what do you say? Wanna go?"

"Some of those slides look like roller coasters."

"That's what makes them so fun. Fear not, I'll be right there with you. Nothing bad will happen."

She hugged him tightly. "Promise?"

"I promise you'll have such a good time, you'll forget about this conversation."

"Okay, I trust you."

He bent over to retrieve the care package. "Get plenty of sleep. I'll call you tomorrow when I'm on my way."

"I trust *you*, but I don't trust the Hubbard mobile for that long of a drive."

"Haven't had any problems since the radiator replacement. Besides, you've done enough driving so let me be the chauvinist…"

"That's chauffeur."

"I guess I was a little off again."

"Not this time; that was waaay off."

"Hey, it's late."

"I know—good night."

Chapter 26

"Arose from a gas station? You really know how to make a girl feel special," Kristin said tongue-in-cheek with batting eyes. "They were just sitting there at the counter, so I figured, why not?" Henry explained, as he steered his van away from the gasoline pump.

"How much was it? A dollar?"

"Those overpriced florists charge four to six dollars for something that's clipped off the same bushes. Does it matter who sells it?"

"Guess not." Her lips disappeared as she held the rose under her nose. "At least it smells nice."

"And it makes a good air freshener for this clunker."

"You can be such a doofus sometimes," she teased.

Upon arrival at the Aqua Dome water park, the pair was surprised to see the abundance of vehicles in the snowy parking lot.

"Guess I was wrong about having the place to ourselves," Henry said, scrambling to find an open space.

"My money's on lots of kids and teenagers being here, not wanting to be trapped in stores."

"Just like us."

Inside the gigantic facility, they parted company for the locker rooms with their duffle bags in hand. Kristin also brought the rose to keep it from freezing in the van. She unpacked her one and only swimsuit from high school phys ed, which still fit her. Changing into the faded blue and black suit in front of a locker, with other women and girls around, reminded her how much she hated the required swimming curriculum in high school. Being the only one in her class unable to swim, she was forced to wear a lifejacket and given special treatment that exposed her fear of water to the rest of the school.

She felt an urge to renege on her commitment to be there. Yet, she knew how much it meant to Henry, and she couldn't bring herself to back out after coming this far with him. Not just in miles from the drive, but in her personal enrichment. *It's only one day, and the water's only waist deep—it's not that much of a sacrifice,* she thought. *Let's do it.* After carefully hanging her street clothes in the locker, she took a deep breath, ready to conquer the slippery slopes ahead of her.

Kristin's hunch was right. The glass covered park was filled with an array of children, teenagers, and young parents. It became obvious that she and Henry would be the most senior of the thrill-seekers there. Alone with his back to the locker area, in superhero-comic-strip-printed Bermuda trunks, Henry stood out like a sore thumb. His presence caused a momentary lapse in Kristin's apprehension about their course of action.

"You left very little to the imagination," she jested.

He swerved to her. "What do you mean?"

"Those"—pointing to his swimsuit—"You look like you're in your underwear."

"Maybe I am," he responded with flittering eyebrows. "Don't tell anyone."

"Oh boy…"

"No, it's more like oh, girl—you look terrific!"

She blinked owlishly. "I don't feel terrific."

He affectionately took her hand. "C'mon, let's get our feet wet. We'll start at the bottom and work our way up the mountain."

As they headed toward the lazy river, Kristin scanned all the slides within her mobile vantage point. Some of them didn't seem so bad, while others looked downright frightening. *What exactly did he mean by the mountain?* she wondered. *Is he expecting me to go on those gargantuan contraptions?* Yet, her boyfriend was more in sync with her nervousness than she knew, hence his choice to start with the lazy river—the ultimate in relaxation.

"Grab a doughnut, Sharpie." He pointed to the stack of inflated inner tubes. "They're going like hotcakes."

"And we'll both end up with spare tires around our waists."

"That's funny!"

"Just laughing in the face of danger."

"There's nothing to be scared of here." He led her into the water and mounted her on the tube. "Just lie back and let all your troubles float downstream. I'll be right behind you."

Henry let Kristin go with the current as he hopped onto his tube and paddled himself to her. They joined hands for the long ride around the circumference of the park. Kristin relaxed as the drifting water soothed her nerves, even with the occasional bumps and splashes from other patrons in passing. By the time their therapeutic journey ended, Henry popped the question.

"Ready for adventure?"

"Willing and able."

"Let's rock 'n' roll!"

Starting with the smaller slides and shorter lines, they embarked on a wet and wild exploration like a pair of youngsters running free. It was the most exhilarating rush of Kristin's life—the element of danger, with the escalation of each slide, electrified her. The unknown twists and turns in the dark pipelines caused her to scream at every opening, but with Henry at the helm of their rafts, she felt safe—even on some of the more insane slides, like the colossal funnel called the Waterspout.

Their afternoon of childlike innocence reached its climax at the launch of the tallest slide in the park—the Ski Jump. Due to the height and force of the rider, the depth of the water tank needed to break the fall measured ten feet. With the dinner hour looming near, much of the tourist crowd had dissipated. Henry convinced Kristin this would be their final slide before calling it a day. His constant yammering distracted her from noticing the full gravity of the slide's trajectory until it was too late.

There was no tube for this ride, which meant they could not go together. Sliders went one at a time on their backs with their arms crisscrossed over their chests.

Kristin shuddered. "This one looks scary!"

"It just looks worse than it really is."

"I'm not sure I want to do this one."

"Oh, now's not the time to start chickening out. You came this far, right?"

"Yeah…"

"Well, it's like getting a shot when you're afraid of needles. Just close your eyes and don't look."

His blasé attitude sent a shiver up her spine. She didn't agree with the analogy at all. This wasn't anything close to a shot in the arm, it was more like a shot in the foot—*for him.*

"You're next, sir," the lifeguard said to Henry.

Getting into position, he grinned at Kristin like a daredevil. "See you at the bottom."

The lifeguard placed his hand on Henry's shoulder. "One…two… three!" He pushed the janitor down the steep slide of running water.

"Bombs away!" Henry shouted on the way down.

Kristin watched as her man went airborne with a whaling screech at the foot of the slide in just seconds. The sight of him summersaulting in the air before plunging into the pool made her woozy. It was as if her stomach went along for the ride with him.

"C'mon, Sharpie!" he yelled to her from the pool deck.

She froze like a block of ice.

"Don't be scared! It's fun!" he continued to holler.

All her fears rained on her like a tropical storm. The sound of his voice faded away as the sound of the running water on the slide increased. Time stood still for her. Other customers began to form a line behind her.

"Miss?" the lifeguard asked her. "Are you all right?"

She trembled *yes,* when she really meant *no.*

"Would you like me to walk you back down the steps?"

"What happens if you're not here?"

"I'd have to close the ride temporarily."

She turned to see all the kids eagerly waiting to take their turn. Kristin didn't have the heart to dampen their spirits due to her personal distress. Her sense of fairness to them compelled her to bite the bullet, despite the emotional consequences. She could still hear shrieks of her nickname echoing from below, along with "What's taking so long? Hurry up! Quit overthinking it!"

Shaking like a leaf, Kristin stepped into the launchpad to lie down. "How long till I get to the bottom?"

"A few seconds," the lifeguard responded. "Are you sure you want to do this?"

She quaked. "Y-y-yeah."

"Last chance?"

"I'll just take my lumps."

He placed his hand on her cold shoulder. "One...two..."

"How deep is the pool?"

"Ten feet...three!" He shoved her down.

"I can't swim!" she screamed for dear life, as the water washed her away.

The few seconds down the slide became an eternity, and she saw her whole life flash before her eyes. Kristin squealed so hard her voice cut out. She could feel the air beneath her backside from the force propelling her off the launchpad like a cartwheel. Her limp body splashed into the tank rock solid. Henry dove into action as if he was an Olympic champion to save her. He pulled her up and swam with her to the ladder.

A patrolling lifeguard ran to assist getting her out of the pool. They lay Kristin's lifeless body on the deck for the lifeguard to pump her lungs.

"Sharpie! Sharpie!" Henry cried, hovering over the lifeguard.

"Stand back, sir!" the lifeguard ordered.

"I'm sorry! I'm sorry; it's all my fault!" Henry wailed. Tears quickly dominated the wetness dripping down his quivering cheeks. "I should've listened to her!"

"Who are you sir?"

"Her boyfriend."

The paid lifesaver felt Kristin's chest starting to heave. "She's coming out of it."

In seconds, Kristin coughed profusely, spewing the chlorinated water out of her mouth.

"Ma'am, can you hear me?"

She faintly nodded to the lifeguard, as he sat her up. Henry wrapped a towel around her, and both men carried her to a chaise where they eased her into the chair.

"Thank you," she gasped to the lifeguard, without acknowledging Henry.

"Thank your boyfriend; he's the one who fished you out in the nick of time."

"I'll deal with *him* later," she responded in a weak voice.

"Are you going to be okay?" the lifeguard asked.

"Yeah…I think so."

"I can call an ambulance to take you to the hospital."

"What for?"

"To make sure you haven't suffered any injuries."

"Maybe he's right," Henry said. "You should see a doctor."

"I don't need a doctor; I can feel my strength coming back. I just want to go home."

"A doctor exam would be a good idea, Sharpie."

"You shut up!" she barked with an angry finger pointed at him like a dagger.

"I don't want to get in the middle of this," the lifeguard said. "If you're feeling better, I'll leave you two alone. Stay out of the water and rest for a while. Let the office know if you need further assistance."

"I will. Thank you again, sir," she said graciously.

Henry shook the man's hand. "Yes, thank you."

Kristin waited till the lifeguard was out of sight before going ballistic on the person she blamed for her traumatization. "Sit down, Henry."

In obedience, he sat at the foot of the chaise unaware of what was forthcoming. He extended his arms to her.

"Don't touch me!" She slapped them away.

"I can't tell you how bad I feel about this—"

"How bad *you* feel? What about *me*? You know I can't swim!"

"Please believe me…I was never gonna let anything happen to you."

"How brave of you," she scowled. "I told you about my fear of drowning and that didn't seem to faze you at all, did it?"

The weight of Kristin's fury squashed Henry like a bug. He knew he was guilty of negligence. "I'll spend the rest of my life making this up to you—I swear."

"Swearing is a bad habit, and so are you."

"What does that mean?"

"It's over. I don't want to see you anymore."

"Well, you gotta see me at school," he attempted to joke.

"I can also end that if you'd like."

"No," he whimpered.

"Then consider this goodbye."

"I know you're mad and blame me for what happened, and I take full responsibility for coaxing you into something you clearly weren't ready for, but we can get past this. I know we can…we've been through so much as it is—it can't end like this!"

"What did I say was a big issue for me? I'll make it easy to refresh your memory—trust, Henry, trust! I told you in no uncertain terms that you are to never give me a reason to mistrust you again."

"And I've asked you to trust me too. Should I remind you of some of the above and beyond things I've done that I didn't have to?"

"That was before there was an *us*."

"What's the difference? I haven't lied to you about anything since the furniture store."

"Trust is more than just simple honesty; it's also about security and safety. You just lost it all in one failed act."

Blood drained from Henry's face.

"Stand up! I need to get my things and get out of here."

Kristin wielded herself straight to the ladies' locker room.

Henry chased after her.

"Don't follow me," she warned.

"How are you planning to get home?"

"I'll call for a ride."

"That'll cost a fortune."

"Considering this date nearly cost me my life, what's a few more dollars." She stopped short to stare him down. "I suppose I should thank you for saving my life, but then, you would not have had to do it had you not pushed me into it."

"I will never get the visual of what happened out of my head, and I'll never forgive myself either. Right now, all I wanna make right is us. I wanna spend the rest of my life with you, and I'll move heaven and earth to do it."

"Sorry Superman, this is one part of me you cannot save. I'm not meant to get married and have a family."

The towel draped over Kristin's shoulder flew in Henry's face like a cape, as she whisked away from him faster than a speeding bullet—not to be seen again.

Alone in the cold outside the park entrance, Henry discovered the rose he'd given Kristin wilting in the snow. He knew she didn't throw it in the trash because she wanted him to find it. The meaning behind her symbolism beat him over the head—it was her way of saying their love just died like a rose in the snow.

Chapter 27

'Tis the season to be melancholy, fa-la-la-la-la, la-la-la-la! So much for the yuletide carol Kristin and Henry hoped to be singing together at Christmastime. The celebrated couple's relationship went from comfort and joy to silent night faster than Santa Claus down a chimney. Neither of them had ever believed their wonderful life together would be stolen by the Grinch of misgivings.

Betrayed by the man whom she'd grown to trust, Kristin rushed out of the water park hysterical, wet, and half-dressed. Only her coat, jeans, and boots covered her moist swimsuit. The rest of her clothes were wadded up in her bag, along with the rose she strategically planted in the snow. She wanted to be long gone before Henry made it out of the locker room. Her mind was made up, and she wasn't going to give him a prayer of a chance to influence her decision.

Kristin shivered all the way home in the backseat of a stranger's car, unable to discern whether the chills upon her body came from the dampness of her clothing, the fright from her harrowing experience, or both. Her thinking was as clouded as the wintry sky.

"Please turn the heat up," Kristin pleaded to the Uber driver.

Fortunately for her, the driver was a woman—had it been a man, she wouldn't have accepted the ride.

"It's all the way up, dear," the middle-aged woman responded.

"I am not your dear, and I'm freezing back here."

"I'm sorry, miss; didn't mean to offend you…but I'm starting to burn up and will have to crack open the window if you insist on the heater being on full blast."

"Please don't open the window; I can't take more of the cold."

"It's a long drive to Perrinsville. Would you like to use my parka as a blanket? That way I can cool off."

"Yes, I think so."

"Okay, let me pull over."

The driver swerved her vehicle to the side of the highway to remove her heavy coat. In handing it over to her passenger, she couldn't help but notice Kristin's ghostly face.

"Are you all right?"

"No." She blanketed her torso with the opened coat.

"Do you want me to take you to the police?"

Kristin shook her head. "No, nothing like that happened."

"You look petrified."

"I just lost the love of my life."

"Oh, okay. I understand."

"I just want to get home."

The driver steered her car back on the road. "Would you like to talk about it? We've got plenty of time."

"I'm sorry, but I don't know you, and I'm a very private person."

"Objectively speaking, sometimes talking to a stranger is better than talking to a friend."

"This isn't one of those times for me. Please just drive; I don't want to talk."

"Then do you mind if I play some Christmas music on the radio?"

"I don't care."

The woman reached for the power button on her radio, as Kristin morosely stared at the snow-covered scenery outside her window. The speaker behind her head suddenly came alive in midchorus—"jingle all the way…"

On the flip side, Henry dashed through the snow, in his van, crying all the way home. Her disappearance blew every speck of confidence he had into a dust storm. He beat himself up all weekend over how badly he had muddied the water of her devotion to him. Unlike his other faux pas, this one reached a level of epic proportion that he couldn't comprehend. She was more than his first girlfriend; she was that million-to-one shot at an unimaginable future. He couldn't fathom life without her, and he became desperate to repair the damage he had caused.

The gravity of her temper normally grounded him from any action until a reasonable cooling period elapsed, but not this time. He needed to patch the hole in their relationship's roof so the impassioned rainfall between them wouldn't leave a permanent water stain. Adopting the Fast Freddie syndrome, he called her incessantly with long-winded messages of apology she never heard. The volume of calls only increased her resistance to him, to the point that she shut the phone off for much of the weekend, making it abundantly clear she did not want to hear from him, let alone see him. He didn't dare show up at her house unannounced.

* * *

Henry arrived at school early Monday morning to set up a Christmas tree in the front office. Dressed in the designer threads Kristin picked out, he hoped to get her attention, as she couldn't avoid him at work. In his desperate frame of mind, it was a gamble worth betting on, since she would have to cross his pathway. Janet assisted in the holiday decorations by running the garland throughout the room and placing the poinsettias she had purchased over the weekend. Her steady stream of questions pertaining to the long weekend were answered by his recounting of Thanksgiving day only—he had no intention of venturing into the aftermath of their black-eyed Friday.

By the time they finished, Kristin materialized with her baggage and coffee mug. Henry ducked behind the tree, so she wouldn't see him just yet.

"Merry Christmas, Kristin," Janet greeted with a pleasant smile.

"Good morning; merry Christmas to you too."

As Kristin fiddled with her keys to unlock her office door, Henry sprang out from behind the tree.

"Merry Christmas, Sharpie."

She turned on her heel. "It's Dr. Sharp to you Mr. Hubbard."

Noticing the look of shock on Janet's face, Henry attempted to save *his* face. "Hey, that was pretty funny, being so formal."

"I'm not joking," she retorted stoically.

"Let me help you with the door." He pulled his key from his pants pocket to unlock the door and let her in, eyeing Janet and hoping she wasn't hip to their friction. "You know, this is how we first met. Kinda fun to reenact the scene."

"I'm not reenacting anything with you." She entered the suite and set her items on the desk, aware that Henry had followed her. "Let's get one thing straight between us—"

"I'm all ears."

"Then hear this because I'm only going to say it once. Any and all interaction between us is going to be strictly business."

Henry's mouth drooped.

"If you cannot accept that," she continued very sternly, "I will accept your resignation. Is that clear, Mr. Hubbard?"

"C'mon, Sharpie, you don't have to be so formal."

"Yes, I do; and you are not to call me that name again—I don't want to hear it. I'm a PhD and deserve the respect I've earned. Are we clear?"

"I guess so."

"You guess so?"

"I mean, yes, Dr. Sharp."

"Good…and by the way, you are overdressed for custodial duties."

He checked himself out.

"Starting tomorrow, I want you to report in your old clothes. You're here to work, not impress the ladies."

"You're gonna take back the man you created?"

"He died in the water three days ago."

"I'm not dead."

"You are to me."

"I cried like a baby all the way home from the water park."

"That's your problem, Henry. You don't know how to take things like a man."

"So, I'm just supposed to forget the past few weeks and go back to the way it was before our relationship?"

"Look, if you cannot comply with my request, I will mandate that dreaded uniform again, which by the way, I will expect you to repair."

"You're gonna strip me down while you keep all the dressing I helped bring out of you."

"I like myself—I just don't like you anymore."

"You just keep getting colder by the minute. I don't know who this is standing in front of me anymore."

"Your employer…who will fire you if you don't get back to work."

Henry exited her office visibly dejected.

Janet was aghast after overhearing their entire exchange. "What the heck was that all about?"

"Long story Goody Two-shoes…maybe another day."

He walked out of the executive suite with his head hanging below his slouched shoulders. Outside the glass door, Miss Perew led her fifth-grade students single file, past him on their way to the art room.

"Morning, Henry," she said, fresh as a daisy.

"Mornin'," he mumbled.

Many of the kids waved hello to him. His normal response to their brightness was marred by a shadow of gloom. Never before had he thought about avoiding the unassuming happiness of the schoolchildren. Now he barely acknowledged them with a feeble thumbs-up and half smile. A boy near the end of the line broke ranks with his class to approach his idolized handyman.

"Mr. Henry?"

"Yeah?"

"I have a drone with a couple of propellers that don't turn. Can you fix it for me?"

"I'd like to, but I don't think I'll have time."

"But you always fix our toys."

"I know, but I'm very busy these days. Maybe sometime after the holidays."

"I can't wait that long; I wanna play with it now."

"I'm sorry, Ryan; it'll have to wait."

"Then I'll just beg my mom to buy me a new one for Christmas—bye."

Seeing the deflated youngster rejoin his class, Henry knew he had popped the boy's balloon just as Kristin had sucked the air out of his lungs. He stood speechless over the lies he told little Ryan for no good reason other than to escape from the reality of his broken heart. He didn't know how to deal with the turmoil he was experiencing, and he couldn't bring himself to pass that on to the kids who meant so much to him.

* * *

Winning Kristin back became a preoccupation with Henry on and off the job. The next two weeks were difficult, not just for him, but for Kristin as well. Her aloofness depressed him to the point that he avoided her. He couldn't bear the thought of running into her at any given moment. His fantasies of her running to him with love in her arms faded with the passing of each day. He reverted back to his old self-image: plaid flannels over colored T-shirts and tattered jeans with dangling keys. The gel was gone from his scruffy hair, and the beard stubbles returned to his cheeks.

Meanwhile, Kristin continued to look spectacular, always dressed to the nines. She never let go of her need to keep up appearances at all costs. It didn't take a child prodigy to figure out their fashionable romance had gone out of style. Their contrasting visuals fueled the rumor mill once again. The whispered scoffs among the school staff reached her ears with discontent. She hated their fake concerns and smiles to her face, knowing they were laughing behind her back about the man whom she had considered marrying. *Henry might be a lot of things*, she thought, *but at least he's not a phony.*

The sting from her tribulation began to fade by early December. The past couple of weeks had given Kristin pause to re-examine her feelings for Henry. She truly did have a forgiving nature, but the scars from her wounded history guarded her heart from further vulnerability. She couldn't allow herself to fall under the spell of his charm again. Her best defense was continued abstinence from him.

Yet, the pain of their breakup didn't just impact them; it spread to the children whom they served. The students at Perrinsville Elementary had grown to love their principal as much as they did their janitor. Seeing the two of them separated dulled the vibrancy that had existed in all the classrooms prior to Thanksgiving. And with the Christmas season in full swing, the wish list of toys to be fixed began to mount on Henry's workbench.

The kinship he treasured had become worthless. No sooner would he start to tinker with a toy than he would give up in frustration. It was during one such incident when his exasperation was observed by his best friend after school.

"Easy guy," Eugene said, upon entering the caretaker's quarters.

Henry swiveled over to him. "Sorry, Baloney, I didn't mean for anyone to see that."

"Good thing it was me and not a student."

"I'm just not the same anymore."

"No kidding. Everyone's noticed, especially the kids around here."

"I know. I don't want to hurt them, but I'm completely lost without Sharpie."

"She seems to be holding up pretty well…all things considered."

"She's a lot stronger than me. I don't know how to be like her and keep it together on the job."

"She's an introvert and you're an extrovert. She knows how to hide her emotions, while yours are written in big neon lights," Eugene explained.

"So what do I do? I'd give anything to take back that waterslide catastrophe."

"You got to admit: that was a very traumatic experience for her."

"I know."

"Then give her time. You can't expect her to get over it so easily."

"I kinda have…but what about me?"

"What about you?"

"I'm dying a slow death," Henry confessed. "I can't take the alienation from her. No matter what I've tried, she won't give me the chance to express my sorrow. Every rejection is a new punishment."

"Have you tried poetry?"

"C'mon, Baloney, you know I'm not a poet."

"If the words are coming from your heart, yes, you are."

"How would you know?"

"They're working miracles for me."

"Oh, that's right…your secret girlfriend. She likes poems?"

"She loves them," Eugene answered proudly.

"I didn't know you had it in you."

"Neither did I until I tried."

"So, who is this woman of mystery?"

"I'm not ready to disclose her yet."

"There's a funny pun in there somewhere. Is it Perew the Shrew?"

"Nope."

"Krack-a-lackin' Krackett?"

"No."

"How 'bout that new one who replaced Tater Tots, Miss Kendall?"

"You can guess till doomsday, and I won't tell."

Henry threw his arms up. "Why is this such a secret?"

"She wants it that way."

"Why?"

"Like Kristin, she's got her share of problems to resolve before she's ready to come out with everything. You of all people should be able to relate to that scenario."

"You win; I won't ask anymore."

"Thanks." Eugene glanced at the clock on the wall. "Got to go home and change for my dinner date."

"You really think a poem will work?"

"As long as you're not dumb enough to start it with 'Roses are red, violets are blue…'"

That night, Henry cleared a spot on his kitchen table to compose the most meaningful words he could think of in a spiral notebook. Page after page of dissatisfaction was ripped out of the spiral binding to be crinkled up and tossed over his shoulder, landing wherever on the floor. Nothing felt right to him. He laughed about Eugene's comment on how not to start a poem. Then a light went off in his head. He remembered the optical message Kristin left him with the rose in the snow—that's it! He used her symbolism as a figurative basis to construct a rhyming tale he titled, "Like a Rose in the Snow."

The next morning, he placed the handwritten sheet on her keyboard, so it would be the first thing she'd see upon her arrival. After sitting down with her coffee, Kristin picked up the unsigned note she assumed at first glance might be from a student. The opening line said otherwise and couldn't be easily discounted.

Like a rose in the snow, our love fell into the cold
Two hearts in peril and so many things untold
Your trust was broken by my selfish deed
I want to repair it, because it's you that I need
Like a rose in the snow, I'm empty and dying
Without your smile, I'm all alone and crying
What can I do to make things right
I pray about it every day and night
Give me a chance and lend me your ears
I'll do everything in my power to ease your fears
I love you, Sharpie, this you must know
Without you I am nothing, like a rose in the snow

The intelligent beauty of Henry's words brought tears to her eyes—the ice had thawed—she could no longer suppress her feelings. "I still love you, Superman, but I don't feel safe with you anymore," she muttered. Oh, how badly she wanted him back, but not at the risk of her personal security. She applauded his lovingly devised effort to restore her faith in him, but it wasn't enough. At the very least, she needed to let him know he'd been forgiven.

"Janet!" she shouted.

"Yes?"

"Please find Henry and ask him to come to my office."

"Will do."

Anticipating a summons to the principal's office, Henry had remained stationary in his workshop. When Janet showed up to escort him, he hopped off the stool like a schoolboy going to recess.

"Did she say why she wanted to see me?" he asked.

"Nope. But I don't think it's anything to worry about. She sounded normal."

During Janet's absence from the office, Kristin took out her compact to touch up her smeared eye makeup. It was important for her to look together, even though she was coming apart inside. This would be the closure she knew they both needed if they were to continue functioning in the same building.

When Henry entered, she requested he close the door and have a seat. "I'm at a total loss for words right now," she said, visibly jittered.

He gulped with butterflies in his stomach. "You read my poem, I take it?"

"Yes, I did, which is why I wanted to see you."

"Hope it wasn't too corny, I've never written a poem before."

"You thought it was corny?"

"I'm just being facetious in case you didn't like it."

"Didn't like it—I loved it!"

Henry's eyes sparkled with hope. "You did?"

"It was the most intellectually clever piece of simplistic literature I ever read."

"I think I need a dictionary interpretation of what you just said."

"You're a romantic genius."

"Now *that* I understand."

"Please forgive me for the way I've been treating you. I'm so ashamed of myself."

"That's okay. Am I forgiven?"

She nodded sensitively.

Henry stood up, as did Kristin, awaiting his warmhearted embrace.

"Thank you so much, Sharpie—I love you."

"And I love you."

He pulled back with refreshed excitement. "Great! Are your parents still coming in next week? I'm looking forward to meeting them."

"Hold your horses, cowboy. Please sit back down."

They both resumed their seats.

"Yes, they are still coming for the holidays, but you won't be meeting them."

"Huh...what?"

"I can't go back to you."

Henry paled. "What do you mean?"

"I don't trust you."

"But you just said…"

"I said I still love you—yes, I do."

"But you don't trust me?"

"No."

"That makes no sense. How do you love someone and not trust 'em?"

"I don't know. That's what I'm trying to sort out."

"Then what's the point of this?"

"To give us closure. After reading your words, I had to let you know that I've forgiven you. It wouldn't be fair to keep that a secret."

"So is this your elaborate way of leading into the 'we can still be friends' speech that I once told you no guy wants to hear?"

"To quote you, 'kinda sorta.'"

"Then I guess I need to tender my resignation—effective immediately."

His knee-jerk reaction stunned her. "W-why? I don't want you to quit your job."

He got up to remove the ball of keys from his belt. "I have to. Being in love with my employer, who doesn't trust me, is un-appropriate."

"You mean inappropriate," she correctively kidded. "You're always off just a little bit."

"Un-appropriate, inappropriate…they're both things that don't work—like us."

He tossed the keys on her desk and split the scene without a goodbye. She chased after him in a panic, stopping short at the doorjamb to catch Henry and Janet in a lengthy goodbye hug.

"I can't believe you're leaving us after all these years," the secretary said, choked up.

"I don't think I have to tell you why."

"I understand. I'll miss you."

"Same here."

They separated with tears of sorrow.

"The kids will be devastated," Janet cried.

"I haven't exactly been very good to them lately, so hopefully they'll adjust."

Kristin was ridden with guilt. "Please reconsider, Henry; I don't want you to go."

He ignored her, staying focused on Janet. "Bye, Goody Two-shoes. Keep Fast Freddie on his toes."

"I've got him minding his p's and q's."

"Great. See you around town—ciao."

"Happy trails, *pawtner*."

Watching Henry vacate the building he had maintained for countless years, shocked and devastated Kristin. She returned to her desk weeping—*What have I done?*

Chapter 28

It was time for Kristin to add the spirit of Christmas to her plain home. With the visit of her estranged parents a week away, she realized how unprepared she was for them. Her days of decorating each room proved therapeutic in keeping her mind away from the demoralization of Henry's untimely departure. Never did she imagine he would just up and quit. She felt totally responsible. In a peculiar sort of way, she came to understand how he must've felt when she walked out on him at the water park—something he never expected her to do either.

Retrieving all the boxes labeled "Christmas stuff" from her basement, including the artificial tree, she gave every room its own motif. The kitchen was everything Santa Claus, the dining room featured snowmen, the master bedroom became a winter wonderland, and of course the living room was reserved for the Nativity scene. Her attentive care to every detail—including the outdoor decorations—spread the project over several days.

The last room on her to do list was the spare bedroom she had converted into a home office. This was delayed on purpose, as it would be the accommodation for her folks. Other than a desk, file cabinet, and bookcase, the room was pretty bare. With a little rearranging, there would be plenty of space for an extra queen-size bed. She remembered seeing a few nice ones at Countryside's Discount

Furnishings the day she went there with Henry.

Having gotten past her unpleasant experience at the emporium, Kristin revisited them over the weekend to purchase a solid mahogany sleigh-bed set, similar to her own bed. It was more than she wanted to spend, but then again, it was for her parents at Christmastime.

"The bed and mattresses will be delivered Monday afternoon," the manager said.

"What time?" Kristin asked.

"Between two and four."

"I'll have to leave work early then. Can the delivery guys set up the bed?"

"That will be delivery guy, we only have one guy making deliveries."

"Is he capable of moving heavy furniture by himself?"

"Oh yeah, he's very strong. It will be no problem for him to do the assembly too."

"Will it take him long to do it?"

"Nope. He puts our furniture together all the time, so he's pretty fast."

Frigid temperatures bit into Monday afternoon, as Kristin awaited the delivery of her new bed. She sat near the Christmas tree at the center of her picture window, hoping to spot the delivery truck. Two o'clock came and went as did three o'clock. In the minutes prior to four, she started to fret. Picking up the phone, she called the store for an update.

"You're his last delivery, Dr. Sharp," the clerk explained. "He's probably just running late. It's a Monday."

"I understand. Thanks for letting me know."

After hanging up the phone, she decided to eat an early dinner, not knowing when the driver would show up. As she prepared to cook a chicken breast and chopped vegetables, the doorbell rang. *Must be the deliveryman.* The store's truck had been parked alongside her front curb. Opening the door, she saw a tall man bundled up, with Countryside's Discount Furnishings embroidered on his cap and coat. His face was concealed by a tight scarf and tinted glasses so he looked more like a prowler than a legitimate delivery driver.

"I'm here to set up your bed," the man announced in a muffled voice.

"Yes, I've been expecting you."

"All the pieces are in my truck, so I'll be making a few trips."

"That's fine. I've got my dinner on the stove, so will you be able to juggle the door by yourself?"

"Shouldn't be a problem. Where is it going?"

She turned to point. "The last bedroom down the hall to the left."

The man tipped his visor and headed for the truck. Kristin remained at the door long enough to observe his removal of the headboard from the back of the vehicle. Satisfied he was carrying the correct item, she retreated back to the kitchen to turn the flames up on her burners. During the course of her meal prep, she heard the man traveling in and out of her door several times. Once he brought the last piece, the mattress, he proceeded to construct the bed as requested.

Having a strange man in her house, was a bit risky, but Kristin kept her phone close at hand with 911 on speed dial. She also had a burning-hot skillet to use as a weapon if needed.

"All done, ma'am," the man reported by the front door. "I need you to sign the receipt for the delivery."

"Be right there. I'm getting your tip."

She reached for her purse that hung over the back of an empty table chair. After extracting her pocketbook, she took out a ten-dollar bill to give as a tip and grabbed her phone. On her way to the door, she noticed the man was gazing out the picture window. His scarf was stuffed in his coat pocket, and his glasses were fastened to the end of the clipboard in his hand. The incoming light beaming through the window silhouetted him enough to conceal the gold tint in his blond hair, below the rim of his cap. In other words, she had no idea whose back faced her.

"Thank you so much, sir."

"My pleasure." He turned slowly to reveal a familiar face.

Kristin's eyes about popped out of their sockets. "Get out of my house, Freddie—I'm calling the police!"

"Please don't do that," he pleaded in a subdued demeanor. "I'm not that same scary dude anymore."

"Why should I believe you?"

"Look at what I'm doing for a living. I can't afford to lose this job. I'm really sorry for the wrong I did to you."

"Let me repeat myself. Why should I believe you?"

"I went from being a football star to a high school coach to a grade school gym teacher, to a furniture delivery driver…and if I get fired from this gig, I'll have to start asking, Do you want fries with that? All my demises were the direct result of my inflated ego. It took the agony of what I did to you to understand what a self-centered monster I was. I'm seeing a counselor who's helped me out quite a bit. I almost called off today when I heard about your order."

"So why didn't you?"

"Because my *counselor*, for lack of a better term, said the best healing medicine is forgiveness."

"Smart man."

"Actually, it's a woman."

"Oh?"

"Since all my problems are about the way I treated women, who better to guide me on the errors of my ways than a woman."

"I'm inclined to agree with that assessment."

"I'm really working hard to turn my life around, and I'm hoping you'll wipe the slate clean by forgiving me."

Even though she didn't particularly care for his unethical means of accessing her, she believed his humility was genuine. After what she endured with Henry, it would be hypocritical for her not to accept his apology.

"All right, you're forgiven."

Fred's pearly whites gleamed. "You have no idea how much warmth you've given me on such a cold day."

"Nicely said."

"Truth be told, I practiced it on my way over."

"You were that confident I would accept your apology?"

"No, but on the chance you did, I wanted to have a pleasing response."

"And if I didn't?"

"I had a line for that too."

She gave a slight smile at his wit. "Getting back to business, don't you have something for me to sign?"

"Oh, yeah…" He handed her the clipboard and a pen. "Just sign at the bottom."

She signed and attached the ten-spot to the board. "Here you go."

"You didn't have to tip me."

"What kind of a customer do you think I am?"

"A gracious one." He stepped to the door and placed his palm on the brass handle. "I heard about your breakup with Henry Hubbard."

"I'm sure it's all over town."

"Any chance you'd be open to seeing me sometime?"

"My forgiving you doesn't mean I want to date you."

"It's Christmas…I was hoping for a miracle."

"What about Janet?"

"What about her?"

"Aren't you seeing her?"

"Yes and no."

"What does that mean?"

"Yes, I'm seeing her, but no, not in that way."

"Then what way is it?"

"She's the one who's counseling me," he revealed.

"But I thought…"

"I said counselor for lack of a better term. I never said it was a professional counselor. She knows how I feel about you."

"And she told you to seek my forgiveness?"

"Yes."

"Interesting…I have a lot to think about."

"I best be on my way. Happy Holidays."

"Merry Christmas, Freddie."

Chapter 29

Geoffrey and Melinda Sharp cruised past the "Welcome to Perrinsville" sign in their radiant silver Cadillac Escalade. It was nearly the end of the journey for the senior couple who had traveled across state lines to visit their daughter. They couldn't wait to reunite with Kristin and meet the man of her dreams. In many ways, this year's season of giving served as an absolution of their long history of neglectful discontent. Their road to recovery, as a family, was about as long as the mileage between their current residences. And because of the actions of an eccentric man unknown to all of them just a few months ago, they reached their endgame destination.

The sound of car doors closing penetrated the walls of Kristin's home, letting her know *they're here!* She stepped into the bathroom for a split second to check her appearance in readiness for their reunion. The reality of their arrival made her jittery from head to toe. Apologizing over the phone was easy, but doing it in person was another matter. She took a deep breath on her way to the door in sync with the bell chimes.

Kristin welcomed her sixtyish parents, who looked as wintry as the weather outside. "Hi, Mom, Dad…please come in."

Melinda hobbled in first with her aluminum four-pronged cane. Geoff followed close behind carrying their suitcases. Kristin closed the door and hugged them both before another word could be uttered.

"Thank you for inviting us," Melinda said.

"Thank you for coming."

"Well, look at *you*," Geoff remarked, pleasantly surprised. "I almost wondered if we'd come to the wrong house."

Kristin blushed.

"Oh stop," Melinda interjected. "Don't embarrass her."

"I was just noticing how fabulous she looks. Can't I compliment my own daughter?"

"Please don't make a fuss," Kristin implored them.

"I do have to agree with your father. You have all the beauty of a woman in love."

"When do we get to meet the guy who got our little girl to let her hair down?"

It hadn't taken Kristin's folks more than half a minute to bring up the topic she dreaded most—Henry. She had successfully avoided the subject of him during their recent phone chats for the simple reason that they were brief. But today, it was in her face, and there was nowhere to run. She couldn't keep them in the dark during their stay until the New Year. They had just gotten there, and now was not the time to drop the bomb on them about her dramatic breakup.

"Let me take your coats."

The elder Sharps shed their heavy outerwear for Kristin to hang in the hall closet.

Geoff surveyed the living room. "You've done very well for yourself. I'm impressed."

"The house is very Christmassy," Melinda commented.

"She's got your talent for perfection," he added. "Remember how you did our home when she was growing up?"

"I gave every room a different theme."

Kristin picked up their luggage. "And I've also continued the tradition here. Let me show you to your winter wonderland room just like mine."

Geoff and Melinda fancied the accommodations prepared for them by their daughter, particularly the new sleigh bed.

"I thought I'd just bunk on the couch," Geoff said.

"I wouldn't do that to you, Daddy."

"I appreciate all the trouble you went through to make us comfortable. Can't help noticing the red mahogany finish, perfect for this time of year."

"Why don't you and Mom get unpacked, and I'll get a pot of coffee going."

"Hot chocolate for me, if you've got it," Melinda requested.

"Okay."

Geoff's eyes widened. "Make it two, Krissy."

"Three hot chocolates then…"

Giving her parents plenty of time to unwind, Kristin disappeared to the kitchen to boil water for the coco mix. *So far, so good.* While much of their alienation had been remedied over the phone, having her parents under her roof felt slightly awkward. Strangely, she equated it to Henry *always being off by just a little bit.*

Over the next hour, they caught up on all the things that had occurred since Kristin's move to Perrinsville—of course she omitted all the bad news. Any time Henry's name came up, she spoke only of the happy days gone by.

"I'm getting pretty hungry," Geoff announced.

"Any good places you recommend?" Melinda asked Kristin.

"Yep, I know the best restaurant."

"What kind of food do they serve?" her mom asked.

"How about I tell you what they don't serve…"

Her dad raised his peppery-gray eyebrows.

"…anything that comes in a package you can just tear open," she chuckled.

Geoff laughed. "Your mom *still* cooks that way."

Melinda bit her lip. "Very funny—let's go."

At the diner, Kristin showed her parents the lemonade trick she learned from Henry. She did it so automatically, just like the jab at her mother, proving how much of Henry had been ingrained in her. Geoff, particularly, marveled at her transformation. He had always carried a cloud of guilt over his head for the way she grew up. As the predominate male figure in her life, he knew he stank as a father. It troubled him to see her trapped in a closed-up state of her own making, due in part to him and his wife. He couldn't wait to give his blessing to the man behind the magic.

Too satiated from their juicy burgers to order dessert, Kristin flagged the waitress for their check. "This is on me."

"Oh, please let me get it," Geoff offered.

"Nope. You're my guests; it's my treat. I won't take no for an answer."

"If you insist," Melinda chimed. "Thank you."

The waitress returned to their booth with the check. "I'll take that whenever you're ready."

Kristin nodded as the young lady left. Going through her purse to get her pocketbook, she sensed the presence of someone breathing on her shoulder.

"Can I help you?" Geoff addressed the blond man sporting a faded tan.

"You must be the parents," the booming voice acknowledged.

Gosh no, not him, not now! Kristin cringed.

"Are you Henry?" Melinda asked.

"Heck no, I'm Fred—Fred Pace."

Kristin jeered. "You have a natural knack for showing up at the most inopportune times."

"Aren't you going to introduce me?"

"Ah yes, where are my manners…these are my parents: Geoffrey and Melinda Sharp."

They nodded politely—*pleased to meet you.*

"Can I join you?"

"May I join you," Kristin snapped at him.

"She's so cute when she corrects me." Fred wedged himself into the empty seat next to her. "It's got to be the principal in her. I have a thing for women in authority."

"You do?" Melinda asked.

"Oh yeah…"

Kristin spiked her boot heel into Fred's toes.

"Ow!"

"Are you in pain?" Geoff asked.

Fred glanced at Kristin staring daggers at him. "Just an old football injury that flares up without warning. You know what I mean?"

"Yes, I do. I'm a personal injury attorney."

"He has one of the biggest firms in the Northeast," Melinda boasted.

"Then maybe you can give me some expert advice on how to win your daughter back."

"Win her back? I don't understand."

Geoff turned to his daughter. "Krissy?"

"It's a complicated story," Kristin dodged.

"I'll simplify it," Fred said brazenly.

Kristin's mind went into panic mode. *Oh, geez—what's he going to say?*

"It was love at first sight, and I blew it."

Geoff and Melinda were bewildered by what they heard for the first time.

"Your daughter has a lot of class, and I have none."

Got that right! Kristin thought.

"She taught me the error of my ways, and I'm a better man now, ready to come back if she'll have me."

"Sorry, Charlie…" Melinda started out.

"I'm Fred."

"Krissy already has a boyfriend who we're looking forward to meeting," Geoff asserted.

Fred's nostrils twitched as he turned to the object of his desire. "They don't know?"

Kristin wanted to slide under the table.

"Know what?" Geoff asked.

"You want to tell them, or *may* I?"

"Please go, Freddie," she mumbled. "You've done enough—again."

"You've been a bit evasive whenever Henry's name comes up," Melinda reminded her.

"I broke up with him the day after Thanksgiving," Kristin muttered.

The disgrace in her daughter's eyes triggered Melinda's long-lost motherly compassion. "Oh, Krissy, why didn't you tell us? You didn't have to hide it."

"I avoided telling you because I'm ashamed."

"I can't say I blame her," Fred butted in.

"Please tell the court why you don't blame her?" Counselor Sharp questioned contemptuously.

"If you want me to confess, I couldn't fathom the thought of a gorgeous babe like her fawning all over a dweeb like Henry Hubbard, when she could have a real man like me."

Geoff sneered. "I've had about enough of your annoying arrogance to last a lifetime. I think you better leave."

Melinda echoed her husband's sentiment. "Yes, I'd like you to go too."

Fred cleared himself out of the booth, focusing on Kristin. "I'm sorry, babe. I believe honesty is the best policy."

"You're a Goliath oxymoron," she branded him.

"It was nice meeting you folks." Fred nodded, then turned to Kristin.

"I'll see you later."

Kristin dropped her head in her hands, as Fast Freddie trotted to the carryout counter for his doggie bag.

"What a jerk!" Geoff vented. "And very deserving of the label you just gave him."

Kristin sniffled. "I still love him."

Melinda looked confused. "*That* guy?"

"No, Mom—Henry."

"Why did you break up? Did he hurt you?"

"I don't want to talk about it in public," Kristin moped. "I'll tell you the whole story when we get back to my home where I can speak freely."

Chapter 30

All the visuals of holly jolly throughout the school failed to camouflage the blue Christmas materializing in the hearts of the student body. They missed the glow of their custodial angel. Peace on the playground and goodwill to all the children were his hallmark—he really did make their wishes come true.

The sullen atmosphere plaguing the classrooms became insufferable. Janitorial duties were shared by the faculty and student volunteers—no one wanted a hired replacement for Henry. They held back their tears in the hope that he would return someday. Kristin struggled to get through her daily hall patrols. The lack of his presence haunted her. It took many days of building courage for her to set foot inside his vacant workshop.

Scattered toys, desperately needing repair, lay in waiting on his disorganized tool bench. Kristin sat on his stool, for the first time, to get a feel of his importance. She studied the complexity of the playthings and tried to repair a few of them that looked easy. Her efforts proved the only thing of ease was increased frustration, along with a broken fingernail. Only Henry could resurrect them from the make-believe graveyard. She mourned his loss with a waterfall of sorrowful tears.

On Crazy Christmas Hair Day, Kristin displayed her holiday spirit with a homemade wreath of tiny presents woven into the top of her honey blond locks like a crown. The creation came courtesy of her mother. Melinda's talent for crafting could've rivaled Martha Stewart had she pursued it professionally. Kristin eagerly anticipated Janet's reaction to her hair decoration.

Not to be outdone in the tradition of wackiness, the secretary colored her hair emerald-green, pulled it up into a cone shape, and added ornaments to resemble a Christmas tree.

"Very nice," Kristin noted, standing alongside Janet's desk.

"Thanks."

"I would never have thought to put *myself* under the tree," Kristin giggled.

"I guess that's the difference between us."

"Do you like mine?"

"It's nice." Janet narrowed her eyes. "I'm sure you'll win first prize."

Something's up. Kristin was taken aback by Janet's despondent tone. "Is everything okay? You don't seem like your usual self."

"I'm fine; just don't have much to say."

"You know you can tell me anything. I'm your friend."

Janet peered at her. "For a PhD, you really lack common sense."

"Where's this going?"

"Figure it out…it's what doctors do."

"I miss Henry too. I'm sure he would've been the biggest hit today."

"This has nothing to do with Henry."

"Then what's the problem?"

The phone rang, ending their escalated exchange.

"It's the nursing line; I have to take the call."

"Fine. I have a busy morning anyway." Kristin retreated to her office, mystified by the coldness coming from the warmest personality on staff.

In the passing hours, Miss Goody Two-shoes sidestepped her boss at every turn. The tension couldn't have been more obvious to Kristin.

When Janet returned from lunch, she was cornered at her desk for a showdown.

Kristin launched into offense. "Let's clear the air right now."

Janet placed her hands on her hips as if to say, *Bring it on.*

"You've been giving me an attitude from the minute I walked in—why?"

"I told you to figure it out."

"I don't have time for games, so why don't you spell it out?"

"F-r-e-d-d-i-e."

"What about him?"

"All he talks about is *you*."

"I can't help that."

"Oh yes, you can; you can kick him to the curb again."

"He's still at the curb as far as I'm concerned."

"Well, he's singing a very different tune."

"Enlighten me."

"You're giving him a second chance."

"I forgave him for the scandal he masterminded—that's it. He told me that you persuaded him to ask for my forgiveness. He said you're counseling him."

"My *counseling* is a romantic relationship with him," Janet clarified.

Kristin felt a lump in her throat. "He didn't tell *that* to me."

"He went on and on about meeting your parents."

"He crashed our party at the diner and made a stupendous fool of himself."

"All I know is that he thinks he's got a shot with you again, and I'm back to ground zero."

"Do you love him?"

"Ever since high school."

"I personally think you deserve better, but believe me when I say that I have no intention of stealing him away. I really do wish you all the best with him," Kristin pledged with the utmost sincerity.

Janet recognized her honesty. Deep down, she knew Fred was an old dog who'd be difficult to tame. She couldn't blame Kristin for his deception. "Will you help me get him back?"

"Well…"

"I wouldn't blame you if you said no."

"Well, everyone deserves love—even Fast Freddie."

"Is that a yes?"

"Only if we're friends again."

The women shared an affectionate hug, unaware their crazy hair had inadvertently clipped together. Their act of healing was interrupted by the switchboard ringing. As they separated, they realized their heads were stuck together like glue—*ow, ow…*

"Wait a second," Janet said, trying to find the connection with her fingers.

Kristin jested about their predicament. "I've heard about putting your heads together, but this is ridiculous."

"That's just what Henry would say if he saw this."

"Well, I thought I'd say it in his absence. Can't let a comedy bit go to waste."

The secretary was unable to find the root of the entanglement. The persistent redial ringing caused her to stress. "I hope that call's not urgent."

"Sooner or later it'll go to voice mail."

The phone stopped.

"See…" Kristin spoke too soon—the ringing started again.

"We need a mirror," Janet declared. "There's one in the nurse's station"—she pointed with the tip of her hair tree—"this way."

"I'm *sticking* with you."

The ladies carefully made their way to the nursing room.

"I sure hope nobody sees this," Kristin continued.

"I wish that phone would stop—*c'mon give it a rest!*"

At the medicine cabinet's mirror above the sink, Janet spotted the problem and, like a surgical pro, freed them with minor damage to their holiday dos.

"Ahhh, that's one crisis averted," Kristin sighed, inspecting her hair in the mirror.

"This better be Publishers Clearing House calling to tell me I won five grand a week for life." Janet raced to answer the phone. "Perrinsville Elementary, Miss Goode speaking…Hey, Eugene, was that you blowing up the phone?…*What!…Aw no.*"

Kristin sensed bad news by the shudder in Janet's voice. She dashed back to the reception desk with her stomach in more knots than her hair.

"How is he?…Yes, I'll tell her." She dropped the receiver to dab her runny nose with the cuff of her sweater sleeve.

"What happened?" Kristin begged to know.

"There's been an accident—Henry is in the hospital with a concussion."

Kristin's legs went numb. "I *need* to be with him."

* * *

"How's he doing?" Kristin asked Eugene in the hospital room where Henry lay unconscious.

"Thanks for coming. I didn't know who else to contact. Henry has no family."

"I know. I'm glad you called."

"Sorry I didn't call you directly, but I thought you'd be tied up."

"I kind of was with Janet, but that's another story. How is he?"

"We're waiting for him to wake up to check his memory."

"What happened?"

"I went to bring him lunch, and he was on his roof, stringing Christmas lights around the chimney. When I called him to come down, he slid on a piece of ice and flew off like a ski jumper…"

Kristin became wide-eyed at the coincidence of his calamity.

"…he clipped the ladder and fell on top of it, hitting his head hard. He was out cold."

"Oh, my gosh!" she anguished.

"I called nine-one-one, and here we are. This whole thing is my fault."

"How? It was an accident."

"I distracted him when I yelled out, and that's how he slid. It never would've happened otherwise."

Eugene's remorse flew right into Kristin's face. His chilling words sent her back to the water park. The similarity between the incidents freaked her out—what had happened to her had now happened to him. It was a real teachable moment for the principal. She finally understood the regret Henry carried and why he gave up everything that meant the world to him. The sight of him lying helpless in the hospital bed was painful enough, but to hear the details of how he got there was gut-wrenching. She knew Henry never meant any harm to her, but she couldn't get past her own stubborn insecurity to let him back in the door again.

Kristin's destiny lay right before her eyes—it was her turn to save him! "May I be alone with Henry?"

"Of course…yes," Eugene answered dispiritedly.

She placed her hands on his shoulders. "You mustn't beat yourself up over this; it was beyond your control. There's nothing more you could've done to prevent what happened from happening. It was meant to be for a reason."

"I wish I knew what it was."

"You're looking at it." She hugged him. "Thank you, dear friend.

When he recovers, he'll thank you too."

"That depends on how mad he is about his clothes being cut off him—his Superman T is no more."

"He doesn't need a T-shirt to be our man of steel."

Eugene laughed. "You totally get him. His future is with you."

"You made the right call."

"As he would say himself—good pun. Nice hair by the way."

Kristin smiled as he left the room. She then pulled up a chair next to the bed. Before sitting, she leaned over him to gently kiss his cheek.

"I hope you can hear me," she said in a tender voice. "I'm going to read a story to you."

Placing her purse on the mobile table at the foot of his bed, she pulled out a small children's book featuring a boy running with a glass of water on his head—*Hooray for Henry*.

"You remember when I told you that I ordered a used copy of your favorite book online? Well, it got lost in the mail, so I forgot all about it until yesterday when it miraculously arrived. And the timing couldn't have been more perfect."

She seated herself comfortably. "I stopped home to get it on my way here. It'll be my first time reading it." Prior to getting started, she flipped through the yellowed pages to study the illustrations. Struck by the uncanny resemblance between the two Henrys, she clearly saw the backstory dimension to him as she began to read the words aloud. "Today…"

By the time she finished reading the story about a little boy who never quit trying to win a prize at the picnic, she was brought to tears when fictional Henry was crowned the winner of the last contest. Closing the faded cover, she added her own happy ending, "Hooray, Henry, you've won your grand prize—*me!*"

Setting the book aside, Kristin clutched his hand to pour her heart out. "I've never stopped loving you, Henry. My love for you is stronger now than it's ever been. And I feel *safe* with you. I'm so sorry for what I've done and pray that you'll take me back. I want to marry you and start a family and live happily ever after." She raised his limp hand to her tear-stained cheek. "You're my real-life Willy Wonka meets Indianapolis Jones story."

Seconds later, Kristin felt a slight squeeze of the hand growing in strength.

"Don't you mean *Indiana?*" Henry whispered groggily.

Her tears changed from sorrow to joy, as she let out a quick chuckle. "Yes…yes."

"You're always off by just a little bit, but that's what I love about you," he muttered to parody her catchphrase about him.

Kristin inched closer to Henry as he slowly opened his eyes. The wreath around her head dominated his blurred vision.

"I must've heard the wrong story. I see the ghost of Christmas present."

She laughed with a sniffle. "And I have a lifetime of presents for you."

He pointed to the miniature packages attached to the wreath. "I've always heard good things come in small packages, but this is over-the-top—literally."

"Welcome home, Henry!" She leaned in to hug him as best she could.

"I love you, Sharpie."

A nurse in scrubs walked in to end their scene. "Ahh…ahh…ahh… this man has a concussion and needs lots of rest."

Kristin snapped to attention. "Oh, sorry."

"Are you family?"

"Actually I'm…"

Henry interrupted. "This is Dr. Kristin Sharp. She was just dispensing the best medicine for my full recovery."

Kristin shied away in modesty.

"There's no doctor like a love doctor," the nurse joked. "Now that you're awake, I need to get the real doctor in here."

"I should probably go," Kristin said to Henry.

"Please don't."

"Listen to your love doctor," the nurse cut in. "You got a head injury, and will need a lot of rest. Besides, your doc looks like she's got her reminder to go Christmas shopping tightly wrapped around her head."

Henry started to laugh, then stopped with a painful grimace.

"Are you hurting?" Kristin asked.

"Only when I laugh," he whimpered.

"I'll come back tomorrow."

He puckered for a smooch—she obliged.

"Where's Baloney?" Henry asked Kristin.

"I think he's in the waiting room. He feels totally responsible for this."

"That's absurd. It was an accident."

"I'll tell him you said that when I see him."

"Better yet, tell him I know what the 'agony of defeat' on ABC's old *Wide World of Sports* intro feels like—he'll get it."

"I get it too," the nurse tittered.

"I'll have to look that one up on YouTube," Kristin replied, gathering her purse and the children's book. "Do you want me to leave the book?"

"If I read it, it won't sound as beautiful as the way *you* read it."

"You *heard* me?"

He winked. "Every word."

She bit the inside of her cheek. "It figures."

"I didn't want you to stop; I wanted to know how the story was going to end."

"Did you like the ending?"

"Couldn't have written it any better if I tried."

"Aw, that's so adorable," the nurse remarked. "But it's really time for the lady to go."

Henry turned to his sweetie. "Better go before my dry humor earns me a sponge bath."

"*Wah wah waahh.*" Kristin mimicked.

"That's a sad trombone," Henry explained to the nurse.

"I know what it is, and your jokes are falling flat. Give me your arm please."

Kristin backed up toward the door. "I'll call to check on you tonight."

Henry waved *bye* to her, with his free hand, while the nurse proceeded to take his vital signs.

Kristin proceeded to the waiting room to look for Eugene. He wasn't there. But someone else certainly was—Fred.

She was horrified to see him there. "What on earth are you doing here? Where's Eugene?"

In his store coat and cap, Fred tossed the sports magazine he'd been reading to approach her. "He split when he saw me. We had a few words."

"About why you're here?"

"We didn't get that far. He blamed me for all of Alma's misery. Not sure why he would care. She couldn't stand the sight of him."

"You still haven't answered my question."

"About why I'm here."

"Yes."

"Janet told me what happened, and I came to support you."

Kristin's brows tensed. "You came to support *me?* The patient is down the hall!"

He shrugged. "I know that."

"So what scam are you pulling now, Freddie?"

"No scam. I came to see you."

"Do you know why I'm here?"

He nodded. "Henry."

"Do you even care what happens to him?"

"Please, I don't have ice in my veins."

"You're right, you don't—they're clogged with apathy. You haven't asked about Henry at all."

"I was going to get to him soon enough."

"In case you're wondering, the *dweeb* is going to make a full recovery."

"That was a cheap shot. I didn't deserve it."

"And Henry didn't deserve any of the cheap shots you fired at him either. Why do you enjoy picking on him?"

"Because Henry Hubbard is not a man. He's just an overgrown kid."

"You know something? I really like your flawed analogy."

Fred puffed his conceitedness. "You do?"

"Oh yes, I really like that it's flawed because you got it backwards. The overgrown kid is *you!*"

Fred's boatload of confidence suddenly sprang a leak.

"Henry Hubbard *is* a real man," she continued. "And he's going to get the girl. I plan to marry him and have babies with him. Put that in your Thorndike-Barnhart."

"What's that?"

"Look it up in the dictionary," she said flippantly.

"Just tell me what's so appealing about that sideshow kook?"

"There's an endearing quality to him that guys like you will never understand. Henry connects with kids better than any parent or teacher I've ever known. He's been blessed with a special gift that the rest of us will never get. If that makes him a sideshow kook, then I can't wait to become missus sideshow kook."

"Okay, maybe I misjudged him all these years. Let me make it up to you."

Fred extended his hand to her.

Kristin thwarted him with a swift arm block and step back. "Don't touch me."

"Sorry."

"Don't you have furniture to deliver?"

"Yeah…"

"The legs on the tables and chairs aren't going to walk themselves to your customers, but I'm going to walk out of here." She turned to leave.

"Wait…please…" he shouted.

Kristin halted with her back to him.

"I need to make a confession."

She was unmoved.

Fred thrust himself in front of her. "I'm a fraud. My arrogance is just a cover up"—he bowed his head—"I'm very lonely. Women always dump me."

"That's your fault."

"Please tell me what am I doing wrong. I'll believe what you tell me."

"You assume women will just fall over the alpha legend of Fast Freddie. You grossly underestimate us."

"What can I do to win a woman like you?"

"Be wise to what's good for you."

"What's good for me?"

"Janet Goode—stop doing her wrong. She loves you *and* your legend. Always has, always will."

Chapter 31

"Henry's back! Henry's back! Yay! Yay!" the students shouted jubilantly at the first sight of their sorely missed caretaker. They surrounded him outside the school's main entry to give him a rock star's welcome. The joy from their hearts was warm enough to melt the snow. Kristin stood by idly to let him bask in the glory. His first day back on the job bore witness to the true meaning of Christmas giving just before the holiday break.

Reclaiming his throne at the workbench of broken toys, along with Kristin's love, aided Henry in his speedy recovery at home. The concussion kept him out of commission for only a week, but during that period Kristin took time off from work to be at his bedside every waking moment of the day—going home in the evenings to be with her parents after Eugene showed up for the overnight watch. Kristin liked playing nursemaid to Henry—it gave her a sense of what to expect in a marriage. She took advantage of his incapacity to add her *touch* to his bachelor pad. It took the entire week, but she succeeded in sprucing up the place room by room—except the bedroom where he recuperated—that intrusion, she felt, might be too personal.

Awakened by the fragrance of fresh flowers, Henry crawled out of bed to venture beyond the bathroom for the first time since coming home from the hospital. Following his nose, he rubbed his blurry eyes as he rounded the corner to the living room. Staring him right in the face was a vision of Kristin pruning the decorative floral arrangements she had strategically placed around the room.

"I must be in the wrong house," he claimed.

"Meet your new home, lazy bones. How are you feeling?"

"Like I'm in Bizarro World. Where did you get all the flowers?"

"Not from a gas station," she replied whimsically.

"Ho-ho."

"I picked them up at a craft store on my way here."

"I didn't know they sold flowers."

"Only fake ones."

"You mean…"

"Ah-hah—they're fake."

"Coulda fooled me."

"I did."

He took a big whiff to inhale the pleasant aroma. "Then how come they smell so nice?"

"Plug-in air fresheners, one in every room—except your room. I'll leave that to you."

He wandered around befuddled by the reorganization of his home. "You know, the only one who ever really cleaned this house was my mom."

"Well, I once read in *Psychology Today* something about wives becoming mothers to their husbands. Now that *I* did all the hard work like a happy homemaker, I'm not going to refrain from asking the burning question I wanted to ask the first time I set foot in here."

"So, ask," he said with a shrug.

"Why did you ever let this place get so trashed?"

"Have you ever heard the common saying about someone who pours coffee all day?"

She playfully crossed her arms and rocked on her heels. "Uh-huh. The last thing you want to do when you get home is pour coffee."

He gave her a thumbs-up.

"You always have an answer for everything," she said.

"It's what keeps me in business."

"You would've been out of business had I found anything *living* under some of the piles I had to shovel."

"Good thing I keep a shop vac in the front closet, huh?"

"For industrial strength cleaning—that's what it took."

Henry placed his arm around Kristin's shoulder. "I love you for it. Can't promise it will stay this way, but…"

"As long as I'm around, it better."

"How long do you plan on being around?" As if he didn't know, but he wanted to hear it anyway.

"The rest of my life."

"Is this the part where I get down on one knee?"

"It would be nice, yes."

He dropped to a knee and caressed her hand. "This isn't exactly the way I pictured proposing to you."

"Me either…but I'll try to overlook your bathrobe and slippers."

"Then close your eyes and pretend I look like Prince Charming."

"And I look like Cinderella."

"You kinda do after all the cleaning."

"Very funny. Get on with it."

"I don't have a glass slipper, and I don't have a ring handy, but I can promise you the fairy tale will come true…"

"Please don't break into a rendition of 'Young at Heart.'"

"You know that song?"

"I haven't stopped my research on old-time music—there's a Frank Sinatra channel on the satellite. So, before you go off on an enumeration of song titles older than us, please just ask the question…I'm sure you know the ending to this chapter."

"Only if the beginning starts out, 'She trembled with excitement from the fire he sparked with four little words fueling his passion: *Will you marry me?*'"

"Well…you may never have a future as a romance novelist, but you *will* have a future with a new wife—YES!"

Henry hopped to his feet to give her an award-winning kiss.

"You best get dressed so you can meet my parents. I want to tell them the good news."

He stroked his whiskery cheeks. "Guess I better shave and wear one of those nice outfits you picked out."

Kristin held up her hand. "Please don't."

"You don't want me to make a good impression?"

"I don't want you to make a false impression. Somehow, your quirkiness didn't seem right coming out of designer labels. Flannel suits you just fine," she emphasized.

"Not that it's a complaint, but does that mean I'm free to be *me* again?"

"I wouldn't have it any other way. It's better that you be comfortable in your own image—not the one I created."

"I did it for you."

"I'm glad you did, so everyone got to see the handsome man I knew was hidden under that chaotic exterior. But I don't want you to be someone you're not—except maybe for me once in a while—*after* we're married," she stated unequivocally with batting eyes.

* * *

"Mom, Dad…this is Henry, my *fiancé*." Kristin beamed. The moment of truth had finally arrived—right in her living room.

"Glad to meet you." Geoff offered his hand to Henry. "Welcome to the family."

"Good to meet you." Henry shook Geoff's hand firmly. "Should I start calling you Dad?"

"Hold on, son; we're not there yet," Geoff kidded.

Henry turned to Melinda for a hug.

"Thank you for giving our daughter back to us." She squeezed him.

"I didn't do anything," he replied humbly.

"Oh yes, you did. We didn't think we'd ever hear from her again when she moved away. You changed all of that."

"Sharpie just needed to find herself first. I just helped steer her in the right direction."

"What did you call Krissy?" Geoff asked.

"Sharpie."

"He calls me that all the time," Kristin inserted.

"It's a cute play on our name, Geoffrey," Melinda opined.

"Is that the reason why?" Attorney Sharp continued.

"Kinda sorta…"

Kristin braced herself for Henry's unpredictably predictable explanation.

"Your daughter is like a fine-tip pen—*right to the point.*"

The elder Sharps glanced at each other as if to say, *That's a new one,* before letting out the ice-breaking laugh Kristin hoped to hear from them. It was important to her that they fully embrace Henry's offbeat personality. She could no longer live in a realm of phoniness to please others, especially with family. Their chuckling spoke volumes about their genuine approval of her choice in a husband.

"I also left a permanent mark on his heart," Kristin added.

"That too," Henry agreed in his best Maxwell Smart impression.

Melinda peeked at her daughter's bare hand. "Where's your ring?"

"Oh, Mom, we just got engaged an hour ago."

"Why don't we all sit down?" Geoff suggested. "I'd like to hear your wedding plans."

Kristin escorted Henry to the sofa where they sat together. Her dad dragged one of the end chairs across the room to sit next to his wife, in front of the happy couple.

"Well, Mrs. Sharp—"

"Melinda, please."

"And call me Geoff."

"Well, Melinda and Geoff…I was thinking of giving Sharpie my mother's wedding ring—after I tear my house apart to find it."

"There goes my labor-intensive home improvement," Kristin said under her breath.

Melinda cocked her head. "Ah, don't you think you should let Krissy pick out what she wants?"

Geoff gritted his teeth. *"Melinda!"*

"It's okay, Daddy…Mom, I'm fine with his mother's ring. I still have Grandpa's wedding band that you gave me after he passed away in my jewelry box, so they'll complement each other. Besides, we don't have any time to shop for rings."

"You don't have time because?" her mom asked unambiguously.

"We want to get married on Christmas Eve," Henry answered.

"That's in two days?" she wheezed.

"We're aware of that, Mom."

"How do you expect to pull that off?" Geoff quizzed. "It takes a long time to plan a wedding. Are you going to elope?"

Henry and Kristin turned to each other—*Hey, that's an idea*—to create a little suspense before coming clean.

"We discussed our plans on the way over and…" Henry started to explain.

Kristin finished his sentence. "It's going to be a dream wedding for both of us."

Melinda was not convinced. "I don't see how?"

"Everything we need to pull it off is on hand." Henry twisted to his fiancée to initiate a pseudo-private conversation to get a rise out of her parents. "Except for your dress. Oh, and the minister."

Kristin played along with the ruse. "Oh, yes…I think we can get the minister at the church where Bob goes."

"Oh, good thinking."

"We should start attending services there."

"I agree, it would be a blessing."

"Amen."

"How's your dress coming along?"

"I've got the bottom end of it in my closet, just need the top half. Do you think Sheldon can help?"

"Shelly can design anything—he'll have it done same day. Call him in the morning."

"How about your tux?"

"I've got one tucked away just for this very occasion. It might be a little outdated, but it'll do."

"Does it have tails?"

"No, it cuts off at the waist."

"But you'll look like a waiter."

"That's because I'll be waiting on you the rest of my life."

Their lips met with a kiss in contrast to the chin rubs and neck tugs of the older generation's astonishment. Henry's eyes bulged at the sight of their baffled expressions. He elbowed his fiancée, who was still occupied in the stillness of their magical moment. Feeling the nudge, she opened her eyes to his thumbing in her parents' direction. Slightly embarrassed by the audience's reaction to her romantic hamming, Kristin's ears burned behind her honey locks.

"Oh, sorry, got a little carried away. We have everything under control."

"Would you like me to open the window for some fresh air?" Geoff asked.

"What for?"

"I think your dad wants us to cool it," Henry deduced.

"I want my daughter to be happy, but let's not get ahead of ourselves rushing things."

Melinda pivoted to her husband with a wrinkled forehead. *Really? I seem to recall my father having to slow you down with the option of continuing your personal injury practice or becoming a client. Need I lay out the facts of the case, counselor?"*

Geoff bit his tongue. "Who's ready for dinner? It's on me."

As everyone stood, Henry launched into a grand announcement. "I know this great place where you can get free lemonade."

The Sharps exchanged funny faces and burst into laughter.

* * *

After the morning bell extinguished the hoopla of Henry's homecoming, Kristin broke the news to Janet.

"Henry and I are getting married."

Janet's goody two-shoes slid into dancing shoes with a squeal. "Yay! I'm so happy for you!"

Kristin stabilized her with a friendly embrace. "Thank you."

"When's the big day?"

"Tomorrow."

"Tomorrow? It's Christmas Eve."

"And?"

"And it's totally romantic. Can I come?"

"Only if you'll be my maid of honor?"

"Of course, I will. Am I allowed to bring a date?"

"Why do you ask?" Kristin's intuition had already told her the answer, but she wanted to hear it from Janet.

"Because of who it will be? I heard what happened in the hospital."

"Well, maybe it will finally register with him when he sees me officially off the market."

"I appreciate what you did, and I didn't take him back so easily. He's still got some work to do to make up for the humiliation he caused, but it's a start."

"Then I'm glad I could help."

"So, where's the wedding going to be? How many people are coming?"

"I'm going to give all the details right now."

Kristin stepped toward the PA microphone for a special broadcast.

"Good morning, Perrinsville Elementary! This is going to be my last announcement for this year and my last as Dr. Sharp. Starting tomorrow, I will be Dr. Kristin Hubbard! Yes, you heard me right...Dr. Hubbard. Henry and I are going to be married tomorrow morning at eleven, here in the gymnasium, and you're all invited—students and staff."

The roaring cheers from the classrooms zoomed through the halls like a jet airplane. Kristin and Janet felt everyone's good vibrations. The energy piped into the office was enough to restore a citywide power outage. Kristin continued as soon as the applause quieted down.

"Please make sure to tell your parents to bring you here by ten thirty. There will be lunch and cake after Henry and I become husband and wife, as well as a special toy giveaway—Merry Christmas!"

"Whoo-hoo! A toy giveaway at a wedding." Janet clapped. "What's next?"

"Is it true that Miss Kendall used to be a home economics teacher?"

"Yes, why?"

"We need someone to bake our wedding cake by morning—that's what's next."

Meanwhile, Henry stayed on his stool, working hard to repair all the toys that had piled up in his absence. As much as he wanted to wallow in the hallways, he knew it would take every minute of his day to make up the lost time. The tasks were tense and tedious, as was the depth of his concentration. It all had to be done by dinner, so he could help transform the gym into a chapel with his wife to be—time was indeed of the essence.

"Congratulations!" Maloney shouted behind the busy bee.

Henry jumped out of his skin, sending the toy pieces in his hands flying. "Ahhh!" he yelped, swiveling around to his friend. "Did you ever hear of knocking, dude?"

"I just wanted to congratulate you."

"Thanks."

"I know you forgave me about the roofing accident, but I still feel like I owe you a debt."

"Do we really have to rehash this, Baloney? You didn't put that patch of ice on the roof, so stop blaming yourself. You more than made up for it by spending nights at my place during my recovery, so Sharpie could go home to be with her parents—if anything, we are indebted to you."

"Roughing it on your couch was nothing. You slept like a baby and didn't know I was there."

"I was heavily medicated, but you gave Sharpie peace of mind that I wouldn't be alone if something happened during the night—c'mon man, let it go."

Despite Henry's assurance, Maloney refused to drop the subject.

"Well, I still don't think what I did was very much. I want to do something really big for you to even the score."

"You wanna fall off a roof in front of me," Henry quipped.

"Okay…maybe not that extreme."

"Look, we're gonna settle this here and now"—the janitor stood up to lock eyes with his friend—"are you game?"

"Yeah…just name it?"

"Will you be my best man tomorrow?"

"I was hoping you'd ask," Maloney responded joyfully.

They shook hands on the deal.

Henry returned to his stool. "If you wanted to be my best man, all you had to do was ask—there was no need to put on a charade about owing me something."

"Well, I thought it would be rude to impose myself on you."

Henry pointed to his chest. "It's *me*, Baloney—our friendship goes without saying."

"You're like a brother to me, Henry. I couldn't imagine not being a part of your wedding."

"Now that you are, do we get to finally meet your woman of mystery?"

"Absolutely, I think this will be a fitting venue for her."

"Good. I was beginning to think Sharpie and I would have our first born by the time you unveil her."

"I'm glad that you at least believed me, unlike a few others around here who think she's a figment of my imagination."

"Don't think that it didn't cross my mind as well," Henry chaffed.

Chapter 32

Wedding and Christmas bells rang together on the morning of December twenty-fourth. In keeping with the tradition of the bride and groom not seeing each other until the ceremony, Henry and Kristin, along with her parents, spent hours the night before transforming the school's gymnasium into a wedding chapel. The wall mounted tables used for lunch provided enough seating for the student body, and there were just enough folding chairs to accommodate the staff and other guests near the rear doors.

Underneath the basketball net by the front entrance, Henry constructed a wintry arch for their altar from the school's unused stage props and holiday decorations. Kristin and her mother cleaned out the craft store's inventory of fake flowers, bows and ribbons, and other miscellaneous wedding items. Geoff helped Henry gather all the excess toys from his home to be used as centerpieces for the tables and wall décor. They also rolled out the piano from the music room to set near the altar. By the time the scene was finished, the gym looked like a cross between the Chapel of Love and Santa Land.

It didn't take much arm twisting for Kristin to convince Henry to donate all the toys stored in his basement and garage. She knew he'd never part with the ones prominently displayed in his living room, but all the rest could be used as decorations and then raffled off to all of the kids. There was more than enough in his stash for every child at school to take one home. The idea kept the integrity of his commitment to give them away, as most of the children came from lower income families, and to clear a path for Kristin's belongings.

Henry slipped his black long-sleeve T-shirt with a tuxedo print on the front over his gelled hair and trimmed beard. He took out the black slacks he wore on the night of the Mayflower disaster, along with the same dress shoes. The request for this combo came from his fiancée. She didn't want him in any of the fancy duds they bought during their shopping spree.

"They'll clash with my dress, and they're not *you*," Kristin told him.

Henry had no idea what her dress would look like, despite their banter about Shelly's custom designs.

"You'll not be disappointed, I promise you," she insisted.

By the time the groom arrived at the school, he was instructed by Geoff that the executive suite was off limits to him—the bride was there with her mother and maid of honor. Outside the gym, Eugene stood by a row of tables containing the recently repaired toys for "pickup" by their owners. Henry showed up with a spool of raffle tickets for the best man to pass out to the kids.

"Before you hand out any tickets, can you swap out the hankie in your suit jacket," Henry requested.

"With what?"

"A pocket protector…what else."

The computer teacher opened his jacket to reveal a fully stocked pocket protector on his shirt. "I'm locked and loaded."

"And full of baloney," Henry ribbed. "Where's your date?"

"She'll be here. Don't fret; you've got enough to think about."

"Is the pastor here?"

"I sent him to your shop. He wants to go over a few details with you."

"What about the photographer?"

"Brice Hurst said his guy is out of town, but he'll be here to take the pictures himself."

"Hurst the Worst is gonna photograph my wedding?"

"Free of charge. And it will be on the front page of tomorrow's Christmas issue."

"So, I better not cry or pout?"

"He promised not to be naughty but nice."

"What about our music teacher?"

"Mrs. Teabolt will be here on time. You better get going." He gestured toward the big plate-glass windows at the sight of cars dropping off schoolchildren at the curb. "Your guests are coming."

"Ciao." Henry split before the first kid entered the building.

Maloney tore a ticket for the first little boy at the door. "Keep this ticket to win a toy after the nuptials."

The seven-year-old gave him an inquisitive look. "What's are nutshools?"

"Oh…err…ah, the wedding ceremony."

"Why didn't you just say that instead of trying to confuse me, Mr. Baloney?"

"Don't be a wise guy, or I'll have to tell your parents about all the computers you locked up—hmmm?" he threatened with the evil eye.

The boy's pupils dilated. "You win…sorry."

"Spoken like a true champ, and you'll win, too, when your ticket is called."

Shortly thereafter, a herd of excited children stampeded the gym, forcing Maloney to tear the tickets faster. *Whoa…Cool…Awesome…*were just a few of the enthusiastic reactions from the kids flooding into the makeshift fantasyland to the tune of Christmas carols performed by their music teacher on the piano.

At the stroke of eleven, the packed house restlessly awaited the commencement. Mrs. Teabolt suddenly changed chords from festive merriment to a romantic ballad.

Henry signaled to the minister outside the front entrance. "Hey, that's our cue."

They filed in to applause, as if the curtain had been lifted to the opening of a theatrical play. Laughter ensued when the groom faced the crowd from the altar in his tuxedo T-shirt. He waved to the guests before mimicking the straightening of his cartoon bowtie like a silent film comedian.

The guffaw faded when Henry pointed to the back of the gym. Everyone turned to see the debonair best man escort the spiffy maid of honor down the white runner between the tables. The piano played a few more bars to build suspense for the arrival of the bride. Henry couldn't resist mouthing the chant, "We want the bride!" for the students to rock the gym into a powerhouse.

We want the bride!

We want the bride!

We want the bride!

We want the bride!

Before things got out of control, the music teacher played the traditional opening notes to "Here Comes the Bride." Henry motioned for the kids to stand with the adults.

The grand entrance of the blushing bride, on her father's arm, personified the total summation of her evolution. There was no question that her dress captured the essence of her matrimonial union. The older guests looked stunned while the younger ones were highly impressed. Kristin walked down the aisle draped in a long flowing white chiffon skirt, topped by a white T-shirt with a ruched bodice print on the front and backside.

The corners of Henry's mouth reached his eyes. The sight of his glowing bride knocked him out of this world. He couldn't have been more pleased with her dress and her incredible beauty. The tiny nylon flowers sprinkled in her stylish hair matched the bouquet her mother had created from the artificial flowers they bought. The arrangement accented her sparkling eyes and pearly smile. The electricity between the soon to be marrieds was enough to give everyone the jolt of their lives.

Hurst's attempt to be inconspicuous while shooting pictures failed miserably. Janet had to pull him back when Geoff handed his daughter to her future husband. Taking a front-row seat next to his wife, on the table bench in the bride's section, the Sharp patriarch was bumped by Hurst trying to wedge himself into a spot that didn't exist.

"Excuse me…pardon me…" the newspaper man mumbled.

Geoff was forced to make himself and Melinda uncomfortable to accommodate their unexpected guest.

"I can't scoot over any more, or I'll be on the floor," Melinda whispered.

Geoff scrunched his arms across his torso and turned to the photographer. "This is it, buddy."

Hurst was oblivious to the context of the remark. He was thinking only about the upcoming headline. "It sure is…what do you think of 'Our Royal Wedding, Charles and Diana 2.0' or 'A Soap Opera Wedding, Luke and Laura 2.0'?"

"I think you need to get with the times."

"I'm with the *Gazette.*"

Geoff suddenly realized who was attached to his left shoulder—Kristin had told him about the episode with the paper. He sneered at Hurst, ready to attack, nearly forgetting that it was his daughter's wedding.

"Dearly beloved, we are gathered here…" the minister announced.

Saved by the beginning of the pastoral opening, the publisher escaped a scathing rebuke by the *sharp* attorney who would've sliced him to pieces.

Henry and Kristin joined hands during the traditional script. Their mutual gaze numbed their ears to every word preceding their own vows. Kristin braved it by going first.

"I want everyone here to journey back with me to the day we met—the first day of school. I needed help getting into my office, and there you were. I was worried about my coffee breath, and you eased my worries by telling me about the cold pizza you ate for breakfast, and I laughed. I knew at that moment there was something different about you. I was affected by the bond you have with kids by embracing the kid in yourself.

"I started to fall in love with you the day you gave me a toy from the happiest period of my childhood. I tried denying it to myself because you didn't fit my stupid criteria…I worried so much about what others would think. Yet, you stood by me in my hour of darkness and then came to my rescue—again. You brought out the strong woman in me by connecting with the scared little girl I kept hidden away. You're my superhero—there's no one in this world like you. And I'm glad, because I get to have you for the rest of my life. I love you, Henry Hubbard!"

She turned to the guests. "You know, I always dreamed of being swept off my feet, but I never imagined it would be by a man who pushed a broom."

Everyone's jovial reaction, triggered by the irony of the pun, sounded like a sitcom laugh track. Henry signaled for the students to clap as if there was a neon light flashing, "Applause!"

"She learned from the master," he boasted after the decibel level dropped.

"Henry?" the pastor uttered in a low voice.

"Guess it's show time for me."

Kristin twinkled. "You're always on."

The nervous groom cleared his throat. "Ah-hem…I think everyone here would agree I'm seldom at loss for words because I'm quick with the quips. But this is one of those rare occasions when I'm starting to suffer the effects of being tongue-tied. You see, I've never poured my heart out in public. It's always been easier for me to be a clown than a superhero, until I met you. I was speechless when I first saw you walk by on your way in here on that first day.

"Superman has X-ray vision, and so do I—I saw right through you when we met. I sensed that you knew it too. What I saw that day was a glimpse into the future—our future. I believed the woman standing before me now was somewhere to be found underneath that guarded armor you used to wear. And you weren't the only one in need of rescuing; I was too.

"The path to get here was bumpy, but now it's a smooth ride on the road to the rest of our lives. You *get* me, Sharpie—I love you!"

Lots of "awws" emanated from the audience.

Henry glanced at the pastor and muttered from the side of his mouth. "Can we get to the rings before I start making a fool of myself and not in a fun way?"

"At least you didn't toss in another ring—suffering," Kristin joked to cover her groom's anxiety.

The pastor chuckled before proceeding with the ring exchange. Henry placed his mother's diamond-chip ring on Kristin's soft finger, then she slid her grandfather's gold band onto his coarse finger. Both fit the members of their hands perfectly, as if they were meant to be saved for this day.

When the pronouncement of their nuptial reached its crescendo—*you may kiss your bride*—the Hubbards received a standing ovation. Kids cheered "Hooray" while the adults wiped their teary eyes. The pianist started the "Wedding March." Hurst leaped to his feet to snap a picture for his front page.

In an unusual move in their unique wedding, Henry picked up his wife to carry her down the aisle to the back of the gym. The *oohs and ahhs* drowned out the music that no one was listening to anyway. Setting Kristin down, Henry climbed on a chair to address the crowd.

"Attention Perrinsville! My wife and I"—he lowered his chin to Kristin's elated smile—"I can't believe I just said that." Looking back up, he resumed, "We want to thank you for coming and would like you to stay for a hot dog lunch—kids first—courtesy of our kitchen staff and the wedding cake baked by our own Judith Kendall. During the cake serving, we will be drawing the kids' raffle tickets. When you hear your number called, you can claim any toy of your choice in this room. It's our gift to all of you. We love you all—Merry Christmas!"

The kids went crazy with glee!

Kristin pulled Henry by the hand outside the gym for the adult reception line. They were joined by Janet, Eugene, Geoff, and Melinda. Superintendent Bakewell was first in line to congratulate the happy couple, followed by his secretary, Kathy, and her husband, and so on till the last guest over the age of ten showed up with a veil. Eugene stepped out of line to reveal her identity—Alma Tater.

The Hubbards and Janet braced themselves for the worst.

"Congratulations," she said with genuine authenticity.

She hugged Kristin, then Henry.

"I can't tell you how sorry I am for the trouble I caused, but I'm a new person now, and I wish you both many blessings for a wonderful marriage."

"Thanks…I think," Henry said.

"Can we believe you?" Kristin asked.

Eugene put his arm around her. "You have *our* word."

"Tater Tots is your mystery woman?" Henry questioned, pointing his finger at her.

Eugene nodded. "Bob Bakewell wasn't the only geek in our class who daydreamed about our homecoming queen. I've always had the hots for Tater Tots…err, Alma. Just took a little humbling for her to notice me."

"We have you to thank for that, Henry. When this guy of mine"—she squeezed her boyfriend's spindly bicep—"is ready, I won't be Mizz Tater Tots anymore. I'll be Missus Baloney Maloney."

Alma's hilarious punch line was a knockout.

Catching her breath, Kristin gently tugged Janet's sleeve. "Where's Freddie?"

"It's a funny thing…while he was getting dressed, the store called him in for an urgent delivery some twenty miles away."

"Well, that's a shame. Can't win 'em all," Henry gloated.

"I don't think it's a legit order, the customer's name sounded like a prank: Bagwood Dumstead, or maybe it's Dagwood Bumstead?"

Kristin raised her eyebrows. "I know that name—*Henry!*"

***

On Christmas morning, Kristin's picture appeared on the front page of the *Perrinsville Gazette* once again. This time it was her happily-ever-after kiss with her husband, under the headline "Toyful Love."

Epilogue

"I don't believe it!" Eugene exclaimed to his fiancée at the sight of the Hubbard house in late June. "The yard is beautiful—not a single weed or wild bush anywhere."

The town's biggest eyesore had miraculously been overhauled from a countryside shack into a mini chateau. The vinyl siding, once covered by layers of filth, now shone like a new car. Hostas and marigolds accented the mulch covered planters all around the frontal view of the house.

"It's obvious who took charge of the landscaping," Alma noted.

With blue and pink gift-wrapped packages under their arms, the couple was led by the sound and aroma of the lively barbeque party in the backyard. Opening the gate of the freshly painted picket fence—traditional white, of course—they were greeted warmly by the glowing hostess sporting a summer maternity dress over her six-month baby bump.

"Thank you both for coming to our open-house baby shower."

"Wouldn't have missed it for the world," Eugene said, observing his old friend slaving over the grill along the back of the house. "Those burgers smell really good."

"I hope you're hungry. Chef Hubb-ar-dee will be ready to serve us soon. He prepared an awesome spread of side dishes last night and this morning, so don't be shy…there's plenty for seconds and thirds."

Maloney licked his chops like a hungry wolf. "I think I'll go see if the grill master needs any help."

He passed off his blue-bowed box to Alma, before vanishing in the haze from the grill.

Alma extended the presents to the expectant mother. "Where do I put these?"

Kristin pointed toward the large tent in the middle of the yard housing several tables and clusters of people mingling with drinks in their hands. "There's a head table there with all the gifts."

"Don't you look like the sunshine?" Bob Bakewell remarked to Kristin upon his arrival, completely bypassing Alma, who cocked her head to him. "Oh, and you too, Alma."

"Nice save," she replied.

"I'm happy for you and Eugene. Sometime at the end of August is the big day?"

"You know it." She turned to Kristin. "I'm going to set these on the table. Excuse me."

"We'll catch up later," Kristin said, as Alma stepped away.

"Are you sure you want me to hire her back?" Bob asked, slightly perplexed.

"Yes, I need someone to cover for me after the twins are born. She's really changed since last year, now that she's found true love with Baloney."

"He's a better man than me. I could never get her to be the meek woman she is now."

"That's because you never know who you're going to fall in love with—I know that better than anyone."

"Are you two ready for twins?"

"As ready as we'll ever be."

"Henry will be a great dad. I don't know of anybody who can bond with children like him."

"That's one of the reasons why I married him." She directed her superintendent to the newly constructed king-size swing and slide playset put to use by several kids in attendance. "Henry designed and built this last month."

"It's a little premature, isn't it? I mean, your kids won't be able to use it for a few years."

"*Our* kids are using it right now."

Bob blushed in humility. "Yes…they *are* indeed your kids. Ah, do you have anything to drink?"

"The cooler's by the food table. I'll take you there."

In their stroll by the tent, Geoff and Melinda waved to get their daughter's attention.

"When's the food going to be ready?" Geoff shouted. "The heat's making me hungry."

Melinda slapped his arm. "Please…"

"Going to check on it now," Kristin announced, as Bob kept on going. She pointed her finger behind his back and mouthed "My boss" to her parents before catching back up with him.

Sweaty from the increased temperature steaming off the stainless-steel grill, Henry flipped his last set of burgers into the large aluminum tray filled to capacity. Janet and Eugene tag-teamed setting up the food line with side trays of homemade baked beans, corn on the cob, potato salad, and coleslaw, along with buns, catsup, mustard, paper plates, plastic utensils, napkins, and so forth. Kristin joined the gang to supervise.

Employing his chef's hat to fan the smoke away from the table, Henry called out to everyone. "Come and get it!"

After the meal, Henry took Kristin by the hand to a gift table overflowing with presents, while the guests enjoyed their cake and pie desserts.

"This is gonna take all night, Sharpie."

"Not if we have some help."

Henry scoped the guests for potential assistants. "I see Fast Freddie is on his third piece of pie."

"I'm glad Goody Two-shoes finally tied him down."

"Hey, that sounds like my line."

She gently rubbed her expanded belly. "Just trying to increase the odds of our babies getting your sense of humor…"

He pecked her lips.

"…along with *my* smarts."

They shared a quick laugh, another kiss, and—Eureka!—"I've got an idea," they said in unison. "Kids love to open presents!"

Henry cupped his hands over his mouth. "Calling all kids! Calling all kids!"

* * *

Six months later, Henry and Kristin tore open the packages underneath their Christmas tree with the newest additions to their family, Henry Jr. and Janene. Kristin insisted their son bear the name of his father, but when it came to their daughter, they agreed on a blended name of their matrimonial witnesses and best friends—Janet and Eugene. The house that Kristin revamped was once again home to a treasure trove of toys—baby toys this time.

Still in their pajamas by late morning, they welcomed the proud grandparents who brought even more presents. Geoff and Melinda couldn't wait to cradle their grandchildren after settling in the living room. Kristin then handed Henry Jr. to her mom and Janene to her dad, while Henry disappeared from the gathering.

"I'm so glad you retired, Daddy, and bought my house. I love having both of you close by…especially this time of year."

"It was a no-brainer, Krissy. Your mom and I know we weren't the best parents, but we want to make restitution by being exceptional grandparents."

"We know the two of you will need someone to watch your precious children when you go back to work," Melinda added. "By the way, where did your husband go?"

"Oh, he went to get a special project he wants to unveil in front of all of us."

"What kind of project?" Geoff asked.

"I don't know, Daddy. He's been working on it for a long time in the garage."

"How do you not know what it is?"

"He's kept it under a covering and swore me not to peek."

"I never let that stop me before," Melinda cackled with a side kick to her husband on the couch.

"We'll find out soon enough; here he comes," Kristin said.

Henry rolled in with a mobile table, borrowed from the school, covered with a painter's tarp.

"I suppose you might be wondering what's under this?" He magically waved his hands over the bulge under the paint-stained covering.

They stared at him with blank expressions.

"Just as I thought; the suspense is killing you. Well, I started to work on this project after Sharpie told me we were gonna be parents. So I wanted to make the perfect toy that our kids can play with when they get a little bit older, obviously, that would help them understand their heritage."

All three Sharps stared, dumbfounded, with no idea what he was about to reveal.

"It took a long time for me to find the supplies to build it, but I finally finished it just in time to dedicate it on our twins' first Christmas. Drum roll please—without dropping the kids."

Geoff and Melinda tapped their toes, as Kristin slapped her knees to simulate the sound.

"May I present to you"—he whipped off the tarp—"'The Story of

Henry and Sharpie!'"

Everyone's eyes widened at the jaw-dropping sight of a doll house resembling Perrinsville Elementary School, complete with two dolls made in the likeness of Henry and Kristin—as they looked on the day they met.

"Merry Christmas!" he cheered.

Kristin sprang up to throw her arms around her husband. "Only *you* can make something so small bigger than life."